IT'S ABOUT TIME

FRANCES SCHEPP RUH

◆ FriesenPress

Suite 300 - 990 Fort St
Victoria, BC, V8V 3K2
Canada

www.friesenpress.com

ISBN
978-1-5255-9176-1 (Hardcover)
978-1-5255-9175-4 (Paperback)
978-1-5255-9177-8 (eBook)

1. FICTION, FRIENDSHIP

Distributed to the trade by The Ingram Book Company

For The Ladies of the Bridge Club
My inspiration and my forever friends

ALSO BY
FRANCES SCHEPP RUH

The Schepp Family Chronicles
Question Everything
Risk Everything

PREFACE

When I finished my second novel, I planned to retire from writing. Even though my intention was to never write another book, this story would not let me go. My original plan was to title this novel Everything Ends both to tell my readers, and more importantly, to remind myself that this would be my final book.

In the late sixties, as mother of two very young children, I was fortunate to join a church circle where I met other young mothers who needed a break from the monotonous and often frustrating job of caring for babies and pre-school children. We met at our church until our children reached school age, and then eight of us began to play bridge together.

Through the years, members came and went. Some moved away, others found jobs, and a few died, but the core group remained together. For over half a century, we've shared all of life's experiences both joyous and heart-breaking. We watched our own, and each other's children turn into adults. We attended graduations, weddings, and welcomed another generation. Later, we shared the problems of caring for and losing our aging parents and the complications of retirement.

A few years ago, we abandoned our bridge games, but we meet at least monthly for lunch, and we still call ourselves "The Bridge Club". When we're with each other, I look around the table and marvel at the many years we've spent together, and I feel inspired by the devotion and the affection that these, my oldest and dearest friends, have for one another.

As this book began to evolve, I would often ask myself, "What is this book about?"

Finally, I realized that it's not necessarily about the characters, but about the stages of life and the passage of time and it was then that I changed the title of this book from Everything Ends to, It's About Time. I cannot stress strongly enough that the characters you meet in this book bear no resemblance in any way to the ladies of my Bridge Club. It's their support and their concern for one another that inspired me and is the same. And now....

Meet the ladies of the Bridge Club

Like many women, they share a bond of loyalty that is often stronger than family ties or marital vows. Here they are: they'll tell you their own stories and when you get to know them, you'll learn their secrets, watch their lives unfold for better or worse and remain with them until death do you part.

PHOEBE FARLEY

In 1940, Phoebe Stevens Farley was born into a family of privilege and wealth. Earlier generations of the family were involved in banking, insurance and real estate expansion. Phoebe and her older sister, Marcia, were protected and indulged throughout their lives. Nevertheless, family expectations and limitations were imposed on them, one of which was to enter into a marriage that met certain economic and social standards. Phoebe complied; Marcia chose a career path, and remained single throughout her life. Marcia was born street smart; Phoebe didn't even know there was a street until she was nearly middle aged.

After college, Phoebe married Jeff Farley, a handsome, well-educated, successful attorney from a family that met her parent's approval. Jeff was madly in love with his tiny, sweet but terribly naive bride. Phoebe had a great affection and respect, for Jeff, and she was pleased that she complied with all of her family's and society's demands, but throughout her life, she was haunted by an early forbidden love that would never let her go.

ABAGAIL GRAY

Abagail married well or at least she thought she did. Raised by a disagreeable, unhealthy middle-class widow, Abagail had no means or opportunity for advanced education or training, and she settled for a secretarial job in an accounting firm. Just when Abagail became discouraged with her lack of advancement and considered looking for a better job, she caught the eye of Stanley Gray, a recent addition to the firm. Abagail was looking for stability, security and a strong father figure. Even though Stan was blustery and a little rough around the edges, Abagail saw him as the best she could attract and, after a whirlwind courtship, agreed to marry him. Abagail was aware of the reasons she was attracted to Stan, but she often wondered why an upwardly mobile man chose an uneducated, plain wall flower like herself. Could it have been that initially, she seemed agreeable and submissive: in other words… easily controlled?

Phoebe literally crashed into Abagail's life. They had a minor fender-bender in a supermarket parking lot. Rather than using insurance, Jeff preferred to cover the damage personally and left the matter in Phoebe's hands. During the exchange of information and conversations concerning car repairs and, against all odds, the tiny pretty, advantaged Phoebe, and the tall, plain and insecure Abagail became the unlikeliest of friends.

Later, a disturbing experience with a strange man led to the phone call that changed the course of Abagail's life and altered the balance of power in her marriage.

HANNAH CONWAY

What was it about Hannah? She's the woman of mystery in the Bridge Club with a secret that no one ever suspected. Hannah never spoke of her childhood. Where did she grow up, did she have siblings and what about her parents? She never mentioned her past, and strangely enough, no one ever asked. She was, after all, a devout Christian, committed to her family and then there was that soft, gentle sweetness about her that no one seemed able to resist. Phoebe and Abagail were touched by her unfortunate circumstances and determined to help her. They were even willing to tolerate her fanatically religious husband, Rob, whose misdirected ambition created desperate financial needs for his family.

TAMMY CRAIG

Tammy, a fun-loving party girl, was perfectly suited for traveling the world with her husband, Jim Craig, an Air Force pilot. Military assignments in foreign countries allowed her to decrease contact with her alcoholic parents and constantly squabbling siblings. Tammy and Jim planned to start a family after they'd seen the world, and when they were ready for a permanent assignment. Fate had other plans for them, and when Jim's plane crashed during takeoff, Tammy was devastated.

The life she planned was no longer available to Tammy, and she found herself disconnected from her family of origin, the Air Force and the friends she had enjoyed there. Life near her in-laws was far from Tammy's life goals, but running out of options, lost and alone, she agreed to Jim's parents offer of emotional support and moved to Springfield. Her in-laws, Millie and Boots, were also wracked with grief and desperate for any connection to their only child.

1969-1970

From a spiritual vantage point our major life task is much larger than making money, finding a mate, having a career, raising children, looking beautiful, achieving psychological health or defying aging, illness and death. It is a recognition of the sacred in daily life, a deep gratitude for the wonders of the world and the delicate web of inter-connectedness between people, nature and things—a recognition that true intimacy is based on respect and love and is the measure of life well lived.

Joan Borysenko A Woman's Book of Life

PHOEBE FARLEY

Looking back, I think roots of our Bridge Club were planted in the church Circle that I joined as a young mother. On the first day that I can still recall, I was already frustrated when I pulled into the crowded church parking lot. Dawdling children and heavy traffic delayed my trip to the monthly meeting. I impatiently rushed my children, Ariel and Adam into the nursery. When I had settled them, I hurried to the meeting and found only one chair left next to a woman I'd never seen before.

She was a large woman; tall, big boned with a big head and thick lips plastered with bright red lipstick. I disliked her the moment I saw her. It wasn't that she was fat…well…maybe she was, but an over-sized hip length jacket of wide gray and camel horizontal stripes made her seem even larger. As a tiny person, five foot nothing, I've always been intimidated by large men. This woman was rather masculine and I was overwhelmed by her. She introduced herself as Bernadine Young but, in an authoritative tone of voice, she told us all to call her Bernie. Normally, a nickname suggests friendship even intimacy. Maybe it was her loud grating voice, but I felt as though it was a command rather than an invitation.

It seemed odd that a woman well into middle age would want to join a group composed mostly of young mothers. We'd all come together earlier that fall to establish a Tuesday morning church Circle that offered dependable, inexpensive child care.

Each month, in the church basement, we arranged a circle of metal folding chairs in a drab concrete block room painted a sickly shade of green. The worn indoor-outdoor carpet, a darker shade of green, smelled damp and musty. At least half the tubes in the fluorescent ceiling lights were burned out. The remaining bulbs sometimes flickered and cast an eerie glow over the room we called "The Swamp."

It wasn't that many of us were involved in other church activities, but the Circle offered a pleasant break from the tiring and often boring business of caring for young children. Despite the dismal setting, I always looked forward to being in the company of supportive women who shared my interests.

After the toddlers were settled in the nursery, we generally spent a large part of our time together catching up on family news, sharing recipes and evaluating various brands of toys and diapers. We were loosely organized which was part of the appeal of our group. In mid-meeting a plate was passed for offerings and we took turns reading passages from the Bible. Our original plan was to discuss the Bible verses over coffee and cookies, but somehow, we never returned to the Scriptures and we again chatted and then ended with a prayer.

On this day, Bernie took over and suggested that we use parliamentary procedure. She was just beginning to discuss dues rather than a free will offering when the leader announced that the children would be needing lunch and naps, and she adjourned the meeting.

The group disbanded quickly, and as I rounded up my two children, Ariel and Adam, Bernie approached me and asked if I could drive her home. She told me that her son had dropped her off on his way to a meeting, and she was sure that someone would be kind enough to drive her home. I looked around, but the room had cleared, and I reluctantly agreed.

I was dismayed when I learned that Bernie lived on an acreage several miles from the church. This was an interruption that I didn't need in my already busy day. As we began our drive, Bernie once again launched into ways the Circle could be improved. As she began to relate her experiences in women's groups in her previous church home, I wanted to kiss my children. Ariel announced that she was hungry and needed lunch right away. Adam expressed his unhappiness with tears and loud sobbing. I did nothing to discourage them.

Soon traffic thinned as did the roadside businesses. We passed a lone cafe, and when I looked ahead, I could see a ribbon of pavement stretching all the way to the horizon. That was the moment I began to tap my ring on the steering wheel.

Once the children quieted down, Bernie began to brag about her son, Ben. She said that he was beginning a medical career in plastic surgery and would be joining the practice of Hendricks and Prettyman. I pretended not to know that Dr. Hendricks was well known and widely respected. Bernie continued, telling me that the doctor's wife was a judge and, as a power couple, they were always photographed at political fund raisers and charitable events. Anyone who occasionally looked at a newspaper would have been aware of the Hendrick's prominence. I kept my mouth shut and tried to appear impressed.

When we turned into a long driveway that led to a large log home, Bernie opened her purse and pulled out a cigarette and lighter. I prayed that she would wait to light up until she was out of the car. The area surrounding the home was ablaze with beautiful beds of brightly colored late summer flowers. Bernie waved the unlit cigarette and began to tell me about her gardening skills and her membership in the Springfield Floral Society. When a car pulled up behind us, Bernie said, "Good, my son's home early. I want you to meet him."

I was stunned when a tall, slender, blond man, who appeared to be in his mid-thirties stepped from the car. He was movie-star handsome and moved with the grace of a dancer. I wondered if he was adopted or if he favored his father. He opened the passenger door of my car and extended his hand to assist his mother. I couldn't help but notice the elegance with which he moved his long fingers.

After Bernie made the introductions and left the car, she lit her cigarette. Ben sat down in her seat and immediately turned his attention to the children in the back seat. He asked their names and ages, and told Ariel he had a daughter Adam's age. Then, he turned to me and thanked me for taking care of his mother. He oozed charm, and I could see that the children were flattered by his attention.

Goodbyes were said, thanks were given and, as I drove away, I vowed to be the first one to leave the next meeting. Adam was asleep before we turned onto the highway, but Ariel intensified her demands for lunch. When we returned to civilization, I broke one of my cardinal rules and drove through a fast food restaurant window for a take-out lunch for Ariel. I hoped to carry

Adam to his bedroom without waking him and fix a healthy lunch for the two of us when he awakened.

I could hear the phone ringing as I opened the door, and I raced from the garage into the house. I tried to balance the receiver, Ariel's lunch and Adam without waking him. I barely recognized my sister Marcia's voice. She was shrieking, "Where have you been? I've been trying to call you forever." Before I could answer she began to cry and between sobs, she said, "Mother's had a heart attack; she's in the emergency room at Memorial Hospital. They say it's serious. You need to be here…come right away."

I dropped Ariel's lunch, and the Coke splattered all over the floor and splashed onto my shoes and pant legs.

"I'll be there as fast as I can," was my reply.

I called my husband, Jeff. His secretary answered and told me he was at lunch and asked if he could call me back later. I said, "Never mind," and hung up. I grabbed Ariel's hand and rushed back to the car. Bless his heart; Adam slept through it all and never woke up until we reached the hospital. Ariel was relentless with her questions and her hunger complaints.

I tried to explain that something serious and bad had happened, and I needed her to be quiet and good. She stopped talking and started to cry. I was almost dragging the children as I rushed to the emergency room.

Marcia ran toward me and said, "I'll take the children, you go in to see Mother."

As I handed them over, I said, "Please call Jeff and tell him what's happened and where I am."

A nurse was leaning over my mother as I entered the curtained space. She turned and very quietly said, "Your mother is taking her last breaths. I'll leave you alone with her. There's a possibility that she could still hear you."

I kissed mother's cheek and held her hand. I tried to tell her how much I loved her and thank her for all she'd done for me, but I was crying too hard. I heard Marcia enter behind me. I turned and said, "You need to say goodbye now."

Marcia's lower lip quivered; she draped her arms around me and whispered, "I already have, and I'm glad you got here in time."

Just then, the nurse approached us and said, "I'm sorry. She's gone." In a few minutes the hospital chaplain appeared. He attempted to console us, and we ended with a prayer.

I asked to see Mother one more time, and when I left her, I saw Jeff running toward me. I fell into his strong arms; he was always there when I needed him. He handled things in a calm and careful way and had always been the strong one who took charge of troublesome situations. Now, though, there was something he couldn't fix.

I felt adrift…I was suddenly an orphan. Father had been dependable but quiet and reserved. Quite honestly, I was never sure how he felt about me. I suspected that Marcia was his favorite child, but that was just a guess…a hunch. Mother was the guiding light in our lives; her love was unconditional. I always believed that, even if I were a bank robber or a serial killer, she would have loved and defended me, just because I was hers. In that moment, I knew I'd never experience that kind of love again.

The days following Mother's death, sadness and loss overwhelmed me. I was nearly non-functional. Jeff stayed home, took charge of the children and worked on the funeral arrangements with Marcia.

As the family filed into the front of the church for the funeral service, I saw the Circle members filling a pew. They sat shoulder to shoulder like a troupe of soldiers ready to defend their territory. During the previous week they delivered countless meals to my home and offered child care whenever needed. Now, their young, beautiful faces seemed to glow in the rays of sunlight that shone through the stained-glass windows. Even though I'd had an immense loss, I felt blessed by them.

ABIGAIL GRAY

I only turned my head slightly, but I could see him behind me on the Macy's escalator. There were about three people between us. Before I could get myself under control, "Oh shit," popped out of my mouth. The woman ahead of me turned and gave me a dirty look. Once I stepped off the escalator, I rushed for the ladies' restroom, and glanced in the mirror on my way to a stall. I thought, *it can't be lust. Who would want a tall gangly woman with drab brown hair and baggy clothes?* I locked myself in a stall and sat down on the toilet seat. My mind raced, *he's everywhere. Who is he? What does he want from me? Does he plan to rob me, kidnap my child or worse? I've seen him watching me in the grocery store and other places. He's even driven by my house at least twice. This is serious, I need help and I need it now.*

Half an hour later, I stuck my head out of the restroom door, looked around and hoped it was safe to come out. I'd noticed a row of phone booths near the entrance to the mall and I headed straight for them. Phoebe answered the phone on the second ring. I had no time or patience for small talk or pleasantries, "Phoebe," I said, "I've got to talk to you. Are you going to be home for a while?"

"Yes, Ab, what's wrong? You sound awful."

"I don't have time to talk. I'll see you in ten minutes."

In scary situations, my imagination always takes control, and while I was driving my mind raced from one awful scenario to another. Every possibility from kidnapper, to rapist to murderer crossed my mind. I pictured my son, motherless, being raised by an inept father who was constantly wringing his hands and saying, "She was right. Why didn't I pay attention?" The one thing I was sure of was that this stranger's presence in my life was no coincidence.

I took a short cut through the university campus adjoining Phoebe's house; something I rarely do. I generally enjoyed the, winding, well-landscaped drive to her home, but on that day, I hit the gas and took the curves with reckless abandon. When I reached the end of the driveway, I could see Phoebe standing on the front steps of her ancestral family home. Her arms were folded across her chest, and she was leaning against a stately white column. Even though she was tiny, she seemed impervious to the wind that was whipping her platinum pony tail over her shoulder. She had a worried look in her large deep blue eyes. Phoebe ran to the car, stood on tiptoe and grabbed my shoulders. "What in the world is going on? You're white as a sheet."

I felt as though I'd been punched in the solar plexus, and when I recovered my breath, I told her about the mystery man and how terrified I was. Phoebe guided me into the breakfast nook of her kitchen and poured a cup of coffee for me. She sat down across the table and said, "Have you talked to your husband or anyone else about this?"

"Stan doesn't take this seriously. He laughs and says it's a coincidence; probably a new neighbor we just don't know yet. He thinks I'm imagining things and making too much out of this. I need someone to believe me and give me some advice. I just don't know what to do."

"How long has this been happening?"

"I've noticed it for the last week. Who knows? It could have been longer, and maybe I just wasn't paying attention."

"Has this man ever attempted to talk to you?"

"No, but I haven't given him a chance. I walk away every time I see him."

Phoebe was quiet for a few seconds, but she reached across the table and took hold of my hand. "The Circle meets next week. Would you mind telling them about this problem. They're all good thinkers…mostly good thinkers… and they might have some ideas that will help deal with this." I nodded and Phoebe continued, "I do think, though, that you should try talking to Stan about this one more time. Maybe today's experience will help convince him that there really is a problem."

All through dinner, I wondered how I'd approach this subject, and when our son, Ryan, was finally bathed, and bedtime stories read and re-read, I knew I had to make one last try to convince Stan that I had a serious problem. I said, "Stan, I saw that man again today. He was behind me on the escalator at Macy's."

Stan rose from his chair, walked to the liquor cabinet and opened a bottle of Scotch. When he had poured a glass, he turned to me and said, "So."

I held back tears, "This is not a coincidence. We need to do something."

Stan raised his voice, "Look Abagail, Every time I go to work, I see the same people in the parking garage, walking in and out of my building, and I see them at lunch. I'm not making a big deal out of it and you shouldn't either. Now, it's time for Hogan's Heroes, and I don't want to hear any more about it."

I was discouraged…no, I was furious.

* * *

The following Tuesday, Phoebe and I were the first to arrive at church. After the children were settled in the nursery, Phoebe said, "How did it go with Stan?"

I said, "He just dismisses me. I don't know what to do."

Others began to arrive, and we immediately started our meeting. The Bible verse for the day was, John 14:27: Peace I leave with you; my peace I give you. I do not give to you as the world gives. Do not let your heart be troubled and do not be afraid.

I listened carefully and tried to find some comfort in those words, but I was in a trance until it was time for the coffee and cookies. Bernie spoke first and suggested we organize a style-show luncheon for the ladies of the church. Phoebe interrupted her and said, "I'm sorry Bernie but one of our members has a serious problem, and she needs advice and possibly help."

Bernie was annoyed. She puckered her large red lips and said, "This is not the place for personal problems; it's a business meeting. If we want Rebekah Circle to be the biggest and best in the church, we should be planning ways to make that happen."

Phoebe said, "I can only speak for myself, but I'm satisfied with our Circle just as it is. This isn't a contest. The Christian thing to do is take care of each other. Now, if no one else objects, Abigail please tell us what's happening to you."

The room was silent and all faces were turned toward me. I stood and told the group about all the encounters I'd had with the strange man. I poured my heart out and when I finished, there were many questions.

The first, "What does he look like?"

I answered, "He's distinctive looking, smaller than average, thin, bald and he has a dark mustache." There were many other questions, some about my husband's reaction, and I hated to admit his indifference, but it was a painful truth.

The last question confounded me, "Have you confronted this man? Why not walk up to him and ask him why he's following you and what he wants from you?"

I said, "I think that could be dangerous."

Bernie surprised everyone when she said, "Not if you do it in a busy public place."

The next afternoon, I realized I needed onions and peppers to finish our dinner. My son, Ryan, was still at his friend's home and I thought I had time for a quick trip to the grocery store. During the drive, I caught a glimpse of the car I'd seen passing by our house several times. Once inside the store, I picked a space a bit back from the windows where I couldn't be seen but had a full view of the parking lot.

Sure enough, I recognized the man with the mustache behind the wheel. He circled the lot twice, parked and started toward the store. I grabbed a cart and positioned myself near the door so I would meet him face to face with the cart between us. When he entered the store and saw me facing him; he stopped. I pushed my cart till it was almost touching him and in a very loud voice said, "Who are you? Why are you following me?"

The man looked around to see if anyone was watching. A moment later, he turned and walked quickly from the store. I watched as he ran through the parking lot to his car. I decided not to tell Stan about this encounter, but I couldn't wait to meet with the Circle. I called Phoebe the minute I got home. First, we laughed; then, she congratulated me and said, "I imagine this is the end of a weird chain of events." How could I have known; it was only the beginning?

Four days later a call came at nine o'clock on a Wednesday morning. The caller was a woman with a very pleasant voice. She said, "Abagail, my name is Cynthia Morris. I hope I'm not calling at an inconvenient time."

I wondered if this was a sales call or a survey. I'm normally not polite with cold callers but there was something about the woman's voice that kept me from hanging up. I said, "Go on."

She said, "This may or may not come as a surprise to you, but I think we're half-sisters."

I was indignant and nearly hung up again, but curiosity took over, and I asked, "And how might this have happened?"

"I was an illegitimate child, born to a very young woman and adopted at birth. I've had some investigation done and I'd hoped to find my birth mother, but I was told that she's dead, and you're her only child."

I was dumfounded and more than skeptical. My father died when I was ten. My mother was a difficult woman, and we had an uneasy relationship. I'd had no grandparents to depend on and, without Daddy, our home was a cold and lonely place. I thought marriage to Stan would provide a safe haven for me, but I soon learned that I was mistaken.

Mother had a long, painful illness, and I hate to admit that after her death the only emotion I felt was relief. Still, I was curious and had to ask myself if I wanted to risk meeting someone who would stir up all those memories, and who might possess all my mother's negative qualities. Curiosity won out; I suggested we arrange a meeting.

Cynthia told me that she would only be in town for one more day and planned to fly home early on Friday. For some reason, I assumed that she was local, and I asked, "Where is home?"

The words, "Syracuse, New York," convinced me of the necessity of meeting this woman as soon as possible. My mother occasionally talked of growing up in Cortland, New York and often described exciting trips she made to nearby Syracuse.

I said, "My son is in kindergarten till noon. We could meet for a short time this morning." We arranged to meet in the lobby of the Radisson Hotel where Cynthia was staying. When I asked how I would know her, she told me she would be wearing a red carnation pinned to her jacket.

No carnation was needed. When I walked into the hotel lobby, I thought my mother had been reincarnated. My father's gene pool must have been dominant. I bear very little resemblance to my mother in build, facial features or personality traits. Cynthia, however, resembled Mother in every way except hair color. She was much shorter than I and her dark brown hair was streaked with gray.

As I walked in the door Cynthia rose and walked directly to me. I was amazed and wondered how she recognized me. I was a little stiff as we hugged and not ready for that yet. We agreed to sit in the hotel coffee shop for our conversation, but I didn't know how we'd even begin.

Cynthia started with a bit about her background. The words seemed to pour out; like water rushing over a damn. I could tell she was relieved to finally open up on what had been a forbidden topic for so long. It seems that Cynthia was adopted by an upper middle class family, and she'd been given music lessons and encouraged in sports. They'd traveled internationally, and she'd earned a college degree.

She said two younger sisters were born to her parents, and she was never told she was adopted. After her mother's death, when the sisters were dividing their mother's jewelry, the younger sister told her she wasn't entitled to any because she wasn't a biological child. It was a shocking, even questionable revelation until a sympathetic aunt provided the details of her adoption. Years later, Cynthia decided to find her family of origin. She said there were many reasons for contacting me, and the strongest was to learn about family history and health.

As I listened, I felt she was the lucky one. Her life had been easier and far more secure and privileged than mine, and I told her so. Cynthia looked down at table and said, "Perhaps, but I'm estranged from what I thought was my family, my husband is dead and I have only my son, Ryan."

I guess this last remark shouldn't have taken me by surprise, but it did. I told her that my only child was a son named Ryan. We compared pictures and found that they were both red heads; the same dark auburn shade as my mother's hair.

Seeing my son's picture reminded me that I was due to pick him up in a few minutes and I had time for only one last question, "A man has been following me. Does this have anything to do with your attempt to find me?"

Cynthia said, "Yes, I hired a local detective. I felt that contacting a stranger was risky, and I just had to find out what kind of person you are. Although he gave you an outstanding report, he must be very bad at surveillance. He called when you caught him, and that's when I decided that I needed to contact you myself. I'm truly sorry if this has upset you, but it won't happen again."

We hugged once more as we said goodbye and agreed to meet the following day, same time...same place.

I knew I had to tell Stan, but I wanted his full attention so I began to think about how to set the stage. I wanted a somewhat crowded place so he couldn't yell at me and expensive enough that he wouldn't suggest we leave in the middle of the meal.

I called Phoebe and told her about Cynthia's call, the meeting and the truth about the detective. There was a long silence, and I finally had to ask, "Phoebe, are you still there?"

"Unbelievable," was the first word out of her mouth. "You have a sister... and a nephew. The girls are going to love this. I hope you're planning to go to the Circle. You will tell them; won't you?"

I said, "Yes," to both questions and then told Phoebe about my plan to tell Stan over dinner Friday night. She agreed to invite Ryan to stay the night at her house.

Early Friday morning I received a distressing call from Cynthia. She said she wasn't feeling well and needed to cancel our meeting and return home immediately. I was more than a little disappointed since I'd had a chance to think about our meeting; it wasn't as much what she'd said, but more her looks and her mannerisms. I wanted to learn more about her and also find out all I could about her son, Ryan. It was rather like having my mother return with a personality transplant.

Cynthia said she'd write to me and possibly call when she felt better. This was such a strange turn of events I could hardly believe it.

PHOEBE FARLEY

When I felt a tug on my covers, I wanted to roll over and go back to sleep, but instead, I opened my eyes and was startled to see Ariel standing next to my bed. Adam was beside her, holding her hand. She was always the spokesperson for the pair, and in a very quiet controlled voice she said, "Mommy, do you think we might be hungry?"

Her words were like an arrow piercing my heart; I sat straight up. I'd had a literal "wake up call." I suddenly realized that I'd been so sad and self-absorbed in the weeks since my mother's death; I'd failed to give my children the attention they needed. It wasn't exactly neglect, but a kind of preoccupation with someone who was gone and failure to realize that I still had people to love and care for. Jeff was my rock, but I was also aware that we had been drifting apart due to my grieving. I vowed to give him the attention he deserved starting that day.

I jumped out of bed, slipped into my robe and said, "How about french toast?"

Both children cheered and I took each of their hands and marched toward the kitchen.

Lately, I'd spent most of my time settling my mother's estate with Marcia. Mother had been in a nursing home for many years, but still there were thank you notes to be written, bills to be paid and accounts closed or transferred. We had finally finished that emotionally draining job, but I was still grieving. My only activity had been the church Circle one Tuesday of each month; but now, I was ready to return to the friends and events that Jeff and I enjoyed together.

As I watched the children devour their breakfast, I asked, "Does a picnic in the park sound good to anyone?" Once again there was a cheer. I wanted to make this a special picnic and spent the morning baking brownies, putting together a Waldorf salad and making their favorite ham and cheese sandwiches. All this activity energized me. I'd finally turned the corner and was back among the living.

I dropped a pen, note pad and calendar into our picnic basket. My intention was to list activities that Jeff would enjoy and make plans for concerts, sporting events and dinner with friends.

* * *

There were several families at the park playground and Ariel and Adam quickly ran off with two boys they knew from Sunday School. I noticed the boy's mother sitting alone at a picnic table. She waved and invited me to sit with her. I had noticed the family at the Sunday service especially her. She was a beautiful woman; not classically beautiful, but she had a soft look to her. Perhaps a better word to describe her would be "lovely." Her fair skin was flawless and her oval face was framed by what I guessed was natural ash blond hair; slightly curly and cut in a mid-length style. I wondered if the shine in her sapphire eyes was due to her pregnancy. I estimated she was about six months along.

She said, "I see our children are friends." Her voice and movements were as soft and gentle as her appearance. I was enchanted. You could attach a pair of wings to this woman and she would look like an angel.

I replied, "I've seen you in church. I'm Phoebe Farley." She tried to cover her amusement, but the trace of a smile crossed her face. I wasn't offended. Most people smile when they hear my name, some even laugh out loud.

She rose and extended her hand, "I'm Hannah Conway; my children are Matthew and Peter."

For a while we chatted about our children and the church and then, I asked, "When is your baby due?"

Tears welled in her eyes and she began to sob. Her crying became so intense that she leaned over the table and cradled her head in her arms.

I walked around the table and put my hands on her shoulders. She stood, turned, threw her arms around me and buried her head in my neck. She whispered, "I haven't felt movement for three days. The doctor says my baby is dead."

I was stunned. I pulled back and looked into her face. "What are you going to do?"

The sobbing stopped, but tears were still flowing, "The doctor said we need to terminate the pregnancy."

"Does that mean abortion or forced labor?"

"I don't know. He referred me to another doctor, an obstetrician."

"What kind of doctor are you seeing?"

"He's…uh…uh family practice, I think."

Just then, I saw our four children running toward us, but I still had one more question, "What does your husband think about this?"

Her answer, "I haven't told him yet?"

We agreed that it was lunch time, and I began to unload the picnic basket I'd brought. I spread out a red and white checked cloth and laid out paper plates and plastic silverware. Hannah had peanut butter sandwiches in carefully folded pieces of waxed paper and a bag of chips.

When the children were seated, Hannah placed her sandwiches on the waxed paper in front of her sons. They looked at their food and at ours and then, they looked toward their mother. I could see that Hannah was tearing up again and I quickly snatched extra plates and utensils from my basket and set them in front of Hannah, Peter and Matt. Then I said, "Dig in."

While my children were immediately ready to eat, Hannah and her children folded their hands and bowed their heads. There followed a very long prayer in which Hannah gave thanks for the beautiful day, the food, and our chance meeting.

When she finished asking for world peace and a blessing on everything within fifty miles of Springfield, her boys stuffed their mouths full of the Waldorf salad and groaned with pleasure. Ariel and Adam seemed to sense the awkwardness of the situation and shared sandwiches with their friends. When the pan of brownies came out of the basket, Peter and Matthew's eyes lit up like Christmas trees, and there was not a crumb left to take home.

As we cleared the table and re-packed my basket, Hannah thanked me over and over for sharing lunch with her children. I was far more interested in her pregnancy and said, "Hannah, I don't want to pry, but what do you plan to do about your baby?"

To my surprise, she smiled and said, "You know the Lord's Prayer says, Thy will be done, and that's what I'm waiting for. If God wants this baby to leave my body, then he'll have to take it out one way or another. I'll just wait for His will to be done."

I asked Hannah if she'd ever considered joining a church Circle and I told her about the Rachel Circle. "That sounds like an answer to my prayers," but once again she looked down at the table, and continued, "We only have one vehicle and my husband needs it for his work?"

"How did you get here today?"

"We walked. It's only two blocks to the hotel where we live."

I was confused, I couldn't imagine why a family with young children would choose to live in a hotel, and I hoped my shock wasn't apparent when I said, "Hotel? Which hotel?"

Tears came to Hannah's eyes again and she said, "My husband is a developer and a contractor. He's building the last few houses in his current development. He sold our house to pay for an option to buy a wonderful piece of ground. We had to sell the house to get the money together to close on this property. It has space for everything: shopping, large homes, and the view is magnificent. There's even enough land for a nine-hole executive golf course. Our living arrangement is only temporary."

I could see that Hannah was tiring and the children were ready to go, but I wanted to make sure that she would at least try the Circle. "I can arrange for transportation for Tuesday. Please say you'll come."

"Yes, yes…the children need playmates, and I need a chance to get out."

"My friend, Abagail, will pick you up at 8:45. She drives a blue station wagon and sometimes she's a little late, but, don't worry she'll get you there on time."

As we said goodbye, Hannah hugged me and whispered, "Please, pray for me."

I said, "Let me drive you home." She agreed and we piled the children into my car.

As I dropped them off, I told Hannah to take care of herself. She said, "God bless you."

ABIGAIL GRAY

The restaurant was elegant, dimly lit and filled with smartly dressed patrons. I'd reserved a center table so we'd be surrounded by other diners. I hoped this would ensure good behavior from Stan. When his Scotch and my Harvey Wallbanger were served, I asked about his day. I hoped the alcohol would relax him a bit. I was amazed when he said, "It was good; actually, very good." I expected his usual reply which was always, "About the same."

I was further amazed when he said, "And how was your day?"

Even though I was curious about his "good day," I wanted to tell him about Cynthia and thought this was a great opportunity. I sipped my cocktail, smiled and said, "I've solved the mystery of the man who was following me."

Stan looked up from his drink, "So, now you know; it was just a coincidence."

I'd been waiting for this moment, "No," I replied, "he's a detective. He was hired to follow me."

Stan blurted out. "A detective!" Then he added in a sarcastic tone, "Really."

His voice was so loud that diners at nearby tables stopped talking and stared at us.

Stan reached for his drink and drained it all in a single gulp.

The waiter appeared and asked for our dinner order. Along with his steak, Stan ordered a refill of his Scotch. "Make that a double," he told the waiter.

Immediately after the waiter left, I began my story about the phone call, my meeting with Cynthia and her confession that she hired the detective. Stan said nothing while I talked, and when I'd finished, the meal arrived. We ate in silence.

Stan suggested Brandy Alexanders for desert and I agreed. After they were delivered to our table, Stan leaned back, threw his arm across the back of his chair and tipped his head to the side. Until this moment, I'd been enjoying this little scenario, but now, I knew what was coming; I'd seen that look before. Stan was planning to burst my bubble, rain on my parade, make me look small and foolish.

He began, "Let's see if I understand what you've told me. Out of the blue, a woman who claims to be your half-sister contacted you. Of course, she has a college aged son named Ryan, the same as our son or so she says. Then, this woman claims she hired a detective to see if you're a good person." Stan curved his fingers to indicate quotation marks as he said, "Good person." He continued, "Strangely enough, the last time you heard from this half-sister she was having a health crisis."

I said nothing; I knew he wasn't finished.

"Have you heard from her again?"

"No, she said she'd write or call me."

"And, you have no phone number or address for her?"

I took a deep breath and tried to salvage the situation. "Stan, I know she lives in Syracuse, close to where my mother grew up. She looks so much like my mother, and her Ryan has red hair; the same color as our Ryan."

"Oh, you met him too."

"No, but I saw a picture of him. He could be Ryan's big brother."

Stan chuckled. "Abagail, my dear, let me tell you what's going on here. This is what's called the long-con. The so-called detective is probably in on it too. He could be Cynthia's husband and there may or may not be a son. At some point, when you've gotten closer, Cynthia will need money for an operation or tuition for the kid, coincidentally, named the same as yours."

I thought offense was the best defense, and I said, "How do you know so much about long-cons?"

"What do you think is in all those detective novels I read?"

Then, I laughed and said, "Sex and murder."

"Let me tell you right now; these people are not getting one thin dime from me. And you…you need to wake up and stay the hell away from them."

Later, when we were home, I asked Stan what was good about his day. He said, "I had an interview with the head of the firm today. It seems I'm a candidate for partnership."

I asked if he had competition. He told me he wasn't sure but didn't think so. I knew that Stan's accounting skills were very good, but he was so lacking in the human relations department that I always wondered how he attracted or kept clients.

*   *   *

When I pulled up in front of the Howard Johnson Hotel on Tuesday morning, Hannah and her two sons were waiting for me. It seems that her boys and Ryan knew each other from Sunday School. Hannah was all that Phoebe had described; soft and gentle but sad. I hoped that she would find support and understanding from the women in the Circle just as I had. I asked how she was doing. Almost in a whisper, she said, "You know about the baby, don't you?" I nodded. Hannah turned her head, looked out the window and said, "Just the same; no movement." Then, she added, "The boys don't know."

I said, "How does your husband feel about this?"

"I haven't told him yet. I plan to do that tonight."

We were the first to arrive at the church. I half apologized for The Swamp, but Hannah seemed not to mind. Bernie came in next. After their introduction, I asked Bernie how her son's medical practice was doing.

She said, "It's slow. Building a practice of your own is difficult even when you're part of a highly regarded group of doctors. Dr. Hendricks is so well known and respected that most patients insist on him as their surgeon." This admission surprised me. Bernie was such a braggart; she hardly ever admitted things weren't going well, especially where her son was concerned.

Hannah looked hopeful for a second and asked, "What is your son's specialty?"

Her shoulders sagged when Bernie said, "Plastic surgery."

The others drifted into The Swamp and Phoebe and I introduced Hannah to them as they arrived. The meeting went as usual, but when we were ready to close with our prayer, Hannah told the group about her baby, and she asked that we all gather around her and lay our hands on her as we prayed. She recited Matthew 18:20, "For where two or three are gathered in my name, there am I among them." Then she looked at each of us and said, "I need all the help I can get."

* * *

Cynthia's letter arrived on Saturday and I was relieved that I was the one who brought in the mail. I pulled out my shirt-tail and shoved the envelope in my waistband so Stan wouldn't see it. After I placed the other mail on the desk, I rushed to the bathroom and hid the letter under a stack of towels. I hated sneaking around and wondered if this was what it was like to have an affair. It was a feeling I disliked, but still, I found it preferable to being the object of Stan's disapproval and ridicule. Time seemed to slow down, and I wondered if I'd have to wait till Monday morning for the time and privacy to safely see what was in Cynthia's letter. I even considered all the warnings that Stan had given me at dinner, and hoped Cynthia wasn't sending a request for money.

About mid-afternoon, Stan announced that he was taking Ryan out to shop for new shoes. Whatever else might be said about the man, he was a caring and involved father.

I made a glass of ice tea, sat down at the kitchen table and tore the envelope open, The letter was written on heavy, high quality stationery, embossed with Cynthia's initials.

> Dear Abagail,
>
> I'm so sorry that I wasn't able to meet with you again on Friday. I was recently diagnosed with diabetes, and I'm insecure about my medication. On Friday morning, I felt a little strange and wanted to be near my doctor in case something went wrong. He made an adjustment in my medication, and I'm much better now.
>
> I enjoyed the time we spent together and look forward to getting to know you. I hope you feel the same.
>
> My adoptive parents were kind and loving people. They gave me the same advantages as my sisters, but I never seemed to fit into the family. My appearance and my temperament were entirely different. I felt like the ugly duckling and I now realize why. I've been wandering around all my life looking for someone like me, someone who makes me feel I belong.

Even though I had a wonderful husband, a very happy marriage, and many friends, there was still something missing from my life. Ryan and I are close, but he's been living on campus for so many years. He only has one more year of law school and I hope and pray he'll decide to practice in Syracuse.

I don't want to force a relationship on you, but when we met, I felt we had a connection, and I'd like to know more about you and your life. I look forward to hearing from you. In case you'd like to call, my phone number is 315-307-5502.

I read the letter twice and dismissed Stan's suspicions. At the moment, it seemed that Cynthia was without ulterior motives and simply wanted a sense of family.

When we met, Stan seemed to be positive and caring, even fun loving. I wondered what happened to that man, and I asked myself *What changed him? Was I desperate enough to overlook other traits or was it all an act?* The bottom line was: I was stuck. I had no education or training and I couldn't afford to support myself, much less Ryan. I'd have to learn to find happiness and fulfillment with my home, my child and the financial security that I had. I actually envied Cynthia for all the advantages she'd enjoyed including a happy marriage. Even feeling like the ugly duckling would have better than life with our mother or life with Stan. I had mixed feelings about my newly found sister. I was intrigued by Cynthia and what a relationship with her could offer, but depressed because I realized I faced a life of walking on egg shells with my husband.

HANNAH CONWAY

When I told Rob about the baby, he slumped onto the end of the bed, shoulders sagging and head down. After a few moments he looked up at me, and he said, "What kind of doctor examined you?"

"Jim, the hotel manager, called him for me. He did it as a favor…there was no charge."

"You used a hotel doctor. Does he have an office? What kind of exam did he do?"

I said, "He came here to the room and listened with a stethoscope. He said he couldn't hear a heartbeat, and I should see an obstetrician to terminate my pregnancy. I haven't felt any movement for several days." Then, I nodded toward the children, "Please keep your voice down."

Rob ignored my request and his voice became even louder. "And you didn't see any need to talk to me first. Let me remind you, this isn't just your pregnancy; it's our pregnancy; this is OUR baby. Now, we, and I do mean we, need a plan. What do you think we should do?"

"We should pray. I've been praying a lot and the Circle ladies at church are praying for me too."

"So I'm the last to know? I'm last in line behind the manager, a hotel quack and a church Circle."

I hung my head, afraid even to meet Rob's eyes. In desperation, I said, "I'd hoped to feel movement again, that it would all be OK, and I'd never have to worry you with it. I know how much pressure you're under, and I didn't want to add to it."

Rob's expression softened. He slid down to the floor, turned and knelt at the end of the bed. He extended his hand to me and said, "Let's pray together, I'm sure we'll get an answer."

Even though I was exhausted, I continued to kneel and pray. I not only prayed for the life of my child, but for a solution to our housing and financial problems. We had no insurance, and a series of medical bills would leave us homeless or living in my in-laws' basement. I asked myself which would be worse.

Finally, I rose and turned down the covers on the bed. Rob tucked me in, kissed my cheek and said he wanted to read the Bible and would be up a while longer. As I drifted off to sleep, I felt something. It wasn't a kick, but more like the point of a pencil being drawn across the inside of my abdomen. I prayed it wasn't gas and drifted off to sleep.

*   *   *

The sound of the shower awakened me the following morning. I pretended to be asleep until I heard the click of the hotel room door. I drifted off again but when I heard the boys moving around, I knew I had get up. I found a note on Rob's pillow. It was written on the back of an envelope.

3:00 AM

My darling wife, Let not your heart be troubled. We're in the loving arms of our savior, and we call him that for a reason. I just finished reading Mark 11:24 "Therefore I tell you, whatever you ask for in prayer, believe that you have received it, and it will be yours." Now I know that if we just keep praying and trusting in our God, we'll have a healthy beautiful child and you will be fine.

I nearly cried when I finished reading the note. While I fed the boys and helped them dress for the day, I tried to believe that our child was alive, but somehow the Bible verse made it seem too easy. I always thought I'd have to pass some sort of test or give up something else to get what I wanted.

I'd hoped we'd see Phoebe at the park, not just for the lunch she might share with us, but I enjoyed her company. She was such a confident person, I felt that she could make anything happen.

While I watched Peter and Matthew play, I thought about my pregnancies with each of them. I remembered how active Matthew was whenever I ate anything cold, and I wondered if that would work with this child. The memory reminded me of the house we lived in at that time. It was small but the boys had a yard of their own, and I was able to cook for them. Now the tiny refrigerator in our room was just enough for milk and a few other necessities; definitely not suited for ice cream. We mostly existed on cereal and peanut butter sandwiches. The hotel wouldn't even allow a hot plate because it created cooking odors. I craved a good pot roast. I could almost smell the aroma of beef roasting with potatoes, carrots and celery.

By mid-afternoon the temperature was rising, and both boys were slowing down. When they returned to our table, I asked, "Anyone for a Dairy Queen?"

Matthew was jumping up and down chanting, "Dairy Queen, Dairy Queen."

Peter was skeptical, "Mom, are you kidding us?"

I smiled and said, "Let's go now."

It took all the cash I had and I even had to count out my last few pennies to pay for our cold, creamy treats. The boys ordered hot fudge sundaes and I literally went for broke with a banana split. I told myself it was therapeutic.

My sons were on a sugar high and ran the rest of the way to the hotel. I could barely keep up with them. Without a word, hot, exhausted and full, we all fell onto the beds. Peter and Matt quickly drifted off to sleep.

I had barely dropped onto my bed when I felt a good solid kick. I laid still, and a few minutes later there was another. I put my hand on my stomach and waited. Eventually, I too fell asleep.

Rob was standing over my bed when I opened my eyes. I looked up at him and said, "Our child is alive and kicking."

He tipped his head back, raised his arms into the air and shouted, "Hallelujah. Praise the Lord." Then he dropped to his knees and prayed silently for a long time.

The next morning, I felt I needed to call Abagail. She had been so good to me and I wanted to let her know about the baby, but the hotel charged fifty cents for each call from a room. I knew Rob would be annoyed if he saw a charge on the bill so I decided to look for a public phone somewhere.

On our way to the library, I stopped at the manager's office to tell him the good news and to thank him for putting me in touch with the hotel doctor.

Jim ushered me to the chair next to his desk. Strangely enough he didn't seem to share my joy about the baby. In fact, he looked serious and determined. "Hannah, uh… Mrs. Conway……I was hoping we wouldn't need to have this conversation but I think you need time to prepare for a move."

I was stunned. All I could say was, "Shouldn't you be talking to my husband about this."

"I only see him once in a while, and I know you better. If he has questions, tell him to come see me."

The joy I'd felt about the baby kicks drained away, and desperation, my constant companion, was back. I hoped maybe I could talk Jim out of this decision. I began, "The boys are quiet and well behaved. Matt will start school in the fall, and only Peter and the baby will be here during the day." I gave it one last try, "Are you evicting us? Why…why would you do that?"

"The answer is no. I'm not evicting you but you need to understand that guests in adjoining rooms will not welcome a crying baby at night, and I can't ask the housekeeping staff to deal with diapers, baby bottles and baby food jars on a daily basis. They're already griping about the possibility. You're not living in an apartment building. This is a hotel; the satisfaction of all guests is important."

"How long can we stay?"

"When you moved in, I was nervous about having a family living in one room, but as you said, you're all quiet and the boys are well behaved. However, a newborn baby is another thing. You can stay until the baby arrives. I'm telling you this now because I want to give you time to make other arrangements. I'm sorry."

Rob was furious when I told him about my conversation with Jim. He said it was disgraceful that he bothered me with this matter in my condition. I told him I was fine and that we'd find somewhere else. He finally broke down and told me that he was already angry and discouraged because he'd just learned that the buyers of his latest new construction home were getting a divorce and planned to back out on their contract for the house. He said, "I have an appointment with a man at the Savings and Loan Company in the morning to see what we can work out."

PHOEBE FARLEY

A chicken casserole was bubbling away in the oven and a nice salad was tucked into the refrigerator. Each weekday I tried to prepare most of our dinner early so I had time to comb my hair, freshen my face and relax a little before dinner. After the children were settled in front of the TV set, I usually mixed a bourbon and Seven up and sunk into the corner of the living room sofa with the newspaper.

As I unfolded the paper, I saw headlines about an offensive in Vietnam, the start of Richard Nixon's campaign and predictions for the coming football season. The days were growing shorter and by the time I turned the page, I had to turn on a lamp.

An article that took up the bottom half of the second page caught my attention. The headline jumped out at me, PROMINENT DOCTOR SUSPENDED. When I finished the article, I took a deep breath and let out a huge sigh. I heard the garage door open and close, and Jeff walked into the room. I handed him my empty glass and asked him to pour another for me.

He said, "You don't usually go for a second."

"I have something really interesting here, something that demands a second drink. You might want to pour one for yourself and sit down."

Soon, Jeff handed me a fresh drink, sat down in a chair opposite the couch and said, "This must be really big news." I read the headline aloud, and Jeff looked quizzical. "So, what makes that bourbon worthy?"

"This wasn't just any doctor," I said with a hint of annoyance. "It was Dr. Hendricks, the lead plastic surgeon in Bernie's son's practice. A nurse thought she smelled liquor on his breath while he was scrubbing, and as he began the surgery, she was sure he was unsteady on his feet. She reported it immediately, but the patient was under, and it was too late to stop the surgery. Dr. Hendricks was removed, and guess who finished the surgery?"

"That wouldn't be our young Dr. Young would it?"

"Bingo! He's the hero of the piece."

As I handed the newspaper to Jeff, he said, "Let's not be too quick to make judgements about heroes. This could really cast a very dark shadow over the practice and result in a big lawsuit against the surgeons and the hospital. If the partners had even a hint about Hendrick's problem and took no action, they could also be involved. Usually, the hospital tries to protect the doctor and downplay the whole situation just to save their own skin. I'd love to prosecute a case like this."

I rose and started for the kitchen just as the phone rang. It was Abagail, and I could hear the excitement in her voice. "Have you seen today's paper? Do you know about Bernie's son?"

"Just what I read. Do you know anything else?"

As Abigail took a deep breath, I could almost feel the juicy details dripping out of the receiver. "My neighbor is a nurse at the hospital, and she told me that orderlies had to drag Dr. Hendricks out of the operating room kicking and screaming. He was really loaded."

"What about the patient?"

"Apparently, Ben was in the hospital seeing another patient. He stepped in, and my friend says he did a beautiful nose job. All of the support people in the operating room applauded when he finished, and the patient will be just fine."

After listening to Jeff's legal analysis, I had to ask her, "What's the hospital doing about this?"

"Well, you know…a lot of PTA. They're trying to downplay it and avoid publicity."

The timer buzzed, telling me my casserole was ready so I said, "Are you planning to go to Circle tomorrow?"

"Yes, I'm picking up Hannah and the boys. Did you know her baby seems to be OK?"

"Yes, but I wish she'd see a doctor."

There was a long pause, and afterward Abigail said, "In light of today's events, maybe she has the right idea."

During dinner, I asked Jeff, "What does PTA mean?"

He smiled and said, "I can't believe you don't know that." Then, he glanced at the children and said, "I'll tell you later."

My precocious Ariel chimed in, "Mom, I can't believe it either, you should know; it means Parent Teacher Association."

Jeff suddenly had a series of coughs that caused him to leave the table.

*   *   *

Abigail and Hannah were already seated when I arrived at the Circle meeting. The rest of the women drifted in, and we agreed to begin with a prayer of thanks that Hannah's baby was alive and kicking. Suddenly, the door flew open, and Bernie made a grand entrance. She closed the door, leaned against it and put her wrist to her forehead. She had our full attention, and she soaked it in like parched earth in a thunderstorm. The drama queen closed her eyes and said, "Please, please excuse me. I've just had the worst day of my entire life." We all stared at her, but no one said a word. Bernie took her seat and was quiet through the remainder of the meeting.

When it was time for our final prayer, Bernie stood and silently looked at each person in the room. It seemed as though she wanted to make sure she had every eye. As the tension built, I was sure she was going to say something about the incident in the hospital, but she caught all of us off guard. Even I was shocked. "I'm asking that we pray for the Hendricks family." Bernie again closed her eyes during a long theatrical pause and then continued, "Last night, Dr. Hendricks, my son's partner, drove his car into a concrete bridge abutment at high speed and he's...he's gone."

After the final prayer, Bernie took her time before leaving and answered many questions. We learned that Dr. Hendricks and his wife had an ugly row when the doctor returned to his home, and it was then, that he sped away in his car, and Bernie did not know if he was intoxicated at that time. We were told that Ben was taking it all in stride, and he and Dr. Prettyman were doing all they could to preserve the reputation of the practice. Someone even asked if it was suicide or an accident. It was then that Bernie took her leave.

ABIGAIL GRAY

Dear Cynthia,

Thank you for your letter. I was happy to hear from you but sorry to learn about your health problem. I was hoping we could meet again Friday morning to learn more about each other.

If you have more questions about our mother or the little I know about her family background, I'd be happy to answer them for you but, I'm sure you'll understand when I say, it's a part of life I'm trying to put behind me.

I told my husband, Stan, about our discovery and he was skeptical about our connection so it may be a while before I can introduce you to him. I look forward to a time when we are able to meet each other's sons, and I'm even more eager for them to meet each other.

I was a receptionist in Stan's accounting firm when we met. He had recently graduated and was just beginning his career. After a whirlwind courtship, I said, "I do," to a generous, supportive, rather charming young man. It only took a few months before I learned that he was none of those things. I found myself bound to a petty, controlling, egotist.

When I read what I'd written, I put the sheet of stationary back in the box and tried to start again. It was difficult to be honest but not negative, and I didn't want to come off as a self-pitying whiner. My pen never touched the second piece of paper. I was hoping to open lines of communication with

Cynthia, but didn't want to seem like a complainer. I sensed the need to give this letter a lot more thought.

*   *   *

Just then, I was surprised by a call from Stan. He said, "Martin Anacott, the head of the firm, wants to take us to lunch at The Springfield Club. Dress up and meet me at the office at 12:15." I guessed that this invitation had something to do with Stan's earlier announcement that he'd been interviewed for a partnership. I'd been told nothing else and didn't think anything would happen so soon. I started to ask if that was the reason, but Stan said, "Gotta go. I have a meeting. Don't be late."

Luckily Phoebe agreed to pick up Ryan when kindergarten let out. Stan never seemed to realize that sitters were still essential for children Ryan's age.

A crisis of confidence hit me the moment I opened my closet door. I'd heard that The Springfield Club was a prestigious all male club and women were only allowed in the dining room when accompanied by a member. My dress-up wardrobe was a little on the skimpy side, and I looked at every garment twice before I chose a navy-blue linen suit and a light blue silk blouse.

It was then, I realized that Mr. Anacott would not extend such an invitation unless he had an important announcement to make. I was almost sure that Stan had the partnership. But then I thought, *is this just an interview before the final decision? What if all of this depends on me? What if I make a bad impression?*

My nerves were in knots when I walked into the office of Anacott & Associates. Stan was guiding a couple out of his office and into the reception area. He was smiling and displayed all the charm I'd seen when we first met. He greeted me affectionately and even put his arm around my shoulders as he introduced me to his clients. I stood alone in the office as he walked the pair to the elevator, but relaxed a little when Stan returned, took my elbow and said, "Let's go. We're meeting the Anacott's at the club."

Fortunately, the elevator was empty and I asked, "What's going on?"

"Meet the newest partner of Anacott &Associates. This morning Martin told me the board voted me in at their meeting yesterday."

I smiled and said, "Congratulations."

"Congratulations to both of us; this will change our lives in so many ways. I can't wait to tell you what's in store for the three of us." I was shocked at

Stan's exuberance and his readiness to include me in the possibilities for our future. He was more like the man I married, and I wondered which of the two was the real Stan.

Except for the strong smell of cigar smoke, The Springfield Club exceeded my expectations. I was led into a world of deep mahogany paneling, rich leather and highly polished marble flooring. The staff was attentive and extremely efficient.

I'd met Martin Anacott at various company functions in the past, but he seemed to have no recollection that we'd met and treated me as if we were meeting for the first time. I remembered his wavy silver hair and his tall, almost military carriage, but now, he wore a pair of gold rimmed glasses on his straight prominent nose. His wife, Joy, was much younger, at least ten—maybe even as many as fifteen years—and very attractive. I'd say, smart-looking rather than pretty. She was impeccably groomed from the top of her blonde french-roll hairstyle to the toes of her expensive spectator shoes. I was especially impressed with her mostly pearl jewelry. She wore a large diamond wedding ring and on her perfectly manicured hand and a Piaget watch dangled from her wrist. Her three-strand necklace, earrings and brace-let were the creamiest pearls I'd ever seen. She was gracious but seemed as if she wished she were somewhere else.

My appearance was in stark contrast. I wished I'd had time to wash my hair. I usually parted it in the middle and let it hang to both sides of my head. The only makeup I wore was lipstick and I felt drab and plain in comparison.

Mr. Anacott told me to call him Martin and he insisted that Stan and I try the Caesar Salad. He promised, "the best in Springfield." I'd never heard of a Caesar Salad much less tasted one, but I was determined to act as though it was a part of my regular diet.

I covered my surprise when a large black man dressed in a heavily starched white jacket and a black bow tie wheeled a cart filled with a large bowl and several smaller containers to our table. Martin called him Simon and asked him to give his guests "the show." And, a show it was. Simon had a Caribbean accent and handled "the show" like a director conducting a sym-phony. Maestro Simon would have been a more appropriate title for him. He named each ingredient as he added it to the bowl with flair. He began with Romaine lettuce; I thought Iceberg lettuce was the only lettuce and had never considered that lettuce might come in many varieties. I had the same thoughts when Gray Poupon mustard was announced. This was only the beginning of my education in gracious living.

I was concerned about the anchovy paste and tried to conceal my astonishment when Simon held a raw egg high above the bowl and cracked it with his thumbs. Good God, how will I eat anchovy paste and a raw egg without gagging. I was determined to stuff it down no matter what and, to my surprise, when Simon placed the salad before me it looked beautiful and appetizing, and I found that I liked it very much.

* * *

As I drove home, I tried to sort out the effects of this partnership. Of course, it meant more money. Stan always controlled our finances and only mentioned money when he told me to cut back on my spending. I doubted I'd ever know how much more we'd have, or for that matter, how much we had, but I knew we'd be very comfortable. The partnership also meant we'd have the means to give Ryan a really good education, maybe even a prep school. While all these elements were positive, I wondered about the social side of life and hoped there wouldn't be a lot of pressure to join civic organizations and do volunteer work.

So far, in my marriage, I'd been able to avoid doing much entertaining, and I'd used Ryan as an excuse for not doing volunteer work. Even before marriage, I felt inadequate for those kinds of activities and wondered how I'd manage if they were required. Then, the thought struck me, *What if Stan left me for a more socially accomplished partner?*

Even though I'd always thought our relationship was somewhat strained and Stan made me feel uneasy, I was surprised that the thought of losing him was deeply disturbing to me.

* * *

The evening left my head spinning. Stan brought a bottle of expensive champagne home with him and boasted that he'd spent twenty dollars for the finest bottle in the liquor store. Earlier, Stan suggested that we grill steak for dinner. I used the good china, and we ate in the dining room. I told Ryan what had happened, but he was too young to really understand.

Later that evening, when I'd tucked Ryan in, Stan and I finished the champagne in the living room. My husband was all smiles as he said, "This partnership is going to change a lot of things for us. You know, each partner receives a membership in The Springfield Club and The Maple Crest Country Club. This means that we'll need sharper clothes and that broken-down station wagon of yours will have to go. It won't bring much as a trade-in, but I think we need a convertible to give the right impression.

I was shocked. Stan had always been so tight with money I was even hesitant to make a long-distance call. I asked, "Can we afford this?"

With a smug smile, Stan replied, "Oh yes, I'll be entitled to bonuses, profit sharing and my salary will be significantly larger. By the way, I think the first thing all three of us should do when we've joined the club is take golf and tennis lessons.

My eye-hand coordination had never been good. In grade school, I was always the last to be chosen for teams in any sport. Since then, I'd avoided sports that had anything to do with hitting a ball, but because of my height, basketball did work for me. I could see how important this was to Stan, and it concerned me.

While Stan was so willing to loosen the purse strings and even a bit tipsy, I thought it might be a good time to see how generous he might be. I said, "Stan, I have an idea about my car."

"What about it?"

His tone of voice was dismissive. I suppose he thought I was too ill informed to know much about cars and car trading. Still, I pushed on, "You know my friend Hannah needs a car and since ours is not worth much, we could give it to her."

Stan frowned and looked at me as if I'd just suggested we rob a bank. "The car has some value even as junk. What's in it for us?"

"The feeling of helping a worthy human being; Hannah is a nice person, and she and her children are having such a tough time living in that hotel. They're trying so hard to get her husband's business on track. It doesn't matter much to us but would be a Godsend to them."

"Maybe we could sell it to them at a cheap price. Do you think they could pay us something for it?"

"Stan, four people are living in one room. They eat very little besides cereal and peanut butter sandwiches. Hannah's baby is due in a couple of months, yet she and the children have to walk everywhere they go. She's using a midwife for the birth because they can't afford a doctor. How can we ask them for money for an old beater that could fall apart any day?"

Stan seemed to soften a little, "Let me think about this. Let's change the subject. Tonight, should be a happy night for us."

*   *   *

The next morning, I felt somewhat guilty about not communicating with Cynthia, and, since I was feeling more positive about my own life, I thought this might be a good time to begin. I started as I had before but made a few revisions and went in a different direction.

> I've wanted to write to you since I first received your letter, but quite honestly, didn't know where to begin. At the moment, my life mostly revolves around my immediate family and our church. Ryan starts first grade next year, and I plan to take an active role in school events.
>
> I was a receptionist in Stan's accounting firm when we met. He had recently graduated and was just beginning his career. After a whirlwind courtship, I said, "I do." I welcomed the security of marriage to a pro-fessional, well-educated man but often wish I'd found a way to go on to school or to get training that would give me more self-confidence. When I'm with Stan's highly educated business associates and their wives or with my friends, I have a strong sense of inferiority.
>
> Just this week Stan was named a partner in his accounting firm, and he's told me to expect many changes in our lives. I welcome his success for the opportunities that it will afford Ryan, but wonder if I can rise to the challenge. I'm going to need a new wardrobe, and I'm insecure even about that.
>
> By way of getting to know one another, I thought you might want to know that my favorite food is anything Italian, and I love cake for dessert. I've even been known to eat leftover cake for breakfast. I've just discovered Caesar Salad and think it's very good. My favorite TV

show is The Forsyte Sage. I'm not very excited about sports, except for basketball which I played on the varsity team in high school. I don't follow any particular team, but I enjoy watching games. Stan loves the Celtics, knows all the stats and idolizes Bill Russell. Basketball is one of the few things we have in common. We are both tall and I hope Ryan will love the game and play when he's older. I intend to encourage that.

Thank you for contacting me. I hope we can stay in touch and see each other again soon.

* * *

A week later, I was surprised when I heard a horn honking in our driveway. Stan was sitting in a new bright red Mercury convertible. He said, "Get Ryan and let's go for a spin in your new car." Stan slid to the passenger side and indicated that I was to drive. The car seemed to float on air and I loved the way my hair blew in the breeze. Ryan sat in the back seat with a smile that went from ear to ear.

As we toured the neighborhood, I wondered why Stan hadn't taken my car for a trade-in and I hoped it meant we would be giving the car to Hannah. When we were back at the house, I asked Stan about his intentions for my station wagon.

"Not a problem," he said. "I talked to Pastor Printzenhoff, and I'll get a nice deduction for donating the car to the church. The church will then give the car to the Conways. What do you think of that?"

I was terribly happy for Hannah but wished it could have been an outright gift given from the heart. I knew that if I revealed my true thoughts Stan might change his mind. Even though we attended church, and my husband professed Christianity, there always had to be something for him in every act. I tried hard to smile and simply said, "Wow." I told myself *After all, he is an accountant.*

TAMMY CRAIG

The moment I smelled the burning cloth, I knew what happened. I pulled my car onto the shoulder of the road and jumped out. The ash that dropped from my cigarette had burned a hole in my favorite Villager A line skirt. When I watched Jackie Kennedy do a tour of the White House on TV, what caught my attention was the cut of her skirt. I'd longed for a skirt like that, and I cherished this one all the more because it was the last thing Jim bought for me. I wore it as often as I could.

The hole was small, and I hoped the burn would be lost in the plaid pattern of the fabric, but when I inspected the burned spot, I knew I couldn't wear the skirt in public again. I said, "God damn it," and immediately regretted it. After all, here I was on my way to church, and I thought, I need to clean up my mouth if I'm going to hang around with a bunch of "holier than thou" church women. What I should have been thinking was, *I need to quit smoking,* but at that time I'd had all the changes and losses I could handle. I'd been a smoker since high school and I couldn't even think about such a drastic move.

Pastor Printzenhoff insisted that I try the women's Circle as a kind of grief therapy. He told me the members were about my age and were supportive and very nice. I'd been pretty much of a recluse since Jim's crash, and since I was new to Springfield, I spent time only with my in-laws. Once Jim was gone, there was nothing to keep me in Wiesbaden, and the Air Force was extremely generous in moving me back to the States. I often thought they were eager to get rid of me because I was a reminder to other pilots of what could happen to them. The base brass said the cause of the crash was pilot error, but there were lots of rumors. Some pilots suspected that maintenance was the real reason.

My dysfunctional family couldn't cope with their own problems much less take on a grieving widow. On the other hand, Jim was an only child and his parents wanted me nearby. They took me in, helped me in every way and I was relieved to at least have them to lean on.

When I pulled into the church parking lot, I took off my sun glasses, pulled down the visor to check my makeup. When I saw three gray hairs in my black curls, I said it again, "God damn it," and then I gave my cheek a little warning slap to remind me to clean up my vocabulary, at least for the coming meeting. I'd never noticed the gray hairs before and the thought seemed to make my lips look even more pouty.

I wandered around the church for a while, and when I finally found the meeting, I was horrified. The room was God-awful. It was windowless, poorly lit and actually stunk. I was sorry I'd bothered to come and was about ready to leave when a woman approached me. She smiled, extended her hand and said, "Welcome! My name is Abigail Gray." When I told her my name, she took me by the hand, "Come with me, Tammy, I'll introduce you to the members." The women seemed so nice and the meeting went quickly. I learned that everyone had children in the nursery except an older woman who seemed out of place. Since I was childless, I felt out of place myself and, thought maybe I could find a better way to spend my time.

At the end of the meeting, a woman named Phoebe stood up and said, "Hannah isn't here today, and I thought this might be a good time to plan a shower for her. We all know she has so little and caring for a newborn in a hotel room will be difficult. We should do something to make her life a little easier. I could have a shower at my house. We just need to find a date so everyone can come."

All the women seemed to like the idea, but I wondered what kind of person would be raising a baby in a hotel room. It seems that Hannah was nearing the end of her pregnancy, and no one wanted to wait. They decided to have the shower in two weeks. Phoebe looked directly at me and said, "Tammy, can you come then?" I was caught off guard and nodded, but knew I could back out and probably would.

As I was leaving Abigail caught me, "We need your phone number and address for our roster." When I told her my address she said, "That's right around the corner from me. We're neighbors." I was pleased to know that and began to think I might go to the shower just to see what the group was like somewhere other than that green dungeon. *What the hell…it might be OK. I never turn down a party. If I can survive the loss of my husband, I should be able to handle a baby shower.*

* * *

I drove into the garage of my new home with mixed emotions. Jim and I always lived in base housing and this house seemed like a palace. It was by far the nicest, biggest and loneliest place I'd ever lived. My in-laws, Millie and Boots, wanted me to have a nice place to live and insisted on making the down payment for me. I told them it was unnecessary, and that Jim bought a large life insurance policy plus, I received a lot of military benefits. I was amazed when they said it would make them feel better. My own family rarely did anything to make themselves feel good except to drink and fight and the thought of giving a generous gift to make themselves feel better would never have occurred to them.

Step by step, I pulled myself up the stairs to the guest room and opened the top drawer of the dresser. I had to blink back tears at the sight of the hand-made baby clothes and blankets I'd bought in Germany when I still had hopes of having a baby of my own. Now, I doubted that would happen, and I gently lifted the garments from the drawer. I didn't know what this Hannah person was like, but I hoped she would appreciate the clothes meant for Jim's baby and mine. The baby that would never be. I laid them on the bed, closed the drawer and rushed downstairs.

* * *

The next day I had two calls. The first was from Abagail. She once again welcomed me to the Circle and invited me to ride with her to the shower. I had a chance to ask more about Hannah and why her family lived in a hotel. Abigail told me that the women in the Circle believed it was only temporary, and Hannah was a darling person that they all loved.

Then, came the questions about my family. I gave Abagail a condensed version of my life in Wiesbaden and the crash. It was still painful for me to discuss, and I wondered if I'd ever be comfortable talking about it. There was no mention of children. I think, by then, Abigail was beginning to get the picture. Before we hung up, I had a chance to say that I'd come to Springfield to be near my in-laws.

The next call came from my sorority sister, Lucy. We were roommates in college and had always been close. She was a bridesmaid in my wedding but I hadn't seen her since Jim's funeral. Lucy was breathless. She skipped the usual niceties and came right to the point, "Tammy, Tammy, I'm so glad you're home."

I wanted to say, "Where else would I be?" but I just let her go on and she did…on and on and on.

"Have I got a deal for us; it'll be like the good ol' days. There's a big concert happening in Woodstock and we've gotta be there. If you can fly into LaGuardia, I'll pick you up and we can drive together, just the two of us. It'll give us a good chance to catch up. I've taken three days off, and it'll be out of this world. All of the greats will be there: we'll have a chance to see Jefferson Airplane, Janis Joplin and Joan Baez. I've even heard the Grateful Dead are coming. What an opportunity!"

Lucy hadn't married and was still very much a party girl. My military life abroad had left me oblivious to the concert scene and disconnected from many of the activities of my earlier life. I was ready for a good time, and I assumed that Lucy had this planned out. I accepted without asking any questions.

*   *   *

When I got into the car with Lucy, the years disappeared and we were just a couple of girls out for a good time. Lucy had a very promising job in the New York fashion industry, but she hadn't changed much since our college days. Her youthful attitude and interests made me realize how much I'd changed. One of the first things she said to me was, "Don't worry, Mary Jane is traveling with us. She's in the trunk." I hadn't smoked a joint since I'd been married and thought it might be fun to try again.

Miles before Woodstock, the interstate was clogged with cars. People of all ages and descriptions were peeling off the highway looking for parking places in fields, ditches; anywhere they could find an empty spot. I asked about hotel reservations, and as we pulled into a ditch next to a Volkswagen van filled with bearded shirtless men, Lucy said, "There must be motels and restaurants close to the concert. Don't worry…. for now, let's rock and roll." We started off on foot following the crowd. As we moved forward, more people joined until there was such a crush of bodies, I could scarcely breathe. By the time we reached the concert site it was late afternoon. Everyone rushed into the area, and I was surprised that no payment was collected. I was hungry and tired, and I said to Lucy, "Look, we need to think about accommodations. We're going to need a place to stay, food and bathrooms. We'd better look for those things before dark. I'm even wondering how we'll find your car again."

Lucy seemed not to care. She dug into her purse, pulled out a plastic bag filled with marijuana and some papers. "Let's see if we can find a place to sit down and roll this shit. This is really good New York stuff. One joint and we won't even care about those things." We found space near a fence and sat on the ground. Lucy was right…the marijuana was really good shit, and I was high after a couple of drags.

Survival skills kicked in, and I held the joint off to the side. By that time, Lucy was too high and self-absorbed to notice or care that I stubbed out my joint and threw it away. We tried to make our way toward the stage, but the crowd was too dense. I saw some people tripping out on acid and others defecating in public. Everyone I met thought this was the best time of their life, and they wanted to talk about peace and love. Somewhere along the way Lucy and I got separated, and I was truly panicked.

About midnight, I was able to make my way to the stage. I was close enough to see Arlo Guthrie finish his show and Joan Baez take the stage. To my surprise, she was pregnant. I estimated her to be about six months along. I watched her for half an hour, and then tried to find Lucy. Eventually, I realized I'd never find her in that mass of humanity. I was exhausted, thirsty, hungry and my shoes were covered with poop and vomit. I starting to lose track of time and realized I had to get out of there.

Just then a skinny bearded man grabbed me and kissed me. I tried to shove him away but he still held me close; his hot breath was nauseating. He pushed his face close to mine and said, "Hey baby, let's make peace and love together." I gave him a hard knee in the groin. As he bent over, I turned and squeezed through a group of people. Finally, I made my way to the outskirts of the crowd and said aloud, "Tammy, you've got to get yourself out of here even if you have to walk to New York."

* * *

The sun was rising as I stumbled away from Woodstock. A couple joined me and asked where my car was located. I was shaking and when I was able to stop, I told them the whole story. I'd lost my friend, had no idea where her car was. I'd had nothing to eat or drink since my arrival the day before and was afraid of passing out. They had only chewing gum and a thermos of cold coffee, but they offered it to me. I took it gratefully. They were from Newburgh, New York and offered to drive me to the Newburgh airport. I hated the idea of getting in a car with strangers, but they looked fairly respectable and I saw no other option. I fell asleep in the back seat and slept till we were on the outskirts of Newburgh.

I asked the couple to drop me at a Sears or Pennys store. My European travel experience taught me one very important lesson; always protect your passport and papers. Fortunately, the cloth pouch I wore around my neck contained my ID and a good amount of cash. I knew I couldn't get on a plane looking and smelling like I did. Even the store clerks raised an eyebrow and kept their distance. I bought an inexpensive set of clothes without trying them on and took a cab to a Holiday Inn near the airport.

After a hot shower, I changed into my new clothes and walked to a nearby hamburger joint. For once, their hamburgers tasted good to me, and I must have drunk a gallon of Coke. I rushed back to the hotel to change my reservations to return to Springfield via Newburgh and then dropped onto the bed. I didn't even give a thought to Lucy, where she was or what happened to her.

I'd run out of cigarettes just before we smoked the marijuana, and when my high wore off, I was focusing so much on food and water that I'd hardly noticed. I planned to buy a pack at the airport, but I was a little late and had to rush to my gate. The plane was filled with smokers, and I really wanted a cigarette. I thought about bumming one from the woman next to me, but she was smoking Salems and I never could stand the menthol taste.

I rushed through the airport remembering the carton of cigarettes in my kitchen. But by the time I got home, I thought, *You've been without a cigarette for more than 24 hours and you're Ok. Let's see how much longer you can last.* I always felt the need to smoke after dinner but when that urge hit this time, I denied it and instead took a walk. Afterwards I called my mother-in-law. She said, "We've been trying to call you and we were getting worried."

"I've been to Woodstock with a college friend."

"Oh," she said, "I'm so jealous."

I was puzzled and all I could say was, "Why?"

She answered, "Vermont is beautiful this time of year and Woodstock is a quaint and very historic little town. I'll bet you had a marvelous time."

I replied, "It's a trip I'll never forget."

HANNAH CONWAY

It was early morning when Phoebe called to tell me about the shower the Circle was giving for me. The kindness and caring that I'd received from these women was such a blessing, but now, I had to wonder if all of the attention was the result of pity. I hoped not, but still, the idea lingered in the back of my mind.

Of course, I was thrilled at the thought of much needed gifts but almost as excited to see Phoebe's home. I'd heard from others that it was huge, historic and beautiful. I hoped that when I announced the news of my new home to the women, they would no longer think of me as a charity case.

A week earlier, I was deeply discouraged when Rob left for his appointment with the man at the Savings and Loan and couldn't imagine what would happen to our family when the baby arrived. He was gone almost all day, and I grew more worried as time passed.

When my husband burst into our hotel room, he almost scared me. I thought he was angry and had come to announce we were homeless. I was about to learn that his news was quite the opposite. He stood silently and turned his head to look at each one of the three of us. Suddenly a slight grin grew into a full-blown smile that seemed to spread all throughout the room. He picked up each boy and swung him around. Then he stopped; looked at me and said, "God is good. Praise the Lord."

I couldn't imagine what had put him in such a joyous mood when we had so many problems, and I asked, "What's happened?"

Rob guided me to the edge of the bed and sat me down. He explained, "I spent the morning with a good Christian man from Republic Savings and Loan. We prayed together about the house I'm building and we decided, since the divorcing buyers refuse to close on the contract, they automatically forfeit their down payment and their claim to the property. The house is in the drywall stage, but it has a furnace and air conditioning, cabinetry, plumbing and appliances. It still needs woodwork, painting and flooring but, we can move in and live there while I finish the construction. I can do most of the work myself on weekends and evenings. A large payment will be due to the Savings and Loan when I finish, but maybe we'll be able to sell it before that happens. We can stay at least a year."

This news was such a gift; I could hardly believe it and if I wasn't so big, I'd have jumped up and danced around the room. "When can we move in?"

Rob frowned, "Not so fast; I've been thanking God all day and now we need to do that too." He motioned to the boys and we all knelt and gave a lengthy prayer of thanks for this great blessing.

I wasn't paying much attention to Rob's prayer. I was thinking about how marvelous it would be to take our furniture and household goods out of storage. I could finally cook good healthy meals for the boys, and we'd have a real home for our new baby. My prayer was already answered, and I tuned into Rob's prayer in time for the final amen.

Rob stood and said, "I think we need to celebrate and there's nothing better than Kentucky Fried Chicken. Let's go out and we can talk over dinner."

That sounded wonderful, but once again I asked, "When can we move in?"

"How about tomorrow?"

The boys wolfed down their dinners and I have to admit, I enjoyed mine and ate more than I should have. I knew I'd pay with a giant case of heartburn, but I was so happy; I really didn't care. As we finished the meal, I began to ask questions about our new home. I'd never seen the house and didn't know exactly where it was located.

Rob told us, "The house is on Culbert Avenue in a really nice suburb. The school is nearby, and people say the school district is a good one. We're not too far from church either. Let's take a look before dark."

Culbert Avenue curved through a sub-division that looked like the set for a Leave it to Beaver episode. We stopped in front of a large two-story traditional home. If I were shopping for a house, this was the one I would have chosen. Happiness and relief came over me all at once and I started to cry. My tears turned to sobs and I couldn't stop.

When I'd dried my tears, Rob led the boys and me into the house. It was all white drywall. Sawdust and drywall dust covered the plywood sub-floor. There was a beautiful family room with a huge brick fireplace at one end. The cathedral ceiling was wood paneled and accentuated with rustic wood beams. While the boys dashed through the rooms, I could hardly force myself to leave the kitchen. The cabinets were beautiful and every top of the line appliance I'd ever seen was there except for a refrigerator.

We told the boys to choose their rooms, and they scampered off. In the end, they decided to share a bedroom. I think they'd been together so long in the hotel that they were uneasy about sleeping alone in a room. I took a good look at the room next to the master bedroom and could see what a nice nursery it could be. Rob and I agreed that he would finish and paint it first.

Several days were required to clean up the sawdust and drywall dust and wash the windows. Doing heavy work like that was difficult for me, but I did as much as I was able. The boys tried to help, but Rob and one of his employees did most of the work, and as each room was readied, they moved our furniture from storage. It was a house, but not quite a home. Bare bulbs hung from the ceiling of most rooms and there were no doors on any rooms…even the bathrooms. Yet, we all loved being there and happily said, "Goodbye," to the hotel where we'd lived for nearly a year.

*   *   *

A few days later, Rob left for another appointment and told me he might be gone for the remainder of the day. I was so busy putting my dishes in the cabinets and organizing pots and pans that I gave very little thought to what he'd said.

Early in the afternoon, Rob's return was much like the day he announced that we could move into the house. The door burst open and he strode into the house like a general who'd just won an important battle. He shouted, "We need to pray!" Then, he dropped to his knees in the middle of the living room, and motioned for the boys and I to join him. His prayer was not as long as one giving thanks for the house, but it was a prayer of thanksgiving. I guessed that it was once again generated by gratitude for our new home, but I could have been more sincere if I'd known exactly why I was kneeling in the living room in the middle of the day.

A world class boxer seemed to be working out in my stomach, and when I couldn't kneel any longer, I moved to the sofa. Rob ended the prayer and sat next to me, "You OK, Babe?" I nodded. "When I tell you what happened today, you'll be much better than OK."

Rob talked in numbers I didn't understand and names I didn't recognize, but from what he said, I gathered that he was able to borrow enough from a bank to exercise the option on the property we wanted.

I said, "Let's see if I understand what you've said. We have a bank loan and can exercise our option to buy the River View property."

"As soon as the loan is processed, we can close and I can begin developing," he said. "I was even able to borrow a little more than we need for the closing so we'll have money to live on till I can begin excavating for utilities and streets. I want you to buy a refrigerator and a washing machine and dryer right away and as soon as woodwork and painting are finished, you can move ahead with carpet and drapes. God is good. This is better than I'd hoped and prayed for."

The very next day, I drove the boys to Sears in Abagail's station wagon. I realized that without her generosity, I'd be taking the bus. I was so tired, I wondered if I'd even have had the energy to manage a trip like that by bus. The weather had grown cold and it would have been doubly difficult for me.

I'd heard about frost free refrigerators and thought it would be wonderful to be free of the tedious job of defrosting, especially since I wanted a model with a large freezer. I pictured myself storing fresh meat in the freezer and also making meals that I could freeze and heat later. This was such a life changing possibility and so much better for the boys. I couldn't wait!

The salesman had other ideas, and he warned me that frost free was unproven, too expensive and I'd be sorry. I actually had to argue with him and finally threatened to go to a different store. Eventually, I got everything I wanted, frost free, big freezer, next day delivery and autumn gold to match the rest of the appliances.

When I told Rob about the salesman's reluctance to sell me the refrigerator I wanted, he said, "Good for you. They probably have a lot of the old models in stock, and they need to get rid of them."

*   *   *

On the day of my shower, I wasn't feeling well, but I was determined to go no matter what. My best maternity dress was so tight, I wondered how much longer I'd be able to wear it. I was feeling some cramps, but remembered I'd had false labor pains a couple of weeks before each boy was born.

The long driveway to Phoebe's house aroused my curiosity, and I was eager to see what her home looked like. As I rounded a bend, I could see a large, beautiful brick home that looked like a picture in Good Housekeeping magazine. I thought our new home was big and beautiful, but this one was in an entirely different class. Everything about it from the two-story columns to the massive front door knocker said, "Old money".

All the Circle members were there, each with a large beautifully wrapped gift. Chicken salad and blueberry muffins were served for lunch. For dessert we had a cake: one pink layer and one layer in light blue. The frosting was white and trimmed in tiny pink and blue candy baby shoes. Phoebe's china and silver were so elegant; I felt like a princess. During the lunch, I announced our move and gave a brief description of the new house. All the guests were interested in frost free refrigerators and everyone seemed to think it was real progress. As they congratulated me, I could almost feel a group sigh of relief.

When we moved to the living room to open the gifts, the pains that I felt earlier returned. There were so many wonderful things for my baby—some practical, others luxurious—I tried to ignore what I realized were actual labor pains.

After I made an attempt to thank everyone, all the guests left except Abagail, Tammy and Bernie. As they were packing up the presents, I stood in the hallway and felt a very strong contraction and then my water broke. I was standing in a puddle, alternately gasping for breath and moaning.

Tammy had just walked into the hall. She looked at the pool of water around my feet and shrieked, "What the hell?!" Then, she clasped her hand over her mouth, moved closer and said, "Damn it, Hannah, I'm really sorry."

Phoebe said, "We need to get you to the hospital in a hurry."

As the contraction ended, I said, "No, no we have no insurance and can't afford a hospital bill."

Abagail said, "Give me the midwife's number. I'll phone her and she can come here." I had to admit that I didn't have the number with me and then Abigail said, "What about your husband? Where can I reach him?"

Once again, I was at a loss. "He and the boys are shopping for winter coats. I don't know where they are."

Abagail seemed the most eager for some kind of help, and she suggested calling the rescue squad. I protested again even though my pains were coming closer and closer together and I could barely talk. I think the last thing I said was, "There's no time."

Phoebe asked if I could make it up the stairs; I looked at the long curving staircase and mumbled, "I'll try." When I reached the top, I needed Abagail on one side of me and Tammy on the other to make it to the bedroom.

Suddenly, Bernie asked Phoebe if there was a phone in her bedroom. Phoebe nodded and pointed to a doorway. Bernie said, "Take her in there and bring some clean towels," and in typical Bernie fashion she said, "I'll handle this."

PHOEBE FARLEY

When Jeff brought the children home, Abagail, Tammy and I were high on champagne. Jeff sent the children to their rooms and walked around the house. He found dirty dishes covering the kitchen counter tops and an unspeakable mess in our bedroom. The three of us were sprawled in a living room surrounded by torn wrapping paper, "What kind of shower did you have?" he asked.

When I stopped giggling, I said, "One of a kind…believe me; there will probably never be another like it. Sit down, and we'll fill you in." Jeff sat on the edge of a wing chair next to the fireplace and stared at the three of us.

Abagail said, "Hannah went into labor during the shower and there was no time to take her to the hospital. We couldn't find her midwife or her husband and we delivered the baby."

Jeff seemed baffled, "The baby arrived at the shower?"

Tammy explained, "Yes she did, at the shower…in your bed."

I realized that Jeff and Tammy had never met so I introduced them. Then I said, "It was an amazing experience. When we realized that there was no time to go to the hospital, Bernie took over. She called her son at his office and demanded to speak to him. The receptionist refused and Bernie said, 'Listen here, I've got a real emergency on my hands. You tell that son of mine that his spoiled patients can wait to get their wrinkles removed and their saggy jowls fixed. I need him right now!'

Abagail spoke again, "Bernie gave the phone to me and I relayed the instructions to her. Tammy and Phoebe ran around getting sterile towels, scissors and dental floss. Dr. Young seemed to think that the first thing to do was to catch the baby and then lay it on Hannah's stomach. That was the easy part."

Abigail hesitated and I spoke up, "It was incredible. There were just the five of us and then suddenly, there was another life, a real person, in the room; a beautiful little baby girl.

"Dr. Young gave Abigail more instructions and Bernie followed them to the last detail and, finally, the baby began to cry."

Tammy added, "According to the doctor's instructions, I washed her, wrapped her in one of the receiving blankets that someone gave as a gift, and then I placed her in her mother's arms."

I continued, "We finally got hold of Hannah's husband, and he was here with their sons right away. Bernie refused to let Hannah or the baby leave until Rob promised to take them both to the emergency room to be checked out before they went home. Later, Rob called to tell us that they were both in good condition, and the nurses and doctors said we did a good job, all things considered."

Jeff stood up and said, "I'll open another bottle of champagne." We were all silent until Jeff returned and then each of us took turns saying what we liked best about the experience. I was impressed with Bernie; I was not surprised that she was in command, but pleased that she wasn't intimidated by the protective receptionist and stood her ground until she got what she needed.

Abigail said she was amazed at how natural the birth was and wondered why we need hospitals, doctors and nurses. She said, "I doubt I'll ever have another baby, but if I do, I might think about using a midwife."

Tammy talked about how beautiful the baby looked and how much she enjoyed holding her. A single tear ran down her cheek when she finished.

Abigail and Tammy wanted to help clean up, but Jeff announced that he and I could sleep in the guest room and he said, "This mess can wait. Tomorrow morning, I'll stay home for a while and help Phoebe clean up." There was a long pause and then he added, "I'll call a cab for the two of you. You're in no shape to drive."

Our family ate party leftovers for dinner and Jeff and I decided to clean up the kitchen after all. Ariel and Adam agreed to pick up the wrapping paper, but not until they'd wadded every piece into balls that they threw at each other.

While we were putting the good china away, Jeff asked, "What about Tammy? Is she a new member of your Circle?"

I laughed and said, "Tammy is new. She's a widow and she lives very close to Abagail." I explained about her husband's death and her move to Springfield. Jeff made some remarks about her being a character, and I suddenly felt a need to defend her. "True, she has a potty mouth, but she seems like a nice person. She pitched in and did her part to help with the birth even though she has no experience with that sort of thing. I think she'll be all right. She seems to be getting acquainted and making a new life for herself."

* * *

Over breakfast the next morning, Jeff asked me to sit down. I could tell from his tone of voice that we were about to have a serious discussion. He began, "I didn't think last night was a good time to tell you about this, but I had lunch with Gary Nyquist yesterday. You know, he was recently elected to the University Board of Regents."

Jeff needn't have continued. I thought I knew exactly what he was going to tell me and I said, "He's after us again, isn't he?"

"Look Phoebe, this isn't personal. It's not just Javier; it's the entire board and this time they're determined. They want to build a new field house and enlarge the stadium."

"So what, they have enough ground. When they bought that land, they promised my father: no lights, no band practices and no nighttime games."

Jeff began to wring his hands, and I knew there was more and it wasn't good. "The Regents plan to expand the program and there'll be all those things: lights, bands, and night games. They're even talking about leasing the stadium to high schools for Friday night games."

"Did you remind Gary about the promises?"

"I did, and he said that the current administration cannot be held to the promises of long-ago boards. Those agreements were done on a handshake and there's nothing on paper."

"This could destroy the value of our property. We just can't let this happen. Can you take them to court?"

"I'm sorry, Phoebe but there's more. They want the house."

"Well, we just won't sell, not for any price. We can live with the noise and the lights. Why would they want the house anyway?"

Jeff let out a long sigh, "With the expanded stadium, they'll need more parking."

I could feel the anger moving from my stomach to my chest. "They want to tear down a beautiful, historic home for a...a parking lot. We just can't give up and give in. We can ask a king's ransom, some price they'll never be willing to pay."

"Phoebe honey, they're talking about eminent domain. If we don't agree to a sale, we may be in for an expensive fight; one we'll lose anyway."

I looked around the room of the house where I grew up, the home that I loved and hoped to live in for the rest of my life and maybe pass on to one of my children. Living anywhere else didn't even seem possible to me. Now my anger moved up to my throat, and I croaked, "What are we going to do?"

Jeff said, "Let's not think about that now. We need some time to let this sink in, and then we can explore alternatives."

"How long do you think we have?"

"A year at most."

Even before Jeff's car was out of sight the next morning, I picked up the phone and dialed my sister, Marcia's number. When she answered, I didn't even say, "Hello." I blurted out, "He's back. This time it's not dormitories, it's a field house and an expanded stadium and they want our house."

Marcia accepted this with a calm I couldn't match. She said, "Make some coffee; I'll be right over."

I put the last of the shower muffins on a plate and got out my every day coffee cups.

When we'd settled into the breakfast nook, Marcia said, "Okay Phoebe, tell me all about it."

I repeated my conversation with Jeff and added, "Jeff says it's not personal and he thinks it's the board, but I know damn well Javier is behind this just like he's been on all the attempted encroachments in the past."

Marcia said, "Let's think this through and see if we can find some answers."

"Answers, hell. I'd like to storm into his office, meet him face to face and ask him what he's trying to prove."

Marcia leaned forward until her hand was on mine, and when our eyes met, she said, "Phoebe... Sis, you'd come off looking like a hysterical bitch and that will definitely give him the upper hand. Promise me you won't do that." There was a minute or two of silence while we sipped our coffee and ate some pastry, and then Marcia continued. "I want you to think about this very carefully, decide what kind of message you want to send him. Write it out. Keep it logical and unemotional and then memorize it. Someday, probably soon, you'll have an encounter and if you still want to, I hope you'll deliver your message in a calm and controlled voice. Here's one more thing I want you to think about. What if the university president were someone else; someone you'd never had feelings for? Ask yourself, would you be this upset; would it matter this much?"

"Marcia, our romance only lasted a little more than a year. It was puppy love, and he was the one who ended it. I was left with the broken heart, and I just don't understand him. It seems as though he has a vendetta and is trying to extract some kind of revenge. It's a power play."

Marcia suddenly sat up tall and leaned back. When her spine was pressed against the back of the nook, she spoke in a whisper, a voice that I almost didn't recognize. "A broken heart is not the result of puppy love. You don't have to hide your feelings from me." Then she spoke in a normal tone of voice and said, "Honey…Sis, I know it all. Now, here's something you should know. I probably should have told you this long ago but I hoped I'd never have to."

"What is it? What could be such a big deal, and why would it matter now?"

Marcia continued, "The night that Javier stood you up, I was coming down the stairs and I heard Daddy talking to him. I only caught the end of the conversation but I heard Daddy tell him not to see you again….to break it off. What he said was that if it got out that you were dating a boy like him your chances for making a good marriage would be ruined. He said he just would not have it."

Javier asked if it was because he was Puerto Rican or if it was because he was a caddy. Daddy said, 'Look Javier I'm not going to beat around the bush about this; it's both. You and my daughter are from different worlds. You're a nice-looking young man, you're a hard worker and I understand you're very smart. I'm going to make an offer. I'll get you a far better job than caddying; I'll also make sure that you get into a top college, and I'll pay your tuition for the first two years. If you're as smart as they say you are, and if you apply yourself, you should qualify for a scholarship for further education.'

Javier asked if you had anything to say about this, and Daddy pretty much told him that you didn't and it was finished one way or another and recommended he take the deal. Finally, Daddy said, 'Think this over. Here's my card; you can call me at my office if you want to accept my offer.' The last thing I heard was the slam of the front door.

I was stunned; I didn't know what to think, and I was blinking back tears. I said, "You've kept this to yourself for a very long time. Did you ever think I should know some of this?"

"I thought I was protecting you. Your romance wouldn't have worked out anyway, and you might have ended up hating Daddy."

"All this time, I thought Javier had lost interest or met someone else. Here was Daddy trying to protect me, and now, it's costing us the family home; the one where we've lived for three generations. I always thought that since you were older, you'd be the one to live here. I'm grateful that you didn't want it, and I've been able to live here since Daddy died. Of course, I'd be upset if it were another president, but Javier's part in this makes it more painful."

Marcia closed her eyes for what seemed like an eternity. When she finally spoke, she was smiling. "I was happy that you wanted the house and you've loved living here, but you know I prefer contemporary styling. Now…let's think about this place."

I knew my sister well enough to know that she was going to be critical, and I braced myself while she waved her hand. "Look around us. Here we are sitting in a breakfast nook. No one has built a breakfast nook since the nineteen-forties. The kitchen is totally obsolete and then there's that free-standing bathtub with the claw feet."

I shrugged my shoulders but that didn't stop her. "Honey, think about how nice it would be to have a built-in tub and a vanity where you could store towels and toilet paper right in the bathroom where it's needed. I'll bet Jeff would like a shower too."

I knew Marcia was right and tension was building. I could feel a throbbing in my temples as I said, "I don't want to live in a house filled with Danish Modern furniture."

Marcia replied a bit defensively, "You don't have to do that. This house is filled with beautiful, irreplaceable antiques. You can build a house to accommodate them, and it would be stunning. I'd like to take you out to see some of the houses that are being built now, and I'm sure that some of my clients would welcome a chance to show you the interior design work I've done for them."

As a last effort I said, "We could remodel and bring this place up-to-date."

Marcia was growing impatient, "That would cost more than the house is worth. The way it's built doesn't even allow for central heat or air conditioning, and you'd still have radiators and those God-awful window air conditioning units sticking out of every room. Then, after you've spent a small fortune, the university would take it anyway and tear it down. I think they've done you a favor, and I hope that you can see it that way too." Before Marcia left, she promised to line up some houses for me to look at.

By the time I reached my bedroom, the headache was full blown. I looked out of the East window and I could see the cupola on top of the University Administration Building and the windows of the president's office on the top floor. I'd only been in the office a few times, but I recalled that former president's desks had faced the door, but Javier had arranged the room so his desk looked directly at our home. I wondered what he thought each time he looked at my house. I remembered Marcia's comment about the university doing us a favor, and I thought, *Maybe it would be good to get out of the shadow of the past.*

ABAGAIL GRAY

Ryan and I spent the last month of summer at the country club. I mostly drove him to golf and tennis lessons and exercised in the gym while he attended swim team practices. I did take a few golf lessons and occasionally played nine holes with Stan and Ryan. However, I didn't have enough confidence to join any of the ladies' leagues. Ryan was excited about his new friends and enjoyed acquiring new skills. All I seemed to get out of our membership was weight loss and a very nice tan.

When school started my life seemed empty and loneliness was my constant companion. To fill my days, I began to spend more time communicating with my sister, Cynthia. We talked and wrote notes to each other several times a week. I dreaded Stan's reaction to our rising phone bills and was relieved when he said nothing. He seemed to accept the idea that Cynthia was now part of my life, and he'd stopped warning me that she was conducting some sort of financial hoax.

I looked forward to the October meeting of our Circle. I hadn't seen Tammy since we delivered Hannah's baby so I invited her to ride to the meeting with me. The Circle members all knew about the delivery and were eager to hear the details. Bernie held court and described every tense moment. Hannah brought the baby and announced that her name was Faith. She talked about the distress she suffered when she wasn't feeling any movement and said she wanted her daughter's name to be Hope, but Rob thought that Faith was more descriptive of Hannah's pregnancy and delivery. They took a family vote and Faith won out.

After the meeting, I went to lunch with Phoebe, Tammy and Hannah. Since our children were now in school for a full day, this was a new and pleasant experience for us. Faith was still portable and slept the whole time. During lunch Phoebe told us about the university's plan to confiscate her home. We were all surprised that nothing could be done to prevent the seizure of her house. She seemed to have come to terms with the idea and said she had looked at several new homes with her sister and thought there could be some advantages to a move. All they needed was a lot in a good location.

I talked about how long and lonely the days seemed and Tammy agreed. Not surprisingly, Hannah laughed and said her days and nights were so full she had no time for herself, and although she loved her family, she envied us the freedom we all had. Phoebe noted that, except for Hannah, the three us no longer needed a Circle that provided childcare. Her comment was a revelation and it awakened me to the advantages of having a school age child. I realized that if I found interesting activities, maybe I could overcome the loneliness I'd been experiencing.

Phoebe said, "Why don't we play bridge. Think about it…there are four of us and we could play in our homes and say goodbye to The Swamp."

Hannah said, "I don't know how to play."

I had only played a few times and didn't really understand the game. As usual, my self-confidence was lower than the thermometer on a January day. I confessed that I'd had some experience, but wasn't really qualified to play.

Tammy seemed thrilled by Phoebe's suggestion. She announced, "Not a problem; I can teach you. Jim was gone a lot when we were stationed in Germany and I practically lived at the Officers Club. The wives played bridge every day and I sometimes gave lessons to new arrivals. Great idea, Phoebe!"

Phoebe wasn't finished. She tossed this question into the air. "Should we invite all of the Circle women to join us or just pick out people we want to spend time with?" All eyes were on her but no one answered. She finally broke the silence and said, "Well?"

Tammy said, "Oh hell." Then she covered her mouth and said, "Sorry." and she continued, "We have four right here and two of you need to learn the game. If we expand, we'll need four more and a couple of subs. Why don't we just get Abagail and Hannah up to speed and then we'll know if we want four more."

Hannah said, "What about Bernie?" We all just stared at her. She didn't give up and tried again, "It's the Christian thing to do. Maybe she could just be a sub."

Still, there was no response.

Planning went into high gear. We decided to meet every Thursday until Abagail and Hannah learned to play and after that twice a month. Phoebe volunteered her home as a meeting place and said she wanted to use it as much as possible before the wrecking ball arrived.

* * *

On our way home, Tammy and I stopped at a garden store and bought autumn flowers and pumpkins to decorate the front of our homes. Suddenly, I saw the entire day as an expression of my new found freedom, and I enjoyed it very much.

During dinner I told Stan and Ryan about my day. Ryan was excited about the pumpkins and eager to begin carving them. Stan seemed detached when I told him about lunch and our plans for bridge, but when I mentioned the university's takeover of Phoebe's house, I had his full attention. He asked a lot of questions about the Farley's plans; more than I could answer. I was intrigued by his interest and eventually asked why he wanted to know so much.

Stan asked if I'd like a Brandy or a Cognac and suggested that we move to the living room. He even helped me clear the table and he fixed the drinks while I loaded the dishwasher. I knew that drinks in the living room meant a serious discussion, and I suspected that our conversation would be related to the Farley's future move.

He began, "You know Abagail, with my partnership, we'll be doing some entertaining, and we need to project a certain kind of image." I knew this was coming, but hoped it wasn't immediate. It wasn't that I objected to a move, but I dreaded the decorating and the decision making. I also knew that if there were opposite opinions, Stan's ideas would prevail. He continued, "One of my clients is a contractor. He recently bought two heavily wooded acres just across the road from the 15th hole of the country club golf course. There's an old barn on the property that could be torn down. The location is ideal, but he wants more than I can afford, and I think two acres is more than we need."

I said, "What's the property like? Is it flat and how many trees are there?"

"It's fairly flat and was once an arboretum. It's thick with trees of every variety. Some will have to be cut down for a driveway and for home sites. There's a shallow creek that serves as the back boundary of the property. It's the same one that we have to drive across on hole number ten. I've cussed that water a hundred times."

"And, you're thinking we could buy the property with Phoebe and Jeff and both build our homes there."

"Exactly, if you agree. I think the idea would be more acceptable if it came from you. Would you call Phoebe and see if we could set up a meeting with her and Jeff and the contractor in the next couple of days? Abagail, this is a prime piece of property and when word gets out, it won't last long. You know, the news about the Farley's house is like a gift. I thought buying this property was the opportunity of a lifetime, but I just couldn't swing it alone and now...now it could all fit together, hand and glove."

First of all, I was amazed that Stan asked for my agreement, and secondly, that he thought I could carry out something that was important to him. Phoebe wasn't home, but Jeff answered the phone. I took a deep breath and mostly repeated what Stan told me about the property. Jeff was very interested and said he'd have Phoebe call to set up an appointment.

* * *

After school on Friday, our family met with Jeff and Phoebe and their children at the property known as Armstrong Woods. Stan introduced us to Don Carleton the current owner and contractor. The lot seemed huge and so full of trees...big old trees; so many that we could barely walk around. The children loved it and took off immediately. Adam and Ariel knew that a move was in their future, but Ryan was unaware that we were even thinking about a move.

Don led us around and showed us surveys and aerial photos of the area. The surveys made more sense and it was difficult to see anything of the terrain just by walking. The barn was near collapse but gave us an idea of what a building would look like on that land. While the men were talking to the contractor, I said to Phoebe, "What do you think?"

Her brow wrinkled, and she replied, "I just don't know. It's awfully dark and maybe it's just too close to Halloween, but I think it's a bit spooky."

The days were growing shorter, dusk was settling in and I could see her point. We could hear the crunch of fallen branches and dried leaves as the children came running to us. Their shoes were covered with mud but their faces were shining in the dwindling daylight. Ryan said, "Mom, this is the greatest place. There's even a creek here."

Adam chimed in, "Yes, I found a frog and picked it up."

Ariel sneered and said, "I told him he was gonna get warts, but he picked it up anyway."

The men were just finishing their conversation and motioned for us to join them. I could tell that Stan was already sold, but I wasn't so sure about Jeff.

Don told Phoebe and I about an architect that he liked to work with, and he suggested we meet with him individually, and give him an idea of what we wanted our homes to look like. He said, "Mrs. Farley, I know your being forced out of your family home and I think Mason can help you recreate the feel of the house you'll be leaving."

On the way home, Stan asked what style of house I was dreaming of. I said, "I've always been satisfied with the home we have and I've never thought much about it." After a moment, I said, "There is one thing I would like and it really hasn't much to do with the house."

Stan seemed puzzled, "What is it?"

"You know, Robin Hill was the name of the estate in the Forsyte Saga, my favorite books and TV show. I'd like to at least name our house Robin Hill or, even better, give that name to the whole property if Phoebe and Jeff agree."

"That's pretty classy; I don't see why they wouldn't."

I expected that Stan would want something heavy and masculine with rough surfaces like wood and stone. When I asked what he had in mind, I was thrilled with his response. "I want lots of glass… I'd like to bring the outside inside. I can see something sleek and low with maybe a flat roof. There's so much land; I think we'll have room for a basketball court for Ryan."

"Can we afford it?"

"All that and more; things are going very well at the firm."

I always found it helpful to approach sticky subjects when Stan was in a good mood. The strategy worked so well with donating my car to Hannah, I thought I'd give it another try. "Stan, Thanksgiving is just a few weeks away and I was hoping that maybe we could invite Cynthia and Ryan for the weekend and the holiday buffet at our club."

Stan frowned, "You know, we're new there and it's important to have guests that are well dressed and know how handle themselves in that sort of an atmosphere. I don't even know what they look like."

"I've only seen pictures of Ryan, but he looks like an adult version of our Ryan and he is a law student. I imagine he'll know how to behave in a country club and he won't show up in bib overalls. Cynthia is attractive, well-educated and well-traveled. From our conversations, I can promise you that neither of them will be an embarrassment."

"Well, OK. Let's see how it goes."

"It's important for Ryan to have some sense of family. I think it's the right thing to do. Thank you."

"Thank me later, when and if it goes all right."

TAMMY CRAIG

Woodstock was becoming a distant memory for me. It was quickly replaced by thoughts of Hannah's childbirth and the feeling of her baby nestled in my arms. I found I was longing for that feeling again. I wondered what Jim's child would have looked like, and I knew what a wonderful father he would have been.

A phone call from Lucy short circuited my baby obsession and transported me back to that awful weekend at Woodstock. Even though I'd occasionally thought about her, I hadn't called because I thought she owed me an apology, and I didn't want to be the first to make contact.

"Tammy, Tammy," she began, "How are you darling? I've thought of you a million times, but haven't had a minute to pick up the phone." I told her I was fine, and she rushed on just like she always did. "Didn't we have a hoot at Woodstock? I told you it would be the opportunity of a lifetime and wasn't it though? My God, I just can't stop thinking about it, and I love telling everyone all about it. It's rock and roll history, and we were there together."

Just about then, I wondered if we'd gone to the same event. I said, "It was truly unforgettable, and I've been wondering how you found your way back to your car."

"I met a great guy, an architect from Washington, DC, named Butch. We dropped a little acid together; let me tell you that was one hell of a trip. After the concert, Butch drove me around for about half a day till we found my car. He's one hot guy." I asked if she'd heard from Butch or if she was seeing him. She said, "He called to tell me he was on his way back to his parent's home in Colorado, and he planned to stay there. He said that when he returned to DC he'd been fired."

Lucy told me she'd changed to a different fashion house and that stretchy stirrup pants were history. She said she was concentrating on designs for bell bottom pants. I thought, *there's no future there*, but wished her great success.

She said, "Those bells are getting bigger every day."

I wondered if she meant bigger in size or in popularity. I later learned it was both. So much for my fashion sense.

Finally, Lucy came to the point of her call. "Listen honey, Thanksgiving weekend a colleague of mine's got a bunch of tickets to Sammy Davis Jr at the Sands in Vegas. He says sometimes the whole Rat Pack joins him on stage. We've got an extra ticket and it sounds like a blast. Do you wanna go?"

Out of curiosity, I asked, "Are you planning to stay at the Sands?"

She came back with, "You know how I am. I like to play it by ear…not be tied down. We can find a room when we get there; more fun that way."

I politely declined and said I had a commitment for Thanksgiving, and I did. I knew I'd be with my in-laws that day. It wouldn't be exciting, but it was far better than wandering around Las Vegas desperate for a room.

Before we hung up, Lucy said, "You OK, honey? You sound different. You need to get out and have some fun." I noticed that Lucy had no interest in how I found my way home from Woodstock.

Lucy's call was a reminder of the struggle I'd had to clean up my vocabulary and to quit smoking. I'd been so impressed with the Circle friends I'd made. My goal was not so much to fit in as to have the same level of dignity and maturity that I saw in them.

*   *   *

A few days later, I had lunch with my mother-in-law, Millie. First, I told her about the shower, then about Phoebe's house, how big and historic it was. When I got to my part in Hannah's delivery, she was fascinated She asked if I was frightened and I said, "It all happened so fast and I was so busy. There was no time to be scared, but I was awed by the whole thing."

Suddenly, tears started running down my cheeks, and I confessed how much I enjoyed holding the baby, and I said, "I'd hoped to give you and Boots grandchildren and now that will never happen. I'm so sorry."

Millie took a minute, then she said, "Tammy, it's your loss as well as ours, but you're young and you may remarry. There's still plenty of time for you to have a family and if that were the case, I'd like to consider myself a grand-mother to your children."

"That's wonderful, but I don't see that happening anytime soon. Don't get me wrong. I love my house, but it's big and empty. I'm slowly making friends, but they're all married with children. Most of the time, I'm lonely… sad, lonely and purposeless."

Millie said, "Have you ever thought about getting a dog?"

"A dog?"

"Do you like dogs?"

I guess, I'd just hadn't thought about it. We never had dogs when I was growing up. Jim and I moved a lot and saw our future with children, but we'd never considered having a pet. I said, "I doubt I'd want some little Yipper wetting on the carpet and chewing up my shoes."

"Tammy, that's not necessary. The puppy stage is difficult, but you could find a young dog that's house trained and past the chewing stage. I have a friend that works at our local animal shelter, and she always talks about the nice animals they have for adoption. They're not pedigreed, but that doesn't mean they don't make good pets. If you tell me what you want, I'll ask her to be on the lookout for you."

I really didn't know what I wanted so I just said, "Maybe, something small."

Deep down, I didn't want any dog. I hoped Millie would forget about the whole damn thing. *Oh, oh, there I go again…gotta watch that.* I planned to go along with the idea but just not like any possible candidate. A dog is not a substitute for a real live child, and I was slightly miffed that Millie even brought up the idea. I'd thought about getting a job to fill my days, but with a degree in chemistry and no job experience about all I could do was teach. I knew I'd need at least a year in school to qualify for a teaching certificate. I felt stuck.

Millie must have thought that my need for a dog was urgent. Just a few days later she called early in the morning. She began, "Tammy honey, I hope you're not busy today. My friend, Sally, called and she's found a dog that really needs a home. I'd love to take you to the animal shelter to meet this little girl." I wondered if Millie used words like "needy" and "little girl" to lure me in. If that was the plan, it worked, and I reluctantly agreed to go.

Sally greeted us at the front door of the foul-smelling shelter. After introductions, she said, "Tammy, this dog is pure potential. We don't know anything about her. We picked her up as a runaway, and it's obvious that she's had a bad time. We think she's sweet and smart, and she'll turn into a great pet with attention and a good home."

As we walked down a row of wire cages, I thought I should show some interest so I asked about the size, breed and color of the dog. Sally answered, "She's mostly poodle, either gray or black. Right now, she needs a bath and it's hard to tell. I don't know what she's been living on, but she's about four pounds underweight. I'd say she's around a year old—way too young to put to sleep."

At the same moment, Millie and I said, "Sleep?"

Just then we stopped in front of a cage. As she opened the door, Sally explained, "We only have enough funds to keep each animal for thirty days. If they're not adopted by then; we have to euthanize them. I turned and looked into the cage, but all I could see were two shiny brown eyes peering out of a dark ball of fur. The dog was in the furthest corner of the cage and appeared not to be moving. We stepped into the cage and still, there was no movement. Sally walked over to the dog and picked her up. The dog started to shake and tried to crawl out of Sally's grasp. She turned to us and said, "Let's take her into a play room so you can get a better idea of what she's like."

I was not impressed. The dog was all bones, her coat was matted and she smelled awful. Sally put her on the floor and still shaking, the dog crept away from us. We sat on wood benches and watched her for a while. I kept remembering what Sally said about her being sweet and smart, but to me, she just seemed damaged. I also wondeed how I could tactfully refuse this animal. Just then, Sally picked her up and put her in my lap. She was warm and soft and she pushed herself as close to me as she could. Still shaking she turned her head and looked up at me with those dark shining eyes. We stared at each other for a moment, and then she put her head down and rested it on my wrist, her eyes closed and I felt her body relax. Sally rose and came toward us. Suddenly, I felt like I did when I held Hannah's baby. I didn't want to let her go. She was mine.

After the paper work was finished, Millie and I bought supplies in the shelter shop. We left with a collar and leash, dog food, treats and a wicker bed filled with a soft cushion. In the car, Millie held the dog, and it was a struggle because she hadn't much of a lap. Millie ran her hands over the dog's ribs, and then she turned to me and said, "Tammy, before you take this dog home, you need to have her checked out by a vet."

"Wouldn't we need an appointment? That could take at least a couple of days."

"I know a vet who doesn't take appointments. We could stop there on the way home."

We pulled into the parking lot of a small, very plain building. A sign above the doorway said Scott E. Barker, Veterinary Medicine. The waiting room was as basic as the exterior of the building. There was an opening in the wall on which hung a set of plastic numbers. Millie had the dog on the leash and she told me to take a number. Seated in the small waiting room, were two other owners with their dogs. My dog was terrified by the situation. She put her front paws on Millie's thighs begging to be picked up. By the time we sat down, she was shaking uncontrollably. The two men in the room were discussing their dogs. One said his dog needed shots for a grass allergy. The other described his dog's back trouble and the need for muscle relaxants. Once again, I questioned my decision.

When our turn came, an older black man appeared at the window and called our number. I expected to fill out paper work and answer questions, but without a word, he opened the lone door in the waiting room and escorted us into an examining room. It was there I met Dr. Scott E. Barker, a man probably in his late thirties. He had a very short haircut and a military bearing; his face seemed to be chiseled. He had high cheekbones, a taught jaw, a straight nose and a very strong chin. I could picture his face on Mt. Rushmore.

Without a word, he took the dog from Millie and said, "Oh, oh sweetheart, you've had a very bad time. I'll bet you've come from the shelter." The only question he asked was the dog's name, and I had to admit we hadn't had time to give her one. I was amazed at the tenderness with which he examined her. The doctor's voice was deep and resonant and, as he talked to her in words of endearment, she stopped shaking and I was almost jealous.

Finally, Dr. Barker turned to the humans, whom he'd ignored until that moment, and he asked which of us was the owner. I said, "I'm the owner. This is my first dog, and I don't really know how to take care of an animal."

With the dog nestled in his arms, the doctor said, "Besides some malnutrition this girl is in pretty good shape. She has ear mites, but I'll give you some drops for that. She should be spade as soon as possible, George can give you an appointment for next week. You should have her cleaned up before surgery." The doctor handed me a card and said, "I work with this groomer. Use my name and tell them I need this done right away. They'll fit you in. Most poodles have their tales cropped as puppies, and I wouldn't do that to a dog of this age, but since I'll put her out, I could easily do it without a lot of trauma for her. Is that's okay with you?" I nodded.

Dr. Barker told his assistant, George, to get a nutritional dog food, ear drops and worming medication for me. I asked about billing, and Dr. Barker said he only took cash; no billing and no checks. Millie and I both had to dig into our purses to get enough money for his fee. He took a roll of bills as big as his fist from his pocket, wrapped our cash around it and secured it with a rubber band. As we were leaving, he smiled for the first time and revealed a perfect row of pearly white teeth. He said, "This dog will be beautiful. Give her a name to match."

*   *   *

Fortunately, my yard was fenced, and the first thing I did when we arrived at home was to put "Stinky," my new name for her, outside. She immediately took care of her bathroom business which was a great relief to me; probably more so to her. The second thing I did was call the parlor for a grooming appointment. Fortunately, they had time early the next day. Stinky sat outside with her nose pressed against my sliding glass door for the next few hours. I filled a bowl with the dog food and one with water. She gobbled the food down like…like…a hungry wolf.

As the temperature began to drop, I knew I'd have to bring her inside. Her smell was beginning to remind me of Woodstock, and I wondered how we'd survive the night. At bedtime I shut her in the bathroom, gave her more food and water and a pile of towels for a bed because I didn't want her smelling up the cushion in her new bed. She whined for a couple of hours. I finally fell asleep, and for all I knew, she might have whined all night.

Friday afternoon, when I picked Stinky up at the Bark Avenue Salon, I thought a mistake had been made. The dog that they brought to me looked nothing like the dog I dropped off that morning. Actually, the dog they placed on the counter seemed to have no reaction to me either. I asked, "Are you sure this is my dog?"

The woman at the counter looked at Stinky and then at me. She checked her appointment book and said, "Yes, she is, and I'm sorry but we'll have to add an extra charge because of the matting and the condition of the dog's toe nails."

The glamorous dog standing in front of me was coal black, not gray and the hair around her mouth was a bright white as was the hair on each of her paws. Her toe nails were painted a metallic pink that matched the bows attached to each ear. The best and most surprising part was the heavenly scent surrounding her.

Once at home, Stinky again retreated; this time she hid under my bed. I thought she might need to go outside, but I couldn't persuade her to come out. A bag of peanuts came to my rescue. I made a path of nuts from the bed to the back door and left it open. Eventually, Stinky surrendered to the treats and followed the trail. That night I introduced her to her new bed and placed it in a corner of my bedroom. All was well when we turned off the lights, and I went to sleep. However, the next morning, I found her curled up at the foot of my bed.

On Saturday, I realized that Stinky was no longer stinky and she needed a name in keeping with her glamorous appearance. I thought *Boots or the more feminine Bootsy, was descriptive, but since Boots was my father-in-law's nickname, I realized he might be offended.* In the midst of my indecision, I recalled Dr. Barker's advice, "Give her a beautiful name," but I couldn't think of anything that fit her transformation.

By late afternoon, I was looking for some escape or entertainment. Football games were on two of our three TV channels and, when I turned the dial to the last possibility; I was disappointed to hear country western music. I dropped onto the couch in resignation and watched The Porter Wagoner Show. Suddenly, Stinky jumped on the couch and inched her way toward me. I reached out, offered, my hand for her to sniff, and began to rub her back. She laid down next to me and closed her eyes. I looked up at the screen as Porter Wagoner introduced a female singer. The first thing that caught my attention was her mammoth chest. Then, my eyes drifted to her tiny waist and hips. Thick blonde hair was piled on top of her head. I looked down at my dog; her chest was deep and her lower body was very thin by comparison. Next, I looked at the top knot of hair between her ears and the bright pink bow and pink nails. I patted my dog and said, "Hello, Dolly."

HANNAH CONWAY

Our first bridge meeting was challenging. Being with my best friends in Phoebe's beautiful home was so much better than a sometimes boring meeting in The Swamp, but I have to admit, I did miss the prayers and the gospel reading.

Tammy was a good teacher; she knew bridge backward and forward and she was patient when she had to explain rules and strategies more than once. Learning to play was such hard work. I arrived feeling eager and energetic. I left feeling like a wet towel that had been wrung out. Faith slept for the first hour but, after that she was always in someone's arms. The women showered her with kisses and cooing; they even changed her diaper. I could see how much they all loved her.

*   *   *

That evening, Rob was a bit too curious about our meeting. When he asked if we played for money, I told him we were still in the learning stage and hadn't really played a game yet. He asked, "When you begin serious play, will you be playing for money?" I explained that we all agreed to each put in a quarter and the winner would take home a dollar. Rob remarked, "Just remember Proverbs 8:20 A faithful man will abound with blessings, but whoever hastens to be rich will not go unpunished."

I said, "Winning one dollar will hardly make us rich, and as for the hastening part, I imagine it will be some time before I'll be the winner."

I wanted to change the subject so I asked Rob if he knew anything about Dolly Parton. He said, "Yeah, she's some country singer. How come you want to know about her?"

"Tammy named her new dog, Dolly, after Dolly Parton. Abagail and Phoebe thought it was hilarious. I just didn't get it."

I remarked about how much I enjoyed Phoebe's beautiful house and how sad that it would be torn down. Apparently, Rob didn't know about the university's expansion plan. He said, "Hannah, are you sure?"

I said, "Yes, I thought you knew. They have a year to find a new home."

Rob said, "This is God's will. I can build a new home for them on the River View property. What a great beginning that could be."

I hoped this news wouldn't lead to kneeling on the floor and praying, but it did. I even wondered *which of us was hastening to be rich.* Fortunately, I had enough sense to keep my mouth shut.

Rob came into Faith's room while I was putting her to bed. He took her from me, settled into the rocking chair and sang her to sleep. After we tucked her into her crib, he said, "Our baby should be baptized soon."

"Yes," I said, "I've been thinking about that. I'd like to have her baptized as a part of the Sunday service."

"You know, Hannah, the man from the Savings and Loan has been such a help. He could have refused to let us move into this house, and he could have listed it for sale right away but he didn't. He even put in a good word with the banker who loaned us the money to exercise the option on the River View property. He could help us a lot in the future too. I think he'd make a good Godfather."

I thought this was outrageous, and I stomped my foot. Luckily, Faith didn't wake up. I grabbed Rob's sleeve and led him into the hall. "Rob, I want Phoebe, Abagail, Tammy and Bernie all to be Godmothers. They brought this child into the world and they all adore her. They deserve this honor."

"Hannah, you may be right, but she'll still need a Godfather."

I surprised myself with my forcefulness, and since Rob didn't have much of an argument; I pushed on. "No, no, no…especially not some man that I don't know, and who has never seen her. We don't know anything about this man. You got your way with her name and now it's only fair that I get to make a decision. We'll have four Godmothers; that's it…end of discussion."

Rob took my rebellion better than I would have thought. After bedtime prayers with the boys, he said, "You know, I've been thinking about this Godparent thing and you may be right. The baptism will give me a chance to open a discussion with Jeff Farley. If I can get him to look at the River View property, I know I can sell him on the idea. It could be a great blessing...for the Farley's, of course."

PHOEBE FARLEY

It was one of those dark rainy autumn mornings when you'd like to curl up with a good book and a cup of hot mulled cider; however, that was far from my reality. I'd dreaded this day for weeks; the closing day for the sale of my house. I was apprehensive because I knew Javier would be present. He would be in charge and, even though I was resigned to the situation; he didn't know that and would believe that he was in control of my future just as my father once was of his.

Parking was always difficult at the university and, earlier, Jeff insisted that he drop me at the entrance to the Administration Building while he searched for a place to park our car. He said, "This may take a while; it's no wonder they want the house for parking. You're the official owner and you shouldn't be late or wet; just don't let them start without me."

When I stepped off the elevator, I could see the silhouette of a man at the end of a long hallway. It was his walk, really more of a relaxed stroll, that I recognized long before I could see his features. As Javier approached, I began to get that almost forgotten feeling. It was a dizzy tingling warmth, rather like the feeling of finishing a second cocktail without the slurring speech or the loss of balance. He extended his hand and when we touched it seemed like an electric current passed through my fingers and into my whole body. I looked up into his dark eyes and felt sensations I'd never felt with anyone else. He held my hand just a little too long, and I could see the trace of a smile on his lips. The memory of summer kisses and moonlight swims flooded over me; I wanted to forget all that, but I wasn't having much success. I wanted to be angry and business like. I remembered everything I said to Marcia about barging into his office, and I recalled her warning.

Without a word, Javier led me into the conference room and pulled out a side chair next to the end chair of a very long highly polished table. As I sat down, he rested his hands on my shoulders and left them there. When I stiffened, he leaned forward and lowered his head till it was next to mine. Our faces were nearly touching, I could feel his breath on my cheek and he half whispered, "I'm sorry, I still can't keep my hands off of you."

I was already awash with emotion and trying hard to remember who I was, and why I was there. In as calm a voice as I could manage, I said, "Apparently, that applies to my house as well."

Javier sat in the end chair of the conference table, his eyes met mine, and he said, "It's a regrettable situation. You should know that the planning was done by the Regents and the final decision was also theirs. Mentally, I recused myself and neither encouraged nor discouraged the action but, it is my job to carry it out. There's no satisfaction in this for me."

I was so confused, I merely said, "Thank you for telling me that. It's not the end of the world."

Javier then said, "It is the end of my world here in Springfield. I'm doing final interviews as a candidate for president of a much larger state university in the South. I meant no disrespect, and I would never have said those things to you if I thought I'd ever see you again, but I wanted you to know the truth. You did…and do mean a lot to me."

I looked into his eyes and said, "I wish you well."

I was relieved when I heard the door of the conference room open. Javier and I sat silently as people streamed in and took seats around the table. Some were Regents; they sat closer to the head of the table and administrative employees were furthest from us. Jeff was the last to arrive, and he sat across the table from me. He reviewed all the papers as they were handed to him and then passed them across the table for me to sign. As I passed them to Javier for his signature, there was no eye contact and not a word was exchanged yet, the air in the room seemed highly charged, and I wondered if others could feel it.

Suddenly, a bolt of lightning sizzled across the window followed by a clap of thunder that seemed to shake the entire room. I jumped a little, and all eyes were on me. Javier covered my hand with his and asked if I was all right. I assured him that I was. He then stood, looked around the room and thanked all who were present. When he reached the door, he turned, smiled for the first time and said, "We can all say that our meeting ended with a bang." And then, he was gone. The highly charged air that had filled the room seemed to be sucked out with him and was replaced by a vacuum. I could hardly breathe.

* * *

The rain had stopped and it was only sprinkling when Jeff picked me up. "How are you," was his first question?

"Numb," was my answer.

"I hope you can stand one more meeting. Our contractor needs to meet with us. He doesn't want us to be seen in public together so I'm having lunch brought into my office. We can eat and talk both."

"What about Abagail and Stan?"

"They're invited too. Don has also asked if his choice of an architect could meet with us."

Abagail, Stan and Don Carleton were all seated around Jeff's conference table. Boxed lunches and cans of Coke were at each chair. We scarcely had time to say hello before Mason Carlisle, the architect, was ushered in by Jeff's secretary. I liked him immediately. He was a little younger than the rest of us and very handsome in an arty Bohemian way. The job title, architect, gave him a kind of cache that evoked skill as well as an aura of mystery.

Don took over. He seemed so serious, I wondered if we'd need to begin looking for someplace else to build our home. He began, "I've asked you here today because we may have a serious problem, and the purchase of your homesite may pose some unusual and delicate problems. I don't want to alarm you. There is nothing wrong with the ground, the zoning or things of that nature."

Stan said, "Cut to the chase; what's the problem?"

Don said, "The problem is tree huggers. If they have even an inkling that we're planning to clear out a few of their precious trees there could be picketing. TV news coverage and public relations damage to all our businesses."

"Armstrong Acres is private property. Right now, it's my property, but it's also something of a local landmark that some people see more as a public park than private property. Old man Armstrong encouraged people to visit "his trees". Many folks have done that, and it's given them a sense of ownership."

We might have thought that Stan was the attorney in the room as he continued to pepper Don with questions. "So, we have a few coffeehouse beatniks parading around with signs; so what? Bulldozers are bigger than a bunch of long-haired pseudo-intellectuals. This'll give them something to write their poems about."

Don looked up and seemed to consult the ceiling for an answer. Finally, he spoke, "A new international group is forming. The name is Greenpeace and its purpose is to disrupt projects like the one we're planning. They have lawyers, and they'll try to bring their cause to public attention any time they can. There could even be personal harassment. The four of you need to know and understand that before we begin. Mason and I have a plan, and if you want to back out after you hear it, we'll understand."

Jeff said, "Stan, do you want to hear the plan?"

Stan looked at Don and said, "Lay it on us."

Don continued, "Jeff, you need to tell me if you think we're going off the legal rails here. Mason will discuss more with you when I'm finished. Right now, we think you two should form a corporation for the purchase, and I hope that Jeff can hide your names in the corporate documents. There's no reason the corporation can't be named after old man Armstrong; that way, it'll attract less attention. Later, you can divide the ownership and each have fee simple title to your part of the property in your own name. Now, I want Mason to tell you about his part in this deal."

From the time he said his first words, I adored Mason. What I liked best was that he looked directly at Abagail and me, and he included us in his remarks. He began, "The five of us need to walk the property and choose a home-sight for each of you. Later, I'd like to meet with you individually and decide what you want in terms of size, style and shape of your homes. I'll make preliminary drawings that will help determine what areas need to be cleared of trees."

I have a friend in the wood business. He sells firewood, and he has a chipper that creates mulch. He tells me that there are a few black walnut trees on the property. The wood from these trees is valuable. If he can take out the walnut trees and haul away the logs; he'll do the entire removal for no charge. Here's the best part, he understands the situation and the need for privacy. We'll mark the unneeded trees as soon as possible, and he'll bring his people in on the worst winter day to do the cutting. Everyone will be preoccupied with navigating snowy streets, and they won't pay attention to what is happening."

Stan interrupted him and said, "Just how valuable are these black walnut trees?"

Mason seemed prepared for the question, "They're worth much more than, say, an oak or a maple tree as lumber. The wood is mostly used for furniture and valued by woodworkers for small household items. The bad news is, they're a nuisance as part of your landscape. They're considered a dirty tree because they drop large nuts. The nuts are delicious," Mason stopped, smiled at Abagail and me, and continued, "they taste best when combined with chocolate. The nuts are covered with a messy…"

Stan interrupted again and said, "Okay, okay…you've made your point. Move on."

Before Mason could start, Jeff said, "What about the barn?"

Mason said, "Here again, as it stands, it's a nuisance, but it has value. There are people who like to panel their basements with weathered barn board. If you want to use the wood, we can move it to a warehouse. If you have no interest, I think my friend would be willing to trade labor costs for the wood in the barn. You've got time to think about it."

I was drained from the morning meeting and felt like I was on a tread mill. I zoned out for the remainder of the meeting and only tuned in when Don asked me a direct question; even then I had to ask him to repeat it. He said, "Have you discussed your plans with anyone, even your children?"

I said, "Everyone knows we have to move, but I haven't discussed this property with anyone. The children came with us to see the home site, but they don't know that we've made a firm decision."

Don then looked at Stan and Abagail. Before he could even ask, Abagail said, "No, I haven't told anyone we're planning to move, and our son thinks we were looking at the lot for the Farleys."

Don stood and began pacing the room. He said, "We've got two possibilities here that could get the word out; city hall and gossip. Lots of clerks and even officials are in touch with reporters and TV people. That's why we need to keep the Armstrong name afloat and delay the building permits until we've cleared the area for the houses and the driveway. I think you understand the need for discretion, but be careful about what you say around your children. I'd recommend that you look at other building sites...take the kids along, and then you can honestly say you're looking at all the possibilities."

Don seemed to be finished and he sat down. Mason stood and approached me. He said, "Mrs. Farley, I want to see your present home as soon as possible. I know this is a difficult transition and I'd like to see what can be done to make it easier for you. My hope is that we'll be able to have a little fun with it."

I said, "Tomorrow afternoon around 1:30?" That was the moment when reality sunk in. This was really happening, actually it was already over; more over than I could ever have imagined.

"Thanks, I'll see you then."

When the two men had gone, I looked at my box lunch and realized I hadn't even touched it. Stan wanted to stay longer to discuss the plan, but I was wiped out. Abagail said, "I've got to pick up Ryan; I need to go." It was a perfect opportunity for me to leave, and Abagail said she would be happy to drive me to the house that was no longer mine.

TAMMY CRAIG

"Dolly…. Dolly." I said it often; accompanied by a treat. Dolly was beginning to recognize her name. During the week we'd spent together, she seemed less fearful and had put on a little weight. In the evening, when I watched TV, she laid on the couch with her head in my lap, and I surprised myself when I spoke to her in baby talk.

Dolly was becoming my friend, and she broadened my world. On our morning walks we met neighbors who were interested in her, and they began to greet us both by name. I timed my afternoon walks to coincide with Ryan's arrival from school. He and Dolly raced around his yard and wrestled in the falling leaves. They both seemed joyful and watching them gave me a great sense of satisfaction.

When I dropped Dolly off for her surgery, I hoped I'd see Dr. Barker again, but George was waiting for us and as he took her from me. He said she'd be in the clinic for twenty-four hours, and I needed to pick her up before eight o'clock the following morning. He reminded me to bring seventy dollars in cash. Before I left, he asked her name and mine, recorded both on a 3x5 index card and he also asked for my phone number and address.

I hadn't realized how important Dolly was to me until I was without her for a day. That evening, Abagail and Ryan stopped by my house. Abagail said Ryan was concerned that Dolly wasn't there waiting for him when he returned from school. I told him about her surgery and suggested that she might need a day or two of recuperation before they rough-housed again. Ryan offered to walk her on weekends if I was too busy.

Soon after Abagail and Ryan left, I got a call from Hannah. She asked if I would be willing to serve as Faith's Godmother. She said I'd be sharing the duty with Bernie, Phoebe and Abigail. How could I say, "No?" I told Hannah that it was not a duty but would be both an honor and a privilege.

The next morning, I was eager to pick up Dolly. When I arrived at the clinic, George was nowhere to be seen. Dr. Barker greeted me and carried Dolly from the examining room to the waiting room. He told me that her stitches would dissolve, and I needn't bring her back until she was due for her next Rabies shot. I accepted his offer to carry her to the car. He told me he liked her name and cautioned me against rough play for a few days. I said, "We haven't played yet, what kind of toy would you suggest?"

"Just put a knot in one of your husband's sport socks. She'll enjoy tugging on it, and you can also toss it for her to fetch."

I said, "I'm a widow. Is there anything else I could use?"

The doctor looked at my bare left hand and said, "I should have realized, I'm sorry. Try a ball or a squeaky toy."

On the drive home, Dolly crept toward me, stretched out and once again put her head in my lap. I patted her with my right hand and looked at my left hand. I realized I had accidentally left my wedding ring on the kitchen counter that morning and I now wondered if it was time to retire it. For the first time, I revealed my marital state without a feeling of sadness. My status as a widow was suddenly seeming more like a fact of life than a deeply personal disaster.

*　　*　　*

Later, Bernie called to say that the women in our Circle thought Faith's baptism was such an extraordinary occasion we should have a reception for the whole church after the service. She said, "The Circle members are willing to do the serving and clean up but, it's up to us, the Godmothers, to spring for the cake and the other refreshments. Don't you think so?"

I did think so, and I agreed to pay my share of the expenses. That was not enough for Bernie, she continued, "We need to give Faith a meaningful gift to commemorate the occasion. I've done some shopping and we can get an Add-A-Pearl necklace for her. It's the perfect gift. The chain and larger starter pearl is fifty dollars. We can each buy a small pearl for around twenty dollars. This is a great buy for cultured pearls. She can have it forever, and we can do it for around thirty dollars each."

It seemed like a good plan but, I felt as though I were lying on the pavement in the path of a steam-roller and I said, "Yes Bernie, it's a nice idea, but will Hannah and Rob be able to afford pearls to fill it in?"

"No problem, Tammy; we can each give her a pearl for her birthdays and other milestones."

I felt as though I was making a lifetime commitment but, when I thought about it; I realized that being a Godmother is a lifetime commitment and I agreed to Bernie's plan. Then, I said to myself, "What the hell Tammy, break the bank. This is a big damn deal. You're already paying for the reception and the gift. Get your hair done and buy a new dress."

*   *   *

If we'd ordered a gorgeous autumn day for the baptism, it couldn't have been better than the one that dawned on the Sunday of the christening. The air was slightly crisp and a few fluffy clouds floated across a bright blue sky. It seemed that every pew in the church was filled. For his sermon, Pastor Prinzenhoff skillfully wove the story of Faith's delivery into Proverbs 17:17 A friend is always loyal, and a brother is born to help in time of need. The ladies of the Circle and their husbands all sat together. The Conway family and the Godmothers sat in the front pew.

As we all gathered around the baptismal font every eye was on Faith. She was dressed in a beautiful baptismal gown I later learned was an heirloom from Bernie's family. Bernie insisted that Hannah borrow it for the day. Faith was adorable; she was awake, but didn't cry as the pastor poured water on her head, and she watched us all with great interest. I was surprised at how much she'd grown since I last saw her.

As the ceremony was ending, I began to look at the crowd. Of the hundred or more parishioners, I recognized only the members of the Circle and Millie and Boots. Suddenly I focused on a familiar face near the back of the church. I hoped it was Dr. Barker, but he was too far away to be sure. I caught myself wondering if he was there with a Mrs. Barker.

The Pastor organized a receiving line at the door of the social room, and I must have shaken the hand of every one of the strangers I looked at earlier. They were all smiling, offered congratulations and asked God to bless me. By the time I chatted with the Circle members, most of the congregation had found seats and were enjoying the refreshments.

As I looked around, I saw Rob Conway deep in conversation with Phoebe and Jeff. Earlier, I noticed that Phoebe didn't seem like herself; her face was pale and expressionless. I suspected it was strain from the loss of her house and the need to find a new place to live. Abagail and Stan were in a corner huddled over a calculator tallying up the expenses for the reception. Bernie told me that she was on her way to a room where Hannah was feeding and changing Faith. Millie and Boots left earlier to meet friends for brunch.

So, there I was, in the midst of a crowd and still feeling completely alone. I sat down at an empty table with a large slice of cake. I'd filled my mouth with the first bite when I heard a deep voice behind me say, "How is Dolly doing?" I nearly choked trying to swallow. I knew the voice belonged to Dr. Barker and I didn't want to greet him with a mouthful of cake. By the time I'd swallowed and licked the frosting from my lips, he was standing next to me. He pulled out a chair, angled it toward me and sat down.

"Dolly is fully recovered, and we're playing every day." I said.

Dr. Barker opened his mouth to speak, and as I glimpsed those remarkably straight white teeth, I found my heart beating a little faster. He said, "It seems you and your friends did a first-rate job of bringing Faith into the world."

I said, "It was an incredible experience, Dr. Barker."

He responded, "Please, call me Scott and may I call you Tammy?"

"Of course, and if you'd like a piece of cake and some punch, the serving table is just behind you."

Scott said, "I'm saving my appetite for dinner, and I'm hoping you'll agree to join me." I was so surprised; I was at a loss for words. While I was trying to decide what to do or say; I was saved by a beep. The pager on Scott's belt went off. He spent a few seconds checking it out, then he flashed that irresistible smile again and said, "I have an idea. A thoroughbred horse is about to go into labor; there shouldn't be a problem, but I promised the owner I'd be there just in case. You're experienced with birth; why don't you come with me and we can stop for dinner on the way home?"

I looked down at my open-toed shoes and said, "I'm hardly dressed for a barn, and Dolly has been alone too long. She'll need to go out."

Scott said, "We both have time to change. Why don't you drive your car home, take care of Dolly and I'll pick you up in half an hour?"

I was still in shock, and all I could think to say was, "You'll need my address."

Scott said, "It's in my files; I'll see you soon." Then, he turned and walked away.

On the drive home, I asked myself many questions. First, What the hell just happened there? Second, Isn't this happening a little too fast? Third, What do you wear to a horse birth? The last and most important question was, Is there a Mrs. Barker?

*   *   *

Thirty minutes later, I was standing in my front yard waiting for Dolly to finish her bathroom business. I'd changed into a heavy sweater and my new bell bottom jeans. Scott arrived; also wearing jeans and a plaid shirt. He left his car and greeted a slightly skeptical Dolly. When he pulled a knotted athletic sock out of his pocket and offered it to her, she grabbed hold of it, and they pulled and tugged for a minute. Dolly let go, and Scott threw the sock across the lawn. Dolly retrieved the sock and dropped it at his feet. She appeared to be asking for more, but Scott picked up the sock, handed it to me and said, "We have to go now."

The mare was stabled in a barn at the local racetrack. When we arrived at the stall, she was lying in a pile of fresh hay. The owners were anxiously watching from outside the stall, and there was no time for introductions. Scott entered the stall and moved the horses tail aside just as a pair of tiny hooves covered in a white membrane appeared. Scott took hold of the hooves and pulled. The mare began to groan, and suddenly there was a colt in the stall. It was rather like Faith's birth; another life appeared so suddenly. Scott peeled off the membrane, looked up at us, and announced, "You have a nice stallion here. We'll expect a lot of speed from this boy." The owners responded with enthusiastic applause.

I introduced myself to the owners and congratulated them on the birth of their colt. They corrected me rather curtly and said that their baby should be referred to as a foal rather than colt until he was a year old.

I was amazed as I watched the foal reach to lick his front legs. His eyes were open, and his head was erect. Within fifteen minutes he was standing and moving around. Scott examined the foal with the same care and tenderness I saw when he was examining Dolly.

While Scott cleaned up and filled out forms, I continued talking with the owners. They seemed more cordial than before, and I imagined that earlier they were suffering from something like parental nerves. Possibly, their attitude may have been as crass as concern for their investment.

*   *   *

Both Scott and I thought we were inappropriately dressed for a restaurant, and he confessed to smelling a little "horsey." We stopped at a drive-in and ordered hamburgers, Cokes and french fries cut like corkscrews. Before the carhop brought our food, Scott said, "What did you think of the delivery?"

"No doubt about it; horses get the best deal. It's so simple; no rushing around for clean towels or boiling water, and the mare didn't seem to be in much pain." Scott nodded and chuckled as I continued, "Human mothers have to wait a year for their babies to walk and that foal was on his feet almost immediately. It just doesn't seem fair."

Scott said, "You want fair, think about this; by the time a human baby hits the terrible twos, that foal will start to train for racing. Before your Goddaughter, Faith, goes to school, the horse that was born tonight may have earned a million dollars. He's from a very good bloodline and could actually do that. Then in retirement...ohhh, retirement... he'll have a great one. The owners will put him out to stud, and he'll have lots of fun and earn even more money. Too bad he'll be an old man at twenty-five and probably die before he's thirty."

The evening ended with a walk to my front door. I thanked Scott for a unique experience and he promised he'd call to set a date for a real dinner. As he turned to walk away, I said, "By the way, is there a Mrs. Barker?"

He said, "Yes, there is; we've been divorced for five years."

PHOEBE FARLEY

Mason Carlisle, our architect, arrived the day after our meeting exactly at 1:30, as promised. My sister Marcia was already there. I invited her to work with Mason because she knew more about putting a home together than I did. Marcia told me that she'd worked with Mason on other projects, and they worked well together.

Mason brought a camera and several sheets of sticky red dots with him. After he'd greeted us, he handed me a sheet and said, "Phoebe, would you and Marcia go through the house, select the furniture that you like best and means the most to you; pieces that you consider keepers. Put a dot on them and I'll follow you and make notes."

The red dot process evoked so many memories; Marcia and I sometimes giggled and sometimes we cried. We chose about half the furniture. While we were time traveling through the house, Mason was photographing and measuring chandeliers and wall sconces. As we moved through the various rooms, he followed along with his camera and tape measure. When we were finished, I asked Marcia what she wanted. She rolled her eyes and shook her head from side to side till her dark hair flew straight out from her head.

The exercise was time consuming and when we were done, I served hot spiced cider and we sat down at the dining room table. Mason said, "Phoebe, I'd like to make you as comfortable in your new home as possible." He was so handsome, earnest and willing; I found myself wishing I were younger.

He continued, "With Marcia's help, I hope to design a house around the pieces you've selected. I also hope to work with the demolition people and salvage enough brick to build a walk-in fireplace in a family room that I think you'll enjoy. A family room is the main thing this home lacks. If you like the idea, we can open the room to the kitchen so you can be with your children while you're preparing meals. I suspect that this home was constructed with heavy beams and joists. If so, we'll re-finish and install them for exposed beams in the cathedral ceiling of the family room and kitchen and I'll try to use these beautiful light fixtures wherever possible. You'll have the best of both worlds; materials from this house and the latest in appliances and plumbing fixtures."

I loved these ideas and began to catch the vision. I noticed that Mason was drawing on a sketch pad as he talked. When he turned it around, I saw a drawing of a comfortable, welcoming family room that I wanted to move into tomorrow. Having pieces of this house incorporated into our new home put my mind at rest, and I found myself eager to see what else he would propose.

*   *   *

Mason left his drawing for me to study, and I showed it to Jeff and the children during dinner. Jeff loved the idea but changed the subject, "I got a call from Rob Conway today. He wants us to take a look at the land he's developing. He's putting a lot of pressure on us to look, and in light of Don's advice, I think we should do that. I made an appointment for Saturday afternoon. Would you call Stan and Abagail and see if they'll go with us?"

Abagail agreed to take Ryan to his flag football game that afternoon so that Stan could look at the Conway property with us. We later learned that the development was to be called Rainbow Ridge. I have to admit it was beautiful and I could picture a home sitting on the edge of a bluff with a view that stretched for miles beyond the river. Rob Conway painted an impressive picture of what the final development would provide in terms of nearby businesses and recreational possibilities.

He told us that God had led him to that spot, and he quoted several Bible verses that were meant to convince us that he was on more of a divine mission than developing property for profit. He assured us that building on Rainbow Ridge would be fulfilling that prophecy as well as securing a perfect location for our home. In a subtle way, he implied that the loss of our home was divinely inspired so that we could relocate to his property. He even zeroed in on Stan and suggested a move might be in his best interest.

I could see the drawbacks to a home on Rainbow Ridge, but still, I wished that Rob had more to offer than raw ground and a dream. On the way home,

Jeff and Stan discussed the meeting. Stan was irritated with the references to religion in the sales pitch. He said, "Do you really think God comes down and shows property to people? Is he a damn real estate salesman? Give me a break."

What the men mainly discussed was the lack of development in the area. Jeff said, "It would be a long commute for both of us to our offices and our wives would be driving miles to a grocery store or a dry cleaners, and we don't even know about the school situation."

I said, "I rather liked the view and can't rule it out completely."

Stan asked if I wanted to live with a well and a septic tank. He said, "Phoebe, you've got too much pioneer spirit. It'll be years before sewer, water and gas reach that far out of town. He hasn't even staked the land for streets. That guy's just blowing smoke."

* * *

Monday, I met with Mason again and we began to develop a floor plan and talked about how we could execute a scaled down exterior similar to our current home. We worked until early afternoon and I was so satisfied with the way our plan was developing I'd almost forgotten the frustration I'd felt when I first learned about our move.

Immediately after Mason left, I got a call from Marcia. She had that same shrieking sound that I heard when she called to tell me about Mother's heart attack. "Have you looked at your evening paper yet?"

"No, I haven't even brought it into the house. Why, what's the matter?"

"Don't, and don't turn on your TV set either. I'll be there in fifteen minutes."

I wandered around the house trying to figure out what had upset Marcia. I called Jeff's office and was told he was in a meeting; that meant he was safe. I knew that if there were a problem with the children; the school would have called me. I couldn't imagine what my sister was so upset about and why she wanted to shield me.

Minutes later Marcia was walking in the front door carrying the newspaper. She said, "You'd better sit down." I did and then she opened the paper and laid it across my lap. Atop a picture of Javier, the headline was printed in large block letters: UNIVERSITY PRESIDENT KILLED IN PLANE CRASH. The words went through me like an electric shock. Marcia sat down next to me, draped her arm across my shoulder and said, "I didn't want you to be alone when you saw this."

My first reaction was disbelief, and I just stared at the picture of Javier. "No," escaped my lips in a whisper and every time I said it, the volume increased until I was screaming. Then the tears came, and I completely folded up. Marcia put her arms around me and said, "Go ahead, honey, let it out."

When I was finally able to stop the tears and sit up, I couldn't read the article. I knew Javier's final moments would have been filled with horror and fire. I hoped that if there was pain it was brief.

I told Marcia about our conversation at the closing and how snippy I'd been with Javier. I confessed, "He told me about his job offer and now, I realize he was saying goodbye and baring his soul. He was vulnerable, and I was a spoiled inconsiderate brat who didn't get what she wanted. How I wish I could go back and relive that moment. I could, at least, have been gracious to him."

Marcia said, "Look Phoebe, you're in for a very tough evening, but you can't let Jeff or the children see you looking like such a mess. You go upstairs, put on some makeup and use Visine to clear those red eyes. I'm going to fix an extra strong glass of your bourbon drink and line up some things you can throw together for dinner. Think about something else, anything else, until tomorrow morning."

As I turned to start up the stairs I said, "Thank you. What would I do without you?"

Marcia said, "You're my baby sister. I love you, and I'd do anything for you."

Jeff heard a radio report about Javier's death on the car radio. When he came home, we discussed the plane crash as you would the death of an acquaintance or a friend of a friend. I mostly just nodded and agreed with whatever Jeff said.

It seems that Javier was flying in a private plane belonging to an alum of the university that was hiring him. Jeff was shocked that he was leaving Springfield; he said he'd heard it on a special radio report. I tried to show surprise as well and asked about funeral arrangements. Jeff said, "Of course, we'll have to put in an appearance. I can take a day off whenever they announce the date." I'll never know how I got through that evening. I spent a long time cleaning up the kitchen and helping the children with their homework, but I was on automatic pilot.

*   *   *

The following week I found that I had to focus on my children and planning the new house. It was a Godsend. Jeff closed the sale of the Armstrong property and after we had walked our new land with Stan and Abagail, Abagail proposed that we name it Robin Hill. Jeff and I loved the idea and although the robins had flown south for the winter, we were certain they would return in the spring. We each selected the area for our homes and fortunately there was no conflict.

My nights were a different matter. During the day, I played a role, but during the nights, I grieved privately. Unlike the time after Mother's death when I was free to express my sorrow and deal with my sense of loss, now, I had to hide my sadness. I played my last encounter with Javier over and over thinking of what I might have said or done to let him know that I cherished the memories of our time together. I often had to remind myself that I had married a wonderful, handsome, caring man, had two remarkable children and that long-ago feelings and experiences no longer mattered.

Soon, Javier began to haunt my dreams. Sometimes, I would dream about his plane falling from the sky and exploding in a giant ball of flames. Other nights, I would dream about our dates, and I would see us holding hands or sipping a single Coke with two straws. I once dreamt that we were inside an elaborate movie theater. Javier passed through a door, told me to wait and that he would come back for me. I waited and waited, and finally, I opened the door and called his name over and over. When I stepped inside the screening area, I found it was empty. After a few weeks, the dreams decreased, and then, to my great relief, they stopped entirely.

Marcia was my rock during this time. She often spent entire days with me. I feared she was neglecting her business, but I needed her so I said nothing.

The day before the funeral, Jeff announced that he had an important deposition and couldn't possibly attend. He said, "We don't know the family and since we've been at odds with the university there's no real reason for us to go. If you think you need to pay your respects; you could go alone."

I was so relieved. I said, "If I go, it might seem hypocritical. I think I'll pass and we can just send a check as a memorial."

ABAGAIL GRAY

As Thanksgiving approached, Ryan was very excited at the prospect of meeting an older cousin with the same name as his own. I was looking forward to seeing Cynthia again and Stan was a little grumpy about making a trip to the airport early on Thanksgiving Day. He was pressing me to get Cynthia's flight information so I called her early in the week.

When I asked about her travel arrangements, she said, "I occasionally have access to my husband's former corporate plane and since I'll be visiting on a holiday, Ryan and I will have the use of it and be landing at a private airstrip." When I put Stan on the phone to take her directions, I thought I might have to catch him. After he hung up, he got a stupid grin on his face and shook his head.

I once asked Cynthia about her husband, and what I learned was that he was a graduate of Rensselaer Polytechnic Institute in Troy, New York. They met when she was a student at Skidmore Women's College. She told me that her husband and his friend liked to putter and tinker around in their garage. She said, "I don't understand much about this sort of thing, but what I do know, is that they invented a thing-a-ma-jig that made circuit boards work faster and better. General Electric needed the device for their role in equipping Polaris Submarines. The sale made it possible for my husband and his friend to incorporate and produce other inventions they'd worked on in the garage."

* * *

Dressing for the Thanksgiving dinner presented an unexpected challenge. I normally wore a black suit and white satin blouse for special events. After my summer of golf and exercise I found that the suit hung on me. I stepped on the bathroom scale and realized that I was twelve pounds lighter than I had been the last time I wore the suit. I tried on several other possibilities and noticed that my entire wardrobe of dressy clothes no longer fit me.

Stan couldn't stop smiling when he brought Cynthia and Ryan into our house on Thanksgiving Day. Cynthia was perfectly groomed and put together from head to toe, and her Ryan was simply an older version of our Ryan. The two had only to look at each other, and they were instant friends.

* * *

Thanksgiving dinner at the club was way, way beyond what I expected. We were greeted at the door by a couple in Indian attire. Waiters and waitresses, dressed as pilgrims, served complimentary Mimosas and Bloody Marys to the adults and soft drinks to the children. We were ushered to a table with a wonderful view of the golf course. The trees were ablaze in autumn colors, and the setting was picture perfect.

Arrangements of hay bales, corn stalks, pumpkins and gourds were tucked into almost every corner of the dining room. Ice sculptures in Thanksgiving themes decorated each of the buffet tables. Those tables were laden with every imaginable variety of food, and a carving station with ham, turkey and prime rib filled an entire table. We began with an ample selection of salads, proceeded to the main course and were eventually led to a room filled with desserts. Both Ryans chose pumpkin pie, Stan and I opted for the carrot cake, and Cynthia abstained due to her health.

Conversation at the table was comfortable and flowed freely. The Ryans mainly talked about sports. Stan asked Cynthia about her husband's business and he told her about our new property and our building plans. Many friends including the president of Stan's firm, Martin Anacott, and his wife came to our table to say hello. Stan could not have been prouder to introduce his sister-in-law and his nephew to them. One would have thought we'd been a family all our lives. Many people passing by our table remarked about their surprise that we had an older son. I was happy that I at last had a family, even though it was new to me, and we all had a lot to learn about each other.

* * *

After dinner Stan suggested that we take a drive past our new property. Even before we reached the location, I noticed many cars parked along the road. I assumed it was overflow from the club dinner, but as we rounded the curve in the road, we could see a crowd gathered along the edge of our land. The people seemed agitated and some carried signs that read, STOP THE CARNAGE or SAVE OUR TREES. I could see Stan's face getting redder, and I was worried that he would stop the car and confront the demonstrators. I think the presence of Cynthia and Ryan was all that prevented that from happening.

When we returned to the house, the boys changed clothes and went outside to shoot baskets. Stan excused himself to make calls, I was sure he hoped to get in touch with Jeff and our contractor, Don, even on a holiday.

Cynthia and I settled in the living room, and I was pleased to have time with her alone. She was curious about the demonstration we'd seen at our property. I told her about our joint purchase with Phoebe and Jeff and about the warning of possible trouble. I added the strategy to lessen the chances. I wasn't sure how she felt about trees or demonstrations, and she didn't say.

We changed the subject, and each complimented the other's son. How could we not; they were so much alike. I also complimented her appearance and confessed my need for a new wardrobe. Stan had even encouraged me to upgrade my closet.

Cynthia surprised me with an offer that seemed too good to be true. She said, "Abagail, when Ryan and I leave on Saturday we're going to New York. He has a girlfriend there, and I'm planning to do some Christmas shopping. Why don't you come along? There's plenty of room in the plane and you can share my hotel room. It's an opportunity to get to know each other better. I'll make some appointments and introduce you to some of the stores and stylists I use. You'll have to take a commercial flight home but, it should be fun for all of us." I was thrilled with the offer but wondered if Stan would agree to the plan.

Later in the afternoon we went to a theater to see True Grit and ended the day eating soup and sandwiches at home. After dinner, Stan showed Ryan and Cynthia the drawings for our future home and explained our plan to remove only the trees needed for construction.

At bedtime, Stan was still fuming over the demonstrators. He said, "If one of those sons of bitches puts as much as his little toe on my property, I'll have his ass thrown into jail." I had to shush him so Ryan wouldn't hear. Stan said he'd talked to Jeff, and Jeff wasn't worried. He added, "Jeff says it's private property, the demonstrators probably know that and they can legally carry their signs and march back and forth for years, but there's nothing else they can do. He thinks he's hidden our names so well, they'll never even know who the owners are until building permits are issued. When the weather turns cold, they'll tire of standing around with no results."

When Stan had exhausted the topic of demonstrators, I told him about Cynthia's invitation to fly to New York. I was uneasy about approaching him with the idea and didn't know what his reaction would be. I was thrilled and excited that he seemed to think the trip was a good idea, and he even offered to make my return reservation. I was hoping that some time during this weekend, he would say the three little words I longed to hear, "I was wrong." Instead I did hear three unexpected words that pleased me almost as much, "I trust Cynthia."

The luncheon I arranged for Cynthia on Friday with Phoebe, Tammy and Hannah went very well. I had written to Cynthia about Faith's delivery and the christening and she was eager to meet the players in that melodrama. My sister charmed them all.

After lunch, Cynthia asked to be driven back to her hotel. She said she needed to make arrangements for our time in New York and reminded me that we had a 7:00 takeoff the next morning. I was eager to pack for the trip and told her Stan and I would pick her and Ryan up at 6:30 in the morning.

*   *   *

I felt like a celebrity flying to New York in a private plane and staying at a posh hotel. It was my first taste of the Big City, and I reveled in every moment of it. During the flight, Cynthia laid out the plans for our trip. She'd made appointments with her hair dresser, and a makeup artist for the remainder of Saturday. Sunday, we had brunch reservations with Ryan and his girlfriend and later the four of us would attend a matinee performance of the Rockettes at Radio City. Early on Monday we'd meet with a fashion consultant at Saks Fifth Avenue. Cynthia left late Monday afternoon open to shop for any accessories I might need to fill out my new wardrobe and, we'd have a farewell dinner at Tavern on the Green. This was all beyond my wildest dreams, but I was determined to enjoy it all and hoped that Stan would understand.

* * *

Antoine, the hairdresser, referred to himself as a stylist; Cynthia had warned me not to address him as a hairdresser. He was a flamboyant character who called me "Dahling" the whole time I was with him. He didn't resort to flattery even though I would have appreciated a little of it. After he sat me down in front of the mirror, he studied my face and ran his fingers through my hair several times. He said, "Dahling, you need to lighten this drab, mousy hair. Please, don't worry…I'm not going to turn you into a brassy blonde, but we'll add enough blonde to give you a nice glow. I need you to trust me. Can you do that?"

I nodded and he continued. "You need to pull that hair back off your face into a smart chignon. Believe me, Dahling, it will reveal your beautiful face and accentuate that long graceful neck of yours. Your cheekbones are high and prominent and we need to show them off too. I wish I knew what your stylist was thinking when she gave you this look."

I was glad I didn't have to tell him that I only had my hair done for special occasions, and that I went to different salons looking for appointment times that worked for me. Since younger woman were wearing long straight hair parted in the middle, I'd hoped this look would make me seem younger. I should have realized that most of the young women I copied were hippies. I did have the courage to voice my one concern. "Antoine, will I be able to maintain this look without you."

"Of course, my Dahling, you'll need a good colorist to touch you up about every three months, but pulling your hair back will be easy. I'll show you how to tease your hair to give you a little height on top and I'll give you a frame to make your chignon a little fuller. You can even wear a pony tail for everyday occasions, but for God's sake, keep it simple. Don't put one of those fussy ribbon thingies on it. Remember, trust me…you're in good hands." Antoine even spread his fingers and held his hands in front of my face to prove his point.

I wondered about the trust issue when Antoine put something like a tight bathing cap on my head and his assistant began pulling strands through tiny holes with a crochet hook. It was a painful process, but I endured it, hoping for a miracle. When she finished, I looked like a cartoon of Albert Einstein. The assistant first covered the stray strands with bleach and then smeared my head with what she said was a toner that would add a soft color to the now blonde strands.

When the toner was washed out, I returned to Antoine. He swung his chair around so my back was to the mirror and he told me I wouldn't see myself again until the entire transformation was complete. When he finished the cut, he put my hair in huge rollers and sent me to the dryer. As I stood up, I noticed the hair on the floor and on my cape was a very nice color I'd never seen before. Thirty minutes and two magazine articles later, I was led back to the chair, but I was still turned and unable to see my face. Antoine seemed to float around me. As he removed the rollers he oohed and aahed and congratulated himself many times. I was dying with curiosity and couldn't wait till he turned me around. That was not to be soon.

A beautiful young woman appeared, and I was introduced to Sofia, the makeup artist. As she led me away, Antoine said, "Sofia will work her magic and I'll see you later for the grand unveiling."

Sofia also turned me away from her mirror, and as she used foundation, rouge, and several eye products. She showed me each one and told me how to use them. I suspected I'd have to buy them all, even if, I didn't like the way I looked. I thought, Cynthia must think I'm really rich if I can afford all of this and what will Stan say?

Cynthia appeared just as Sofia was finishing. When she saw me, she hesitated and gave me a big smile. I wondered if the hesitation before the smile meant a lack of recognition. Cynthia and Sofia led me back to Antoine's chair. When they turned me around, I gasped in surprise and delight. I looked at Antoine and Sofia and wondered how I'd ever thank them. When I got the bill, I knew they'd been thanked sufficiently. I was so pleased; I sat in front of the mirror for a long time and finally said to the trio, "You mean she's been hiding inside me all this time?"

Antoine was quick to take the credit. "Yes…yes, and it only took the genius; my genius and Sofia's too, to find the real you and bring her out. Now, it's your job not to let her hide inside again."

I have to admit, the afternoon so exhausted me that Cynthia and I ordered room service for dinner. We had a long intimate talk as we readied ourselves for bed and I told her about the inadequacy and the inferiority I'd felt with my friends and how this physical improvement would give me more self-confidence. I still wondered if it would make up for my lack of higher education.

Sunday was like watching a movie on high speed. We rushed from one activity to another. Every time I passed a mirror or saw my reflection in a store window, I wondered who that woman was. I liked Ryan's girlfriend very much, and I think Cynthia did too. I was awed by the Rockettes and amazed at their energy and precision.

Monday morning, Cynthia and I slept late and had a leisurely breakfast. Christina, the fashion consultant was waiting for us at the front door of Saks Fifth Avenue. She ushered us in and led us to a special dressing area filled with multiple racks for clothes and a couple of three-way mirrors.

Our initial conversation was more like an interview. Christina asked about my daily activities and my social life. She took polaroid photos of me front and back, sitting and standing. She measured every part of my body and even asked about my shoe size. When Christina asked to see my wrist, I thought she was going to suggest a bracelet. Instead, she turned my wrist over and tapped on the blood vessels above my hand. She looked into my eyes and said, "You're a Spring…yes, definitely a Spring." I must have looked skeptical because she explained. "I can tell by the blue color of your blood vessels." All of this took a long time, and I was rather disappointed that I'd not seen any clothes. I couldn't have known what awaited me after lunch.

Two hours later, Cynthia and I returned to Christina's dressing room. I'd hoped to start trying on clothes immediately, but first Christina seated me in front of a lighted mirror. I thought, Oh no, more makeup. I was relieved when she began to tell me about my coloring. She said "You're definitely a Spring, now I'll show you what Spring's colors do for that blonde hair and those aqua eyes. Large swatches of cloth were thrown over my shoulders, and Christina stood back and looked at each one. She said, "Can you see the difference? You should be wearing warm colors like camel, peach, golden-yellow and golden brown. I could see a difference and hoped to remember all of this, plus instructions for my hair and makeup.

Christina continued, "To convey authority and power, wear your darkest colors: dark grey and navy blue. Use harmonizing colors or bursts of bright colors like raspberry or a muted orange to accentuate your neutrals. I'll give you a chart so you can always take it shopping with you.

The formerly empty racks were filled with clothes. Shoe boxes and purses were stacked everywhere. When Christina had me undress to my underwear, she was shocked that I was wearing a garter belt and traditional nylon stockings. She made a call and a woman appeared with several packages of what she called pantyhose. They seemed like pants and nylon stockings sewn together. As I slid them on, I realized that they also flattened my tummy. I thought how brilliant; why did I not know about this? Christina advised me to wear matching pantyhose and shoes with each basic dark color. "It will make you look taller and slimmer. Remember, you can't be too tall or too thin and you, my dear, will look like a model when we dress you up."

Cynthia disappeared and what followed was exhausting. Christina had at least two outfits for every activity I'd told her about. I have to admit, the way she mixed and matched was brilliant, and I could combine the pieces in many ways to fit into my schedule. When we'd made our final selections, Christina had another rack brought into the dressing room. It was filled with dress clothes and coats. We chose an ivory silk suit for Stan's company Christmas party, a camel sheath dress for the club Christmas buffet and a red dress with one bare shoulder for New Year's Eve. I selected two coats, a tweed with a fur collar for everyday and a double-breasted navy cashmere coat with beautiful brass buttons for dress.

I'd packed a very small bag for the trip and wondered how I'd get all the clothes home. When Cynthia reappeared, she told me not to worry, they'd all be packed carefully and shipped to my home. I loved my new wardrobe and hated to walk away from it, but I did wear the camel sheath and the tweed coat. I left my, shoes, coat, dress and handbag with Christina. She suggested they be donated to charity. I suppose I might have been offended but knew I'd probably donate the entire contents of my closet when my new clothes arrived in Springfield. Since we'd joined the club, I'd been aware of how out of style I was but I just didn't know what to do about it. In earlier years, I was less concerned and wasn't sure we could afford a change or that Stan would even allow it.

Each evening I'd talked to Stan and Ryan on the phone. Most of my end of the conversation was about New York, and I just casually mentioned the beauty services and my shopping spree. Stan was preoccupied with the demonstrators at our new property. He said that one man had climbed into a tree and pledged to remain there for the entire winter. Don, our contractor, called the fire department. The man was removed and arrested for trespassing. Stan said that Jeff persuaded him not to press charges because it might lead to revealing us as the owners. Stan said the number of demonstrators was dropping, and he speculated that the cause may have been the arrest or colder temperatures.

*　*　*

Most tables were filled and there was a quiet buzz of conversation when Cynthia and I walked into the Tavern on the Green. The atmosphere oozed class and success. The decor wasn't flamboyant or garish but restrained and understated. I was generally intimidated when I entered expensive places like this and tried make myself seem small, hoping no one would notice me. However, on this night, I stood up straighter, raised my chin and walked with a confidence I'd never felt before. In an upscale place, for the very first time, I felt as though I belonged. I had to hold back the tears that were about to flow. All my life I'd told myself, it's what's on the inside, not the outside that really counts. Now, I knew I was only half right…it takes both.

When we were seated and cocktails were served, I tried to tell Cynthia how much her guidance meant to me. She leaned forward and in a very confidential tone of voice she said, "Abagail, all I did was make appointments. I know that you're going to face new demands socially and intellectually, and I hope that what we've done this weekend will boost your self-confidence and allow you to blossom in your new roles."

I confessed, "I don't even know where to begin. I know Stan's going to expect a lot from me, and I just don't know how I'll fit into his new world."

"May I offer you some advice?"

"Yes, I'd welcome it."

"I can see that Stan is very ambitious, but I think he's a good man and he feels pressured because he knows he's a little rough around the edges. It seems he just wants the best for your entire family. Now it's time to realize that his world is his, and it's up to you to create your own world. It seems to me that you're intimidated by him, and you appear to be walking on eggshells when you're with him. Don't be afraid to voice your ideas and tell him about your vision for the future."

Everything Cynthia said scared me a little so I just nodded and tried to look confident. "You've graduated from the mother of a preschooler stage of life, and you need to find interests and activities of your own. I'd suggest that you pick out some charity or institution that interests you and join their auxiliary or fund-raising organization. Go to every meeting, do whatever they need and ask to do even more. You'll be surprised how quickly you'll move up and, along the way, you'll learn a lot of social skills, make important contacts and eventually your name will appear on the letter head as a board member."

I'd always been somewhat skeptical of women's volunteer groups and actually thought that the whole concept was exploitive. I said, "Cynthia, isn't that just social climbing?"

"Of course, it is," she answered, "but it's how the game is played. Just because you understand the game and see the real purpose, doesn't mean that you can't play it. Actually, if you set goals for yourself, your understanding and insight can be an enormous advantage.

If an older more experienced woman takes an interest in you, befriend her and don't be afraid to ask for advice about who to cultivate, who to ignore and what organizations will benefit you the most. This may seem calculating, but remember you're giving your time and your effort and you deserve something in return. As a fringe benefit, when you have authority in another arena, you may find that Stan will relax and you'll have more respect from him."

Over coffee and dessert, I asked Cynthia if she had climbed the ladder. She said she had and had advised some younger women, as well. However, she now found that widows were somewhat like a third leg: uncomfortable and useless. Since she planned never to marry again, she'd pretty much retired from the social scene. She said that connecting to me and my family filled a void in her life and she hoped we'd stay in close contact.

*   *   *

During my flight home I thought about everything Cynthia said the night before. It seemed a bit cynical, but it was a glimpse into a world that I would likely inhabit in the very near future and I planned to take her advice and see where it would lead me.

It was noon when the plane landed and I wore my new oversized sun glasses for the walk down the stairs and across the runway. When I entered the terminal, I spotted Stan and Ryan waiting for me. As I approached them, I could see no look of recognition so I just kept walking. A few feet beyond them, I turned and watched the two of them. As the plane emptied, they started to look at each other and when the crew walked into the terminal, Stan shrugged his shoulders and turned around.

Ryan was the first to recognize me. He shouted, "Mom!" He ran to me and nearly knocked me off my feet with the force of his hug. Then, he stood back, looked me up and down, and said, "What happened to you?"

Stan was still standing in place staring at the two of us. When he reached us, he took me in his arms, stared into my face and said, "I don't know what happened, but I like it." His welcoming kiss seemed more ardent than any I'd ever received from him.

HANNAH CONWAY

Bernie's generous offer of a high chair for Faith was well timed. Faith was already eating baby food and I knew that using a high chair would simplify an increasingly messy process. When I picked up the boys after school, they complained about the long trip to Bernie's house, but when they saw a log home at the end of the drive, they were fascinated. Bernie told us a bit about the history of the high chair. It had originally been used by her son and later by her grandchild. I said, "Ben is still young, perhaps there will be more grandchildren. Are you sure you want me to take it away?"

Bernie turned away for a moment and when she faced me again, her eyes seemed a bit moist. "I very much doubt that. Ben and his wife are separated and a divorce is inevitable."

Matthew and Peter seemed ready to settle into Bernie's house. They examined the log walls, warmed themselves by the fireplace and accepted Bernie's offer of hot chocolate. I have to admit, it sounded good to me too, but the sky had grown dark and I'd noticed a light snow was starting to fall. I reluctantly thanked Bernie and assured her that I would return the chair if she ever wanted it. After we said goodbye, I rushed two unwilling boys to our car.

*   *   *

The snowfall increased before we turned onto the main road. At first, I was relieved that the highway was free of traffic, but after a few miles, our car began to slow down. I checked the gas gauge and found the tank was half full. We had only enough power to make it over the crest of a hill, and I coasted off the road on the downhill side just as the engine stopped running.

I regretted my positive thoughts about an empty road and wondered what to do next.

Here I was stranded in the cold with two children and a very young baby. I thought about walking back to Bernie's house but doubted the boys could walk that far without boots. After a short time, Faith started to whimper, and the boys began to complain about the cold. I tried to start the car again, but the engine was completely dead. When I turned the key in the ignition; there was no sound. Snow was beginning to collect on the windshield, and the wipers were as powerless as I felt.

I was wearing a beautiful white wool winter coat that Phoebe gave me, and I hated the thought of exposing it to the snow, but knew I had no choice. When I stepped out of the car to brush off the windshield, I thought I saw a glimmer of light above the hilltop. The light became brighter, and soon, a pair of headlights appeared.

I realized that the approaching car could bring help, or more trouble or could pass us by. I said a quick prayer; "Please God, send someone good to help us." My heart dropped as the car drove past until I saw the brake lights light up. I watched as the car pulled onto the shoulder and backed up to the front of my car.

When a man stepped out of the car and walked toward me, I felt a strange mix of relief and fear. I calmed down when I saw he was dressed in business clothes and looked quite respectable. He said, "Is there a problem?"

"Yes, my car stopped running, and my three children are getting cold. I don't know what to do."

"If it's all right with you, I'll take a look under your hood. First though, I'd like to try the ignition. Your engine may just be flooded."

"Yes, I'll appreciate any help you can give me."

I stood outside the car as the man eased himself into the driver's seat, and I gulped as I thought *He could start this car and drive off with my children. I was almost relieved when no sound came from the engine.*

The man said, "I'm going to turn my car around so I'll have some light to look under the hood." It was almost dark when he shone his headlights on my car. By the headlights of his car, I could see that he was slender, about five foot ten, he had dark brown hair and wore a pair of gold rimmed glasses. I guessed he was around forty years of age. He raised the hood, pushed some things and pulled on others.

He stepped back and said, "I'm afraid I can't do much here, but I can take you and your children into town."

His voice was calm and reassuring and I felt I had no choice. When I opened the door of my car Faith and Peter were crying and Matt was shaking from the cold. The man suggested loading my family into his car to warm the children. I sat in the front seat of my car and picked up Faith. The stranger reached his arms toward me, and I handed my baby to him. *What am I doing? I'm handing my child to a complete stranger.* I guided the boys to his waiting car and noticed that it was a new vehicle which I somehow found comforting. The new car smell combined with warmth of the car destroyed my defenses. I dropped my guard and tried to be grateful for our rescue. I knew I should be saying a prayer of thanksgiving, but I was too relieved and promised myself I'd do that later. I was certain that Rob would have the whole family on our knees for at least half an hour giving thanks.

Our rescuer took a business card from his coat pocket, handed it to me and said, "Oh, by the way, I'm Hugh Fordyce." I told him my name and introduced him to the children. Before he put the car in gear, he removed his glasses and cleaned the snow off of them. Then, he looked at me, and I was struck by his slender, handsome face and the kindness that seemed to radiate from his eyes. I was embarrassed by my thoughts and hoped I wasn't blushing.

As the car started to move, I looked at his card. At the top, in large letters it said, Fordyce & Douglas. In small letters under Hugh Fordyce's name, it said President. I knew I was in good hands, and I did say a silent prayer of thanks.

A few minutes later, I said, "You're in the car business."

My new friend said, "Yes, my partner and I have a Pontiac and Oldsmobile dealership on Eastlake Boulevard."

I'd passed his business many times and knew that it was large and likely successful. I wanted to thank my rescuer, and I began, "Mr. Fordyce, I'd like…"

That was when he interrupted me, "Please, it's Hugh and no need for thanks. I'm just glad I happened to be in the right place at the right time."

As we approached the edge of town, Hugh said, "There's a small restaurant just ahead. I'd like to stop there for a few minutes. We can get some food for the children, and I can call my agency. I think we should have your car towed before the snow gets any deeper."

I wasn't sure we could afford a tow job or even car repairs, but I felt I was in no position to question Hugh's judgement so I agreed to the plan. Faith had fallen asleep, and the boys were cheering at the thought of restaurant food, a rare treat for them.

Inside the cafe, Hugh told the boys to order whatever they wanted and excused himself to find a phone. Matthew and Peter ordered hamburgers, fries and hot chocolate. I thought they were too extravagant and settled for hot chocolate.

I needed a trip to the ladies room, and I handed Faith to Peter and told him not to wake her. When I returned, the food had been served, and Hugh Fordyce was holding Faith. As I approached the booth, he looked up at me and said, "She's really beautiful."

I asked if he had children, and he replied, "Yes, I have a pair of sixteen-year-old twin girls."

I said, "Twins, that sounds like fun."

"It's been a challenge."

Before more was said, the waitress delivered the check to our table.

During the drive to our home, Hugh said, "I'll have a mechanic go over your car first thing in the morning. If you call after ten, I'll be able to give you an idea of what repairs will be needed to get you up and running again."

The house was dark when we arrived, and I hoped that Rob was late and hadn't had a chance to worry about our absence. I tried once again to thank Hugh for all he'd done for us but, he simply said, "I was glad to do it and to meet you, Hannah."

As my sons piled out of the car, I asked, "What do you say boys?"

Peter said, "Thanks for the ride and the food."

Matthew followed with, "Yes, thank you for rescuing us, Mr. Four Eyes."

There was a long pause after which Hugh laughed and said, "Out of the mouths of babes."

*   *   *

Rob arrived about half an hour after we did. He took the news about our car problem better than I thought he would. However, he was furious that I allowed the children to get into a car with a perfect stranger in the middle of nowhere. "Woman, think about what might have happened. You could all be dead or in another state by now. God was definitely with you."

I was growing tired of speculating about what God did or did not want for us, and I raised my voice, "Perhaps, God sent a good person to help us. The alternative was watching my children freeze to death. When you meet Hugh Fordyce, you'll understand why I was willing to trust him."

"Meet him? Why do I need to meet him?"

"Because," I said, "he had our car towed to his agency, and I'm supposed to call him after ten o'clock to find out what's wrong. I imagine we'll need to discuss repairs and at the very least pick up my car. You might even want an opportunity to thank him for saving your family."

Just then, Peter said to his father, "Mr. Fordyce is nice. He saved us and even bought hamburgers for us."

There was no response.

When we'd given thanks for our rescue and listened to Rob quote related scripture, the children were put to bed. Over soup and sandwiches, Rob said, "The reason I was late was because I was signing contracts for the construction of two new homes at Pheasant Run. My friend from the Savings and Loan referred me to these prospects and, we closed the deals today. God has sent us a really fine friend in that man. I'll be able to make payments so we can stay in this house, and we can even get carpet and coverings for the windows."

Naturally, more prayer was required to give thanks for the new construction jobs.

* * *

At 10:00 Saturday afternoon, our entire family was seated in the impressive office of Hugh Fordyce. I suspected that not all customers with car problems received such treatment. Hugh told Rob that the reason our car stalled was that our fuel pump stopped working. He then showed Rob a list of five or six other things that needed replacement or repair to keep the station wagon running safely. I was shocked when I heard the total amount that was needed to repair our car.

Rob said, "Mr. Fordyce, I have a lot of money tied up in a real estate development and I need to keep a close watch on expenses. I'm just not sure we can put that much into an old car. I can pay you for the tow job, but I'm going to have to consult scripture and pray about how to get transportation for my wife and children."

I couldn't read the expression on Hugh Fordyce's face. He might have broken into a laugh or ushered us out of his office; either seemed like a possibility. I was surprised when he said, "Mr. Conway, bear with me. I have an idea."

He picked up the phone and said, "Marty, please go to the back of the lot and bring that black Buick to the front door."

Hugh leaned forward and tapped a pencil on his desk a few times, then he directed his remarks toward Rob. "Occasionally I have a car that I can't put on the lot. For several months, we've been storing a sedan with hail damage. The car has low mileage and is in good mechanical shape; even has air conditioning. Repairing all the body damage would cost more than the car is worth. The coach top has no dents and only the hood and trunk are damaged, but dents don't show much on the black paint. With your car as a trade-in, I could sell it to you for little more than the cost of the repairs on your car, and we can set up a comfortable payment plan that will cover the difference."

For once Rob had nothing to say. He sat in silence staring at the wall. Hugh stood, walked to me and said, "Mrs. Conway, I want you to take the children on a test drive. My sales manager will go with you; if you like the way the car handles, Mr. Conway and I will see what we can do." I handed a sleeping Faith to Rob. Hugh Fordyce motioned to the children to follow, took my elbow and escorted me to the front of the dealership. On the way, he reminded me to call him Hugh.

The car drove like a dream, but what I noticed and liked most was that Hugh opened the car door and moved the seat forward till it was just right for me. One would have thought I bought a new car from him every year.

When we returned to the agency, Rob and Hugh were standing inside the front door. Faith was crying, and Rob was trying to sooth her. Hugh was the first to step outside. He opened the door and took my arm as I stepped out of the car. "Drive all right?" he asked.

"Like a dream," I answered, "but I'm not sure…"

Hugh cut me off, "Your husband and I have made a deal, and all we need is your approval."

My opinion never mattered much to Rob, and I was dumbfounded that he was willing to accept my judgement about such an expense. I was hoping we could drive the car home, but Hugh wanted to keep it for a couple of days to clean it up and make sure it was running right.

On the drive home, I learned why Rob was so agreeable about the car and why he had such a smile after my test drive. He said, "God was surely working his wonders for us when you were stalled in the snow."

I said, "What do you mean? That was a terrifying experience."

Rob grinned and said, "Look how well it all turned out. We have a dependable car for you at a reasonable price, and I've got a prospect for Rainbow Ridge."

I wondered why Hugh Fordyce would want a new home miles from his agency, and I asked for an explanation.

Rob said, "I thought Fordyce might be a prospect for a home, but he said his daughters love their school, and he can't even think of moving them. He does like to invest in real estate and agreed to take a look at our property. I'm meeting him there next Friday."

* * *

Time slowed to a crawl as I looked forward to the Thursday bridge game with my friends. I had so much to tell them, and I always enjoyed time spent in Phoebe's house. My new Buick took the curves in their drive smoothly, and I was eager to surprise the girls with my new car and to tell them about the strange circumstances that led to the trade. I was unaware of how many surprises were awaiting me that afternoon.

The first shock came when I walked in the front door of the Farley house. Many pieces of furniture were missing, the wallpaper had faded spots where artwork and mirrors had hung and some light fixtures were gone. Apparently, the furnishings and accessories covered a multitude of flaws. The worn wood-work, the aging carpet and the cracks in the plaster were all uncovered. Even the drapes were shredded from sun damage. The home reminded me of a once beautiful woman standing in a spotlight with her face wrinkled and worn by age. Phoebe met me at the front door with, "Welcome to my mess."

I did a three-sixty turn in the foyer, looked up at the peeling paint on the ceiling and said, "I can't believe the change. This home was so beautiful."

As Phoebe led me to the living room, she explained. "I hadn't realized what bad shape this place was in and seeing it like this is probably a good thing. I now know that a change is needed, and I'm ready to go."

Abagail was the next to arrive, and I had to do a double take. I barely recognized her. Whatever beauty Phoebe's house had lost seemed to have been bestowed on Abagail. It wasn't just the physical changes, it was her clothes and the way she wore them; the way she carried herself. She looked like an entirely different person, and it was apparent that the tale of her transformation would be of far more interest than how I acquired my new car.

Phoebe wasn't surprised, and I assumed she'd seen Abagail since Thanksgiving. Tammy was the last to arrive and when she saw Abagail, she squealed, hugged her and said, "Well, I'll be damned."

No bridge was played that afternoon, and as we all gathered around the fireplace, Phoebe struck a match and announced that this fire would be the last in her living room.

All eyes were on Abagail as she recounted the details of her trip to New York and all of the wonderful beauty services Cynthia had arranged for her. There were many questions, but the most interesting was about Stan's reaction. Abagail smiled and said, "He loves my look, but in some ways, he treats me like we're dating. I don't think he's quite sure I'm the same person. He's so polite and thoughtful, and he wants to take me out all the time. Who could have guessed that a hair style and makeup would make such a difference?"

Eventually we got around to discussing my new car. I started with my trip to Bernie's house and talked about the station wagon stalling in the snow. When I got to the part about my rescue, there were a few audible gasps and open mouths.

Phoebe said, "You got to spend time with Hugh Fordyce. Lucky you! He's so handsome; most women in Springfield would gladly get stranded in a blizzard just to spend five minutes with him. He's…"

Abigail interrupted her, "It's such a shame about his wife, and there he is, trying to raise two girls by himself."

I was amazed by these comments and asked, "What about his wife?"

Abagail spoke again, "People at the club talk about her all the time. She was very well liked; even loved. Two years ago, she was involved in a terrible car crash, and now she's a vegetable. He put her in some sort of institution on the edge of town. They say there's no hope for recovery."

I had to ask, "Is the institution near Bernie's house?"

Phoebe said, "Yes, I guess it is. I think it's just a couple miles beyond the turn off to Bernie's.

I said nothing, but this answered a question for me. I'd been wondering why Hugh was on a lonely road in a snowstorm. I now guessed that he was returning from a visit to his wife.

Tammy seemed to come to life and remarked, "A handsome, successful and caring man who may be lonely and in need of companionship; maybe I should think about buying a new car."

That comment was not well received and there was an embarrassing silence in the room. I was more than a little surprised by my reaction. It was a deep gut level howl. It snuck up on me and screamed from somewhere deep inside, *Hands off, Tammy. I found him and he's mine. You have no right to him.* This thought shook me to my core, and I wondered why a married Christian mother would even have such thoughts.

Phoebe finally, broke the spell and said, "Tammy, I thought you were dating Scott Barker."

Tammy said, "I'm trying to gradually distance myself from him. It's just not working out."

Abagail wasn't satisfied with that answer and pressed Tammy for more.

Tammy said, "All our dates have to do with animals. Mostly, we go to a barn to watch the colt he delivered being trained. Our most interesting date was a dog show. I'd occasionally like to see a play or go to a concert; even a movie would be welcome."

"What about dinner," I asked, "does he feed you?"

"Usually, we just stop for hamburgers. Our most extravagant meal was at Barbie Q Ribs. All the waitresses look like Barbie dolls and wear roller skates. I can tell you, there's no romance in a joint like that.

Abagail said, "Can't you just say no or tell him what you want to do?"

"He's very insistent, and he kind of disguises the invite. He wants us to be together, then there's always a reason that we end up with animals. Just like

our first date when he asked me to dinner and he needed to deliver a colt…
excuse me, a foal. I was severely criticized for that misstatement."

My curiosity got the best of me, and I asked, "What about sex?" Everyone
looked shocked and stared at me. I could tell they all wanted to know, but
were afraid to ask.

Tammy said, "Scott once suggested we go to a horse breeding. I let him
know there was no way that was gonna happen. Afterward, I wondered if
that was his idea of foreplay. Anyway, there've been a few good night kisses,
but that's about it."

We all advised Tammy to shop around for male company. All the while,
my gut was speaking again, *Not Hugh, please not him.*

As our conversation was winding down, Phoebe left the room and
returned with cards that had each of our names written on them. She looked
at each of us before she spoke. "I won't have space in our new home for all
this furniture, and I'd like each of you to pick out something you like and put
your name on it. The pieces with red dots are what I'm keeping, but the rest
is up for grabs."

We all thought Phoebe might regret the offer and tried to persuade her
to keep all her heirlooms, but she insisted. "Of course, I'll miss some of the
things I've lived with all my life, but I want to know that they're with people
who'll appreciate and care for them. When I visit your homes, I'll get to see
and enjoy them in a different setting."

Phoebe made her point, and we drifted around the house inspecting different pieces of furniture. Abagail was the first to choose a piece, and she
placed her name on a simple marble pedestal. Next, Tammy chose a square
cocktail table with an inlaid burled top.

I couldn't take my eyes off of a large walnut bookcase. I looked and looked
for a red dot but couldn't find one. Phoebe came and stood alongside me. She
put her arm around my waist and said, "You like it don't you?"

I tipped my head onto her shoulder and replied, "I love it, but it's just too
much." The piece was quite tall. The ends were finished with fluted columns
and a pediment with a carved shell motif was mounted on the top. I could
picture it on a long wall in our living room and knew it would be perfect and
we could never afford anything like it for our home.

Finally, Phoebe took the card from my hand and laid it on a shelf. "It's yours."

Holding back the tears, I threw my arms around her neck and whispered, "We hardly have any books."

Phoebe stood back and said, "No problem, we have an attic full of books. I can pretty much fill up the whole thing for you."

Tammy, Abagail and I were almost floating as we approached the front door. I told them that Rob could have some of his employees use a company truck to move the pieces and deliver them to each of our homes.

Phoebe said, "Please do it soon." I was afraid she'd change her mind, and I put it at the top of my to-do list.

PHOEBE FARLEY

Mascara ran down my tear stained face as Rob Conway's truck drove out of sight. It wasn't the loss of the furniture; it was everything: the house going under the wrecking ball, a forced move and Javier's violent death. I seemed to be caught in a vortex of mixed emotions. Even though I looked forward to living in a new and up-to-date home; I just couldn't come to grips with the transition emotionally. I now knew the house was as good as gone, and I hated living with all the exposed flaws. I wondered why I'd never been aware of the growing deterioration and obsolescence and guessed it was denial or family pride.

Then, there was Javier's death; the shock, the dreams and the suppressed grief that followed. I suppose I should have been relieved that I'd never see him again, but the resentment that I felt toward him was overshadowed by the unforgettable memories of a forbidden love. My head throbbed and I wanted nothing more than to run out the front door and never look back.

I called my sister Marcia and asked if we could stay with her for a few days. She said, "Honey, I'm so sorry. I should have told you weeks ago, but you were dealing with so much, I didn't want to bother you. I've sold my house, and next week I'm moving into a condominium. Right now, I have one foot in each place. I wish I could help.

"What's a condominium?" I asked.

Marcia said, "I'll explain later, but it's a new concept that's sweeping the country. You have ownership like you do with a house, but all outdoor maintenance is someone else's responsibility. Jeff can explain it to you better than I can."

I tried to pull myself together before the children came home, and I was doing a good job until Jeff walked in the door. When I saw him, I collapsed into the breakfast nook, sobbed and screamed. I pounded on the table and begged him to get us out of this house.

"Sweetheart," he said, "it'll be months before our new place is ready. Maybe we could stay with Marcia for a while."

Through my tears, I said, "What's a condominium?"

Jeff said, "It's a new kind of carefree ownership."

I said, "Marcia's moving into one. I've already asked, and she's not able to help us now."

Jeff said, "I'll tell you what. I'll check us into the Holiday Inn for the weekend. They have an indoor pool for the children and we can eat out, take in a movie and you can relax a little."

* * *

I was upstairs packing for the weekend when Jeff came into the bedroom and closed the door behind him. He sat down on the bed and motioned for me to sit down next to him. "You know Gary Nyquist?" he said.

"Yes, the Regent who is the bearer of bad news. What is it now?"

"The university no longer wants our house for a parking lot."

"Do they want us to buy it back?"

"No, but now they plan to build a multi-story parking garage on the East campus."

"OK, what then?"

"The new plan is to build an alumni building on this spot."

"So?"

"It will be a memorial to Javier. The name will be The Javier Ruiz Memorial Alumni Center."

While my insides churned, I just stared into space. I wanted the earth to open up, swallow me and take this whole damn house with it. I thought about Daddy and how this ground, once pioneered by his ancestors, would bear Javier's name for all time to come. It was an ironic twist leading to the perfect revenge.

Jeff laid me across the bed and said, "I knew this would be a blow to you, and I wanted to pick the right time and ease into it, but the announcement will be in tonight's paper and I couldn't wait."

* * *

Ariel and Adam loved motel living and spent hours in the pool. We invited Abagail and Stan to bring Ryan to swim with them. Jeff told the Grays how eager we were to move out of the house, and Stan told us that there was good news. It seems the city announced a plan to widen one of the main streets and cut down the adjacent trees. Almost immediately, the Greenpeace demonstrators at our property targeted the new project and moved the demonstrators. Stan heard they were threatening to chain themselves to those ancient Elm trees. He said that with this new development our construction might even be finished ahead of schedule.

* * *

Christmas music and decorations were everywhere, and there was no denying, something needed to be done for the children. I would like to have cancelled the whole holiday thing, but I realized I'd have to go through the motions for them. I threw myself into a shopping frenzy which, at least, kept me away from the house for hours at a time. I saw no reason to attempt decorating the house or planning any sort of celebration.

I did miss Christmas baking, and when Bernie invited me to a cookie exchange at her home, I enlisted help from my daughter, Ariel. We turned on our ancient oven for what I hoped would be the last time and baked several batches of light buttery pink and green Spritz cookies, enough cookies for the party and for our family's Christmas celebration however meager it might be. I promised the children, "Next year we'll have a huge tree and presents that will fill half the room. We'll invite Aunt Marcia and lots of friends, and we'll have trays of food and eggnog too."

* * *

Every inch of Bernie's home was decorated. She even had red and green covers on the door knobs. Most of the women from Rebekah Circle were there and some of Bernie's other friends. We sampled cookies and shared recipes, but I was too tired and emotionally drained to enjoy the afternoon.

I was sitting alone on the couch when Tammy brought a plate of cookies and sat down next to me. "I know this is a difficult time for you," she said.

I blinked several times trying to hold back the tears, but a few escaped and ran down my cheeks, "I've got to get out of that house. The holidays and all the memories are making it harder. I can't entertain, and I see no reason to decorate. I suppose we'll have to look for a rental somewhere."

Tammy dabbed at my tears with a napkin and said, "I have an idea, Phoebe. Why don't you and your family move in with me until your home is finished. I have a big, lonely house, and I'd love nothing more than people coming and going and, best of all, children's laughter filling the rooms. Please say you'll do it." I was too shocked to reply and thought Jeff wouldn't even consider the idea.

Tammy continued, "Promise me you'll talk to Jeff about it. I'm very lonely and this could be good for both of us. Dolly would love it too." There was something so sincere about the invitation; I had to give it serious consideration. I suspected that the offer was more about Tammy's need than about mine.

On the drive home, I did think about the idea, and the thought of leaving the house gave me an enormous feeling of relief. I fantasized about just walking out of the front door, and like Scarlet O'Hara, saying, "I'll think about this tomorrow."

Persuading Jeff to make the move was an easier task than I thought. He must have been eager to end the temper tantrums and crying jags. We agreed to take only our clothes and leave the furnishings in place until we made the final move. Whatever remained would be left to an auctioneer. The children were excited about the move. They loved the idea of being close to Ryan and of living with a dog. My wish was granted, and as we drove away from the house, I said, "I'll think about this tomorrow."

Jeff remarked, "That's OK for now Scarlet, but please remember, we'll both have to think about it in the new year."

The moment after we rang the doorbell, Tammy and Dolly stepped outside and welcomed us to a picture-perfect home. Dolly celebrated the children's arrival and greeted them with a wagging tail and a happy bark. Once inside we noticed three stockings hung from the fireplace mantel: one each for Adam and Ariel, and one for Dolly. Tammy's father-in-law, Boots was on the floor setting up an electric train that circled the tall Christmas tree. Tammy's mother-in-law, Millie was in the kitchen doing some serious holiday baking. Later, Tammy told us that the train belonged to her late husband, Jim, and Boots was thrilled to have an opportunity to assemble it again.

Even before Christmas Day, Tammy and I began planning New Year's Eve. All of the Bridge Club members and their families were included, and, of course, Boots and Millie, Marcia, and as a goodwill gesture, we decided to invite Bernie and her husband. Jeff's gift to Tammy was hiring a caterer and a bar tender.

Christmas Day passed in a blur of gifting and gorging. However lovely Tammy's home was decorated, the celebration seemed other-worldly. I kept picturing my former home in it's cold, dark, semi-empty, crumbling state, and I wondered if it missed us. I kept telling myself *One more week and the holidays will all be over.*

Two days after Christmas, Don, our contractor, called to say construction was stalled on our new house due to the need to reclaim material from our current home. He said he'd been in contact with the university, and they were ready to begin demolition. We had three weeks to clear the house.

* * *

By New Year's Eve, Tammy and I had pulled the pine needles out of her carpet and replaced the Christmas decorations with crepe paper streamers. We stocked up on noise makers, silly hats and found a recording of Auld Lang Syne.

Bernie called early in the afternoon and asked if she could bring her son, Ben. She told Tammy that he was newly divorced, and she didn't want to leave him alone on New Year's Eve. Dr. Ben Young was as handsome and charming as when I first met him and I was flattered that he seemed to remember me.

Hannah and her family arrived late because they don't drink and they wanted to avoid the cocktail hour. They were barely inside the door when Rob started a sales pitch for his River View property. Stan, never the diplomat, said, "You know, Rob, your idea is great, but the place is just too damn far out of town. We bought a piece of ground by the Country Club with the Farleys and we're both building new homes there."

It seemed that Rob wasn't able to cover the negative emotion he was feeling when he asked, "That wouldn't be that wooded ground with all the demonstrators would it?"

Jeff answered, "Yes, it is, but they're gone now, and everything is Ok."

I could tell that both Jeff and Stan wanted to change the subject but Rob wouldn't let it go. "Ya know, I could still do the construction for you. I'm working on two houses now, but I could…"

Stan interrupted, "We bought the land from Don Carleton, part of the deal was that he would build our houses."

Rob wasn't willing to give up and as he spoke, he seemed more contentious, "Hey, I'm still looking for investors. Hugh Fordyce is going to look and he has some big bucks to spend. We could do a limited partnership."

At that point, Jeff had enough, "It's a party. Let's celebrate the New Year and talk business some other time."

As sometimes happens, the group separated into women in one room and men in the other. I told my friends about the deadline on the house and, they were all in on helping me organize and do whatever was needed. I wondered what I would do without them.

Over dinner we tried to prioritize the events of the past year. Everyone thought that our moon landing was the most important for this or possibly any year in human history. Other notable happenings we discussed were the comeback of Richard Nixon, Chapaquidick, Vietnam war protests and all the mothers welcomed the introduction of Sesame Street to the TV schedule. As we finished dessert, my sister, Marcia, said, "What could possibly happen next?"

Before the stroke of midnight, I watched Rob Conway who appeared deep in conversation with Bernie's son. I could tell by Rob's facial expression and gestures that he was pitching his property. Ben had been polite and somewhat withdrawn throughout the evening, but I noticed that he and Tammy often exchanged interested glances. Now, with Rob, he appeared to be indulgent but distracted and was still watching Tammy.

At the stroke of midnight, Jeff placed the needle on the Auld Lang Syne record; couples kissed, men slapped each other on the back and the women hugged. The children were asleep by then and we kept the noise making to a minimum. While we were toasting, kissing and hugging, I noticed that Tammy and Ben were engaged in a private, quiet conversation. At the end, he wished her a happy new year and kissed her on the cheek.

*　*　*

Throughout the next week, I kept telling myself, We're not only in a new year but in a whole new decade. Things have got to be better. Turning a page on the calendar was not the answer; first, there was the old house to be dealt with and also many decisions regarding the new one.

Jeff took two weeks off to help with the house. Marcia decided that at least half of the furniture we were keeping needed repair or restoration, and she made arrangements to send the pieces away. The rest was put into storage. Tammy was with us every step of the way. She and Abagail packed china, linens and other household items to be moved. Hannah helped as often as she was able. Marcia and I tackled the attic which was the hardest part. At least three generations of dusty clothing, paper, toys and memorabilia had to be sorted. In the end, most of it was thrown away or donated, and I wondered why I let it accumulate in the first place. Dirty and exhausted, we stumbled into Tammy's house every evening. Boots was always there mixing our favorite drinks, and it seemed that Millie must have spent the entire day preparing the delicious meals she served. I wondered how I'd ever repay them for their kindness.

Due to our efforts, the house was clear two days before the deadline. Marcia and I walked through our front door together one last time. We climbed the staircase and said goodbye to our childhood bedrooms. I went alone to the room that Jeff and I shared for so many years. We met again in the dining room and reminisced about the many dinners served there, some jubilant and a few sad and silent. When we reached the foyer again, Marcia said, "Do you plan to come back for the demolition?" It was then that I told her about the plan to build an alumni center on our site. She was furious and said, "Oh shit, can we put a curse on this ground?"

I answered, "It seems there already is one."

HANNAH CONWAY

Every time Rob put a business deal together, he swaggered into the house with a smug smile, shouted "Alleluia" and announced that there'd been a new development in God's plan for us. When he strolled in with a double alleluia, I knew something big must have happened. On the day of the double alleluia, he picked me up and swung me around in circles. He finally deposited me on the sofa and sprawled out beside me. Instead of quoting scripture, he looked at me and said, "Guess what happened today?"

"You're building another house?"

"Better than that; think big, Hannah."

"You'd better tell me; that's the best I can think of."

"Well, I took Hugh Fordyce to Rainbow Ridge this afternoon. He was so impressed, he took one look and decided to invest."

"Perfect," I said.

"The Lord moves in a mysterious ways, his wonders to perform, but it's not quite perfect."

"What could be wrong with that?"

"Hugh is kind of a hard-nosed guy. He's in for twenty-five thousand, but he only gave me half." Rob then pulled a check from his pocket. He continued, "Hugh is insisting that I use the money to get a survey and have the land platted into lots. He said that I'll never sell anything unless prospects can see exactly what they're going to own. Hugh wants to see the survey and the plat before he forks over the other half."

I said, "That seems reasonable."

Rob looked down at the check and said, "I was hoping to use the cash for us to live on for a while and to make payments on this house. There'll be some left after the survey work, but not as much as I need."

I was amazed that Rob would do something that seemed….seemed… maybe not dishonest, but maybe a little questionable, and I wondered how he would square that with his religious beliefs, so I said, "You can do that? I mean, use the money for personal expenses?"

Rob frowned, looked at me and said, "Unless you want to move back to the hotel, that's the way it has to be."

* * *

Two weeks later, Rob told me to stop by the auto dealership to pick up an investment agreement that Hugh's lawyer had drawn up. Tammy and Phoebe wanted to spend some time with Faith, so I dropped her at Tammy's home on the way to the agency. They told me to take the afternoon off and enjoy myself.

Hugh was as cordial as always and suggested I take a seat across from his desk while he put the papers in an envelope. We talked about the holidays, and he asked how my car was running. When the subject of family came up, Hugh said, "You know, Hannah, I'm raising two teen-age girls alone, and I could use some motherly advice."

"I'd be happy to help, but I'm not sure how much I know about teen-age girls."

Hugh looked at his watch and said, "There's a nice little cafe around the corner. If you have the time, why don't we walk over there for lunch, and I can ask you a few questions."

Before I could respond, Hugh rose and took my elbow just as he did the day we bought the car. He guided me down a hallway and out the back door of the agency. Hugh said it was a short cut, and I could see that it was, but still, it seemed a little sneaky. Hugh had been so good to rescue me and to find a nice car that I just couldn't say no, especially, if I could help him in some way.

The cafe was small and mostly empty. Shortly after we ordered our food, a chubby middle-aged man entered with a parakeet perched on one gloved hand and a basket hanging from his other arm. He must have been a regular because the hostess greeted him and the bird by their names, Arthur and

Tweety Pie. While Arthur chatted with the hostess, he occasionally kissed Tweety Pie on her head. I could hardly control myself and thought I might have to go to the restroom to laugh out loud.

When the waitress seated the "couple" at a table next to us, there was complete silence at our table. Hugh and I were mesmerized as we watched Arthur take a saucer of bird seed from the basket and place it on the table. Next, he put the basket on the chair opposite himself and moved Tweety Pie to the basket handle. The handle was a perfect height for Tweety Pie to reach her bowl. Hugh's eyes locked on mine and we both knew that we dared not even smile. Arthur leaned across the table and said to the bird, "Are you warm enough, Tweety?" I almost expected Tweety Pie to answer.

As we ate, Hugh and I attempted conversation between Arthur's remarks to his bird. I told Hugh about Faith's birth, and he described his wife's accident and the resulting devastation to him and his daughters. Each time Arthur spoke to Tweety, we halted our conversation in mid-sentence and our eyes met. When the waitress brought our check, Arthur asked Tweety if she was enjoying her lunch. Our eyes met for the final time and lingered just a bit too long.

Once outside, we walked around the corner of the restaurant and began to laugh. I started first with a giggle and then Hugh removed his glasses and broke into a laugh so hearty, he almost doubled over. I laughed until tears ran down my cheeks, and I began to lose my balance. Hugh reached out and caught me by the shoulders. I looked up into the handsome face I first noticed in the car on the snowy night he rescued us, and I didn't want him to let go. He did take a step back and replaced his glasses. I said, "Thank you for the lunch, Mr. Four Eyes."

Hugh smiled and said, "I hope you enjoyed it, Tweety Pie."

We laughed all the way to my car, and when Hugh tucked me behind the wheel, he put his arm on the roof of the car and bent down till his face was even with mine. He said very quietly, "I can't even remember when I've had such an enjoyable time or an honest laugh. I hope we can do it again soon." I smiled but didn't respond. I knew the attraction I felt was out of control and I almost didn't care.

Half way to Tammy's house to pick up Faith, I turned on the car radio. The radio didn't work in the old car that Abagail gave us and I really enjoyed the speakers in this newer car. All along, I'd had the feeling that the car was worth much more than we'd paid, and I wondered if Hugh had taken a loss to make sure that I had safer, dependable transportation. After a commercial, Karen Carpenter started to sing that song, the one I hated. Every time I heard it, I felt like a mouse caught in a trap. She sang:

Before the risin' sun, we fly
So many roads to choose
We'll start out walkin' and learn to run
And yes, we've just begun

I snapped off the radio and pulled over just as the tears began. I sobbed and pounded on the steering wheel. When the crying subsided, I sat for a long time trying to calm down. That awful song reminded me that I hadn't just begun, I was well down the road of life and had no other roads to choose. There would be no flying before the rising sun for me. I was committed to three children and married to a religious zealot with questionable ethics and a pile of debt.

When the pressures of child care and the sacrifices required to advance Rob's ambitions built up in me; I occasionally had a disappearing fantasy. I'd day-dream of walking away from my family, finding a quiet room where I could sleep as long as I needed, have time to read a book, manicure my nails and take long walks. I knew I'd never actually do that but thinking about it seemed to get me through the bad days. My lunch with Hugh didn't exactly match that dream, but it did give me a feeling of freedom and, for the very first time since my marriage, another road to choose. I liked that feeling and I liked him.

I used the rear view mirror to dry my eyes and freshen my lipstick, and I said to my image, "You should be ashamed of yourself; here you are, a married woman with wonderful children, good friends, a nice home and you're attracted to a married unavailable man. You'll probably burn in hell for all eternity for these thoughts you're having."

* * *

When the survey and the plat were finished, Rob once again asked me to take the paperwork to Hugh's office and pick up our check. After our previous trip through the back hallway, I was reticent about being seen at Hugh's office again. I called him and asked what time he had available. Just as I hoped, he suggested we meet for lunch, this time at a French restaurant farther from his office. A quick call to Tammy ensured me that I could drop off Faith for a couple of hours.

In the days since I'd last seen Hugh, I'd given a lot of thought to our meeting and where the relationship was leading. Yes, he was married to a woman who was not a wife in any sense of the word. She could give him no companionship and no comfort, and I was in a three-way marriage with Rob and God. When I was with Hugh, it was just the two of us and every experience didn't have to be interpreted as God's will or God's plan. It was such a relief. I was hoping that Hugh and I could settle for a close friendship that would give us both some of what was missing in our marriages without going any further. Deep down, I knew I was kidding myself.

Hugh was waiting for me at the door of the restaurant with a brief case in hand. The hostess led us to a circular booth and we slid in from each side until our shoulders were nearly touching. Hugh opened his briefcase and after we traded envelopes, we sat in silence for a while. I was just happy to be there seeing him and feeling his presence. Finally, he said, "How have you been?"

"Conflicted."

"I know; me too." There was another period of silence where we both stared straight ahead. Hugh took my hand, turned to me and said, "Hannah, if our meeting like this worries you or makes you uncomfortable, we don't have to see each other again; I'll understand."

"I didn't tell Rob about our lunch, and I won't tell him I've had lunch with you today, If there's a price to be paid; then I'll pay it."

Hugh said, "If it helps, I'll take care of you as best I can and protect you if you need it." No question was asked or answered, but in that moment, a silent agreement was made and sealed with the briefest of kisses.

Hugh ordered salads and escargot for us. It was so exotic and something I'd never tasted or even heard of but, I did find it enjoyable. We talked about our marital history, how we met our spouses, and Hugh told me about how he'd started his business and described the road that led to his success. I wanted to ask about his motive for investing with Rob, but that was a door I was afraid to open.

Before the check arrived, Hugh said, "When can I see you again?" I hesitated just a moment too long, and his confident look faded. "If you've changed your mind......"

"No, it's just that I'll have to make arrangements...find a sitter for Faith. I just don't know. "

Hugh took a card from his pocket and wrote a number on it. "This is my private line. Please call me when you're ready." Then, he opened his briefcase again, removed a book and placed it on the table in front of me. "Tweety Pie, this is a book of poetry that made me think of you. I hope you enjoy it."

I said, "Thank you, Mr. Four Eyes, for the book, the lunch and for being here.

I didn't have a moment alone until the following morning when the boys left for school, and Faith was settled in her play pen. The cover of the book was bright pink, the spine a little faded and the edges of the cover were well worn. The book was written by John Lawrence and titled My Beloved. That alone sent shivers through me. I opened the book and found the corner of page twenty-five turned down. I read:

> I watched you walk away.
> Alone and incomplete, I cursed my fate
> Longed to call out, to follow, to possess.
> You took the sun away.
> Moonless, starless night engulfed me
> I searched for light, for warmth, for the purpose
> That I found only in the depth of your eyes.
> Only you can bring the dawn
> Calm the turbulence of need and loneliness
> Fill the bottomless hole in my heart
> Heal me with your tenderness and serenity.

1980

All human beings go through cycles in their lives, progressing from infant to child to adolescent to adult. While each stage builds upon previous biology and experience, evolving from one stage to the next sometimes requires a dying to what we have been in order to complete our metamorphosis. While the infant does not lament becoming the toddler, or the child mourn the approach of adolescence, women have been portrayed as lamenting our continued maturation into middle life and older adulthood. Older women are supposed to fade graciously—or gloomily—into the woodwork. Yet, as studies demonstrate, the truth is that women continue to develop strength and actually bloom rather than fade with the advent of midlife.

Joan Borysenko, Ph.D. A Woman's Book of Life

Adecade has passed since we last saw the ladies of the Bridge Club, but they still meet for their monthly game. Despite the changes they've experienced, their bond is stronger than ever. Now, it's time to check in and see what's happened to them during the past decade.

PHOEBE FARLEY

Time has been kind to the Farley family. Jeff's law practice is thriving and the family is enjoying their home in Robin Hill. The children are adolescents and Phoebe and Jeff are just beginning to deal with the problems of the teen years.

ABAGAIL GRAY

The makeover and the coaching that Abagail received from her sister, Cynthia, has transformed her into a community leader. More importantly, she enjoys an equal partnership with her husband, Stan. Their son, Ryan, is nearing the end of his high school years and is faced with the task of choosing a college.

TAMMY YOUNG

Tammy's New Year's Eve flirtation with Bernie's son, Ben, led to marriage and the motherhood that Tammy longed for. When Tammy and Ben Young were married, Tammy felt the need to have children while she was still able, and they have a boy and girl. Ben moved the family into a larger home and with the expectation that his daughter, Melissa, would want to spend some time with them. Melissa had an instant dislike for Tammy, and her room remains empty. Tammy tolerates her mother-in-law, Bernie, fairly well but still prefers the company of Millie and Boots, her former in-laws, who act as surrogate grandparents to the children.

HANNAH CONWAY

Rob continues to build custom homes, but Rainbow Ridge remains a barren piece of ground. Even though the city has expanded, development has not reached as far as Rainbow Ridge. Hannah is still involved with Hugh Fordyce, and even though Hugh regularly begs her to seek a divorce; her religious scruples and family loyalty have prevented her from making a decision.

ABAGAIL GRAY

It all came to a head the spring day I saw Martin Anacott's car driving toward our home in Robin Hill. Our winter was long, cold and dark and I was finally able to clear leaves and debris from some flower beds. I welcomed the warmth of the sun and the cloudless sky, until I saw Martin's car approach. It was too late to run into the house and pretend no one was at home.

Ever since I'd changed my style, Martin had been entirely too attentive and outrageously flattering. At first, I ignored his flirtation because he was the head of Stan's firm, and I didn't want to spoil my husband's prospects for success. As time went by Martin became more aggressive; his behavior bordered on obsession and he never missed an opportunity to touch me. Stan seemed not to notice, until I broke down in tears at the prospect of another dinner with the Anacotts.

We did meet them that evening. Martin maneuvered our seating so he was seated next to me, and he often rested his hand on mine when he was making a point. I'm sure his wife was well aware of these advances and had probably experienced them herself before they were married. I felt sorry for her and was sure that under her polished exterior, she was seething. Finally, Stan took notice, and he too, was seething but, uncharacteristically, kept it under control.

Now, as I watched Martin's car coast to a stop, I was alone and vulnerable, faced with a man intent on forcing his attention on me. I picked up a rake and was holding it upside-down in front of me with the prongs facing outward as Martin stepped out of his car carrying a bottle of Scotch.

Martin extended the bottle toward me and said, "This is a single malt, twenty-one-year-old import. I was hoping we could go in the house and sample it together. You know, of course, I only want the best for Stan." I shifted the rake to my left hand and took the bottle but said nothing. After a long pause Martin continued, "Now that I've given you something, you need to give me something in return."

With eyes fixed on Martin, I nonchalantly dropped the bottle on some bricks bordering a flower bed; imported glass flew in all directions as Scotch watered the garden. I said, "Now, I owe you nothing," and I shifted the rake back to my right hand, prepared to use it, if necessary.

Martin looked down at the Scotch-soaked ground and said, "This is such a waste."

Then, he looked directly at me and raised an eyebrow.

I narrowed my eyes and through clenched jaws I said, "Stan will have to clean up this mess." Martin must have understood my intention; he retreated to his car without another word.

* * *

"Son of a bitch," was what Stan yelled when I told him about Martin's visit. I was afraid he might resort to physical violence, but he had a better and more sensible solution. He sat me down and laid out his plan. "I've been working with a tax attorney for some time," he said. "He's unhappy with his law firm, and we've been discussing a possible partnership. We could take on clients who have tax disputes with IRS and companies that have unique tax situations. Having legal and accounting advice together in one firm could be a real advantage. My friend's name is David Kaiser, and he's ready to go. All I have to do is say the word, and I can say goodbye to Anacott & Associates."

I asked Stan, "Can't you just resign and open your own accounting firm?"

"I could, but I've signed a contract with a non-compete clause, and I'd have to leave all my clients with Anacott. Essentially, I'd be starting from scratch."

"Wouldn't you just be doing that anyway?"

"Dave would be able to bring his clients with him, and they would give us a start."

"What about money? You know, Ryan will be starting college this fall, and we've been looking at some top colleges for him."

"I think Ryan's grades and his basketball skills should be enough for a nice scholarship. I've got money put away to cover college expenses, if needed, and we can cut down on travel and maybe put off buying new cars for a while. We'll still need to do a lot of entertaining, and you should keep your high profile in civic organizations."

"That means donations; big ones."

"It's OK. I think we can handle it. Remember, I'm a tax expert and those contributions will make very good deductions."

Stan poured a drink and said, "I'll call Dave tonight, and tell him I'm ready to say goodbye to the asshole that runs my firm. I'd guess we could get office space and be up and running in a couple of weeks."

* * *

The next morning, when the house was empty and quiet, I sat in the kitchen, looking out at the woods that surrounded our home. Robin Hill had become a refuge as well as a home for me. My sister, Cynthia, loved it too and spent a lot of mornings sitting with me at that table, watching the birds and squirrels.

I would have given anything to be able to call her at that minute, but she lost her long struggle against diabetes during the past year. Since she entered my life, a decade earlier, she and her son Ryan had grown very close to my family, and we talked nearly every day. She was my mentor and best friend. She'd been the adviser that helped me grow into an influential member of our community sitting on the boards of charities, museums and the university. Cynthia had transformed a shy, frightened, plain woman into a powerful, self-confident leader. What pleased me most, though, was that Stan now regarded me as an equal partner in our marriage.

Cynthia's son, Ryan, filled a similar role in the life of our son, Ryan, and the two were more like brothers. Within the family, we called Cynthia's son by his initials, R.J., to avoid confusion. Even though R.J. was married and had children of his own, he often flew to Springfield to watch our Ryan play high school basketball and was currently guiding him through the maze of college choices and the application process.

I welcomed the chance to play bridge a few days later. I was eager to tell my friends about the visit from Martin Anacott, but planned not to say anything about Stan's intentions to leave the firm. He and Dave Kaiser had been looking at office space and narrowed the field to two choice locations.

I was even more willing than Stan to make this change and hoped never to have to see Martin Anacott again.

Even though it was not her turn, Tammy insisted we come to her house for bridge that day because she had a problem finding a sitter. Grant, her older child, was in first grade and would be gone for the afternoon and she hoped her two-year-old daughter, Taylor, would be napping during our game. Tammy delighted in naming her children after presidents. I often thought if she had another one, boy or girl, she'd probably name it Roosevelt or Cleveland.

Bernie loved taking care of her grandchildren, but was unavailable that day. She lost her husband soon after Ben and Tammy were married, and it seemed that Tammy, Ben and the children had become her whole life. Tammy handled that situation pretty well and we all admired her for it. She was so crazy about Ben; I think she would have welcomed Attila the Hun as an in-law just to be with him.

The marriage gave me an opportunity to get to know Ben better, and though I liked him, I had an ulterior motive. My jaw line was starting to sag, and my laugh lines were deepening. I thought I might want his services if Stan's new business was successful.

A few years ago, our group decided to serve lunch in our homes before playing bridge. We'd all shared so much and were so relaxed when we were together that nothing was held back. Lately we'd begun to serve wine with lunch; the wine of choice was Portuguese, came in a green oval shaped bottle and was called Mateus. Hannah was loosening up and started experimenting with wine. She began with just a sip and now enjoyed a whole glass. We usually started with a toast, and when we raised our glasses, Hannah always said, "Please don't tell Rob." It made me think that Hannah had a well concealed adventurous streak in her.

Over a scoop of cottage cheese, surrounded by an arrangement of fruit, the topic of conversation turned to the lives of our children. Phoebe confessed that her daughter, Ariel, was upset that the Spring Prom was coming up, and she had no date. Phoebe said that Ariel was even desperate enough to ask her brother to go as her date. I thought she was directing an unspoken plea to Hannah and me to arrange a date with either my Ryan or Matthew, Hannah's older son. I was aware that Ryan had his eye on a girl in his class and planned to ask her to be his date. Spring Prom required a tux rental, dinner and flowers. I knew that money was still an issue for Hannah and Rob and doubted they would be willing to take on the expense of a formal evening.

Hannah confirmed my suspicion when she announced that she was thinking of getting a job. She said that she and Rob realized that more income was needed to send their sons to college and to dress Faith a little better and to give her the same advantages as other girls in her class. Rob continued to build custom homes, but Rainbow Ridge remained a barren piece of ground. Even though the city had expanded, development had not reached as far as Rainbow Ridge. Both Jeff and my husband, Stan, had loaned money to Rob and were disappointed that no grading or prep work for streets had been done as promised. We all suspected that he was using the money for living expenses, but we loved Hannah and her children and wanted them to have the best life possible.

When we were settled at the card table, I told my friends about my experience with Martin Anacott. On several occasions in the past, I'd mentioned my problem with him and asked for advice. Most of the advice I received involved physical violence, and I didn't find it helpful. They were all shocked and wanted to know what I was going to do about it. I told them Stan was planning to handle it, and I was relieved when no more questions were asked.

After our bridge game, Tammy served chocolate chip cookies that her former mother-in-law Millie made for us. She told us that Millie and Boots bought a condominium in Scottsdale, Arizona and would be spending the winters there. She said it was both good and bad news. She'd miss them terribly but visiting them in the winter would be a real pleasure. Although nothing was said, I suspected there was some friction between Bernie and Tammy's former in-laws.

* * *

A few days later, Stan announced that he wanted to show me the office space that he and his new partner leased. He arranged a meeting at the office with the Kaisers followed by lunch at The Springfield Club. I guess I shouldn't have been shocked at the size of the office. I pictured something far more modest than what I saw, and I hoped it would soon be filled with employees and clients, but it was a bit unsettling.

Lunch was a déjà vu experience. It had been a few years since I'd dined at The Springfield Club, but the lobby looked exactly as it did the day I first walked through the front door; minus the cigar smoke. Some time ago, women were allowed to join, but few were ever found in the lounge area. The dining room had been updated but had the same elegant feeling that I'd noticed when we had our original lunch there. Now, Stan and I were much like the Anacotts, the older more experienced couple, and we were introducing a younger couple to a new lifestyle.

I ordered a Caesar Salad and hoped for the same dramatic presentation I'd witnessed years ago but was served an ordinary, far less delicious salad.

I could see that Dave and Audrey Kaiser were filled with all the ambitions and hopes that Stan and I felt on our first visit to the Club.

The luncheon conversation revolved mainly around the selection of a name for the firm. A fall back name was simply joining the names Gray & Kaiser or Kaiser & Gray; Stan jokingly suggested that they flip a coin to see whose name would be first. Finally, we all thought it best to find a name that described the combined services.

Conversation moved on to more personal matters such as family and other interests toward the end of lunch, Audrey's brown eyes had an extra sparkle and out of nowhere, she said, "How about this for a company name, Associates in Taxation and Legal Services? You could use the first letter of each word which comes close to spelling Atlas. It would be ATLS; that symbolizes strength." It was the perfect name for the firm. Stan and Dave looked at each other and nodded.

Dave said, "A picture of Atlas with the world on his shoulders would be a great logo."

Stan added, "Our slogan could be something like Let us take the world off your shoulders or Let ATLS lift the world from your shoulders." Then he smiled, leaned back in his chair and said, "I like it. We're gonna make a great team."

PHOEBE FARLEY

During the weeks before Spring Prom a sense of gloom hung over our home; only tears and envy prevailed. All of Ariel's friends had dates and she had no one to share her misery on the night of the big event.

In an attempt to avoid watching the unfortunate drama unfold before our very eyes, Jeff booked a week for our family at a luxury resort on Sanibel Island on the West coast of Florida. Our hope was first to present Ariel with an attractive alternative to the dance, and second to give her a respectable and enviable excuse for her absence.

Ariel seemed at least neutral with the trip. Who would not have been pleased with the warm water of the Gulf of Mexico, the beautiful scenery and the wonderful food? We swam, sunbathed, walked the beach and discovered Grouper at an interesting restaurant called "The Bubble Room". There were a few other teenagers at our resort and Ariel and Adam played tennis and collected shells with them. In the end, Ariel admitted to having a pretty good time and was eager to show off her tan when she returned to school.

Finally, enough time had passed that Ariel's friends were no longer discussing their dresses, the music, who danced with who and if there was a goodnight kiss or many kisses. After the trip, Ariel was different; she seemed detached, the phone rang less, and she dove into her studies with a ferocity I hadn't seen before. After all, she had a wonderful personality, was extremely intelligent and deserved to have a good high school experience; but it wasn't happening. Just when I was desperate for help but simply didn't know what to do, the answer came from an unexpected source.

On one of those change of season days I've always disliked, dark, low clouds were racing across the sky driven by a high-speed wind. That afternoon I was surprised to find my sister, Marcia, on my door step carrying a bottle of White Zinfandel. As she stepped inside, she handed me the bottle and said, "Hi Hon, I want to introduce you to my new favorite wine." This was unlike my sister, and I could tell by her demeanor that she'd come for a serious discussion.

Before we settled on the sofa in front of the large fireplace in my family room, Marcia ran her fingers over the bricks we'd saved from our former home, turned and said, "I still can't believe it's gone, but how wonderful that you've preserved pieces of it for us to enjoy."

I was in no mood to take a sentimental journey into the past. I put our wine glasses on the coffee table and said, "Marcia, this is not about the wine. What's going on with you?"

Marcia sat down, took a sip of wine and said, "Okay, I had lunch with your Bridge Club yesterday."

I was dumfounded. "And just why would they have lunch together, invite my sister, and not even tell me?"

"They wanted to talk about Ariel."

At first, I thought Marcia misspoke or I'd heard her wrong. There was a long pause while I processed what she'd actually said and then I got angry. "And you went to a pity party about my daughter?"

"Take it easy, Sis. It wasn't pity; it was concern. They love you and they love Ariel and want you both to be happy."

By this time, goose bumps were raising on my arm. "Don't you think her father and I know what's best for our own daughter; this is outrageous."

Marcia took another sip of wine, bigger that time. "Please, remember the time when you first learned about the university wanting your house. You thought the house was perfect, and later, when you took a closer look, you found it was not as perfect as you thought and realized there was a better option."

I was sure my face was beet red, "So you think my daughter is hopelessly flawed and perhaps needs to be replaced."

"Not at all, she's my niece and I love her, but your friends did have some good ideas; they, more or less, elected me as a spokeswoman to tell you what they think. Please, please hear me out."

For the first time in my life, I wanted to slap my sister, but I sat down crossed my arms and simply glared at her.

Marcia continued, "Tammy says her husband, Ben, has wanted to work on Ariel since she hit puberty. He thinks her nose is too…too prominent and he could give her a thinner nose, one that turns up just slightly at the tip. He also thinks she needs an otoplasty which would pin her ears closer to her head. Then, she could wear a pony tail or a very short haircut. Both procedures could be done at the same time."

My mouth fell open; the absolute insolence of this conversation was unendurable, but, before I could say anything, Marcia rushed on. "Ariel's senior year is coming up and unless changes are made, it appears it will be a repeat of this past year, frustrating and unhappy. In a little more than a year, she'll be going through rush and you know how brutal that can be. I'm concerned about her psychological state as well as her social life. School will be out soon, and we have a whole summer to make improvements that could give her a lot of self-confidence.

"Oh, so now she's a mental case as well."

"No, not at all, but she's clearly unhappy, and we have a plan that could change everything for her. Just look what making changes did for Abagail. Her sister's guidance turned her into a beauty and changed the direction of her life. Abagail thinks that Ariel should lose about fifteen pounds, and she offered to take her to New York to let her hair and clothing stylists work their magic on her. Hell, I'd take Abagail up on an offer like that in about two-seconds."

Just when I was about to throw Marcia out of the house, I heard Ariel say, "Mom." I hadn't heard the garage door open and was shocked when I turned and found my daughter standing in the doorway of the room.

"Honey," I said, "how long have you been here?"

"Long enough," was her answer.

Sobbing, she rushed to the sofa and threw her arms around Marcia's neck. "Thank you, thank you," she said through her tears.

Aerial looked at me and said, "Mom, Aunt Marcia is right. I want to do all those things she talked about. Please… please; I'll do anything. You don't know what it's like seeing all those cute girls walking down the hall with boyfriends and sitting together at lunch. They're nice and they talk to me at school but, I'm always on the outside. I get along with boys…they all consider me a friend… but never a girlfriend. I want something different… something better. I don't need to be popular, just accepted."

It was as if the air had been knocked out of my lungs. I realized that my love for people and things always blinded me to the need for improvement. It was a cruel awakening, but Ariel's pleas tore at my heartstrings.

I turned to Marcia and even though it was difficult, I said, "I was probably a little hasty and should have been more in tune with what's happening to my daughter."

Then, I said the hardest words anyone ever has to say, "I was wrong and I'm sorry."

We all hugged and I said to Ariel, "Don't worry, honey. We'll get this done."

Ariel said, "Do you think Daddy will go along with it? It's probably going to cost a lot of money."

I said, "We'll get it done one way or another."

Before she left, Marcia handed a business card to Ariel and said, "You have an appointment with Dr. Ben Young next Wednesday at 4:00." Ariel grabbed the card and held it over her heart.

TAMMY YOUNG

Sometimes, I think I'm the only person in the world who loves Monday mornings, and what could be better than a Monday morning in the spring. Ben and Grant had just left the house. Ben usually dropped Grant at school when he had no early morning surgery scheduled. I knew that soon school days would end, and I'd have two children to care for and entertain each day. Being a mother was all I ever dreamed of or hoped for, and marriage to Dr. Ben Young was like winning the lottery. Occasionally, I thought about writing a note to Ben's ex-wife, Marietta, to thank her for divorcing him.

I'd planned to take Taylor to a nearby playground that day and was just wiping the cereal from her face when I noticed my dog, Dolly, standing in the dining area of our kitchen. She seemed like a statue, frozen in place, with one of her back legs up as if she stopped in mid-step. I turned toward her just as she toppled over on the floor. Her whole body began to convulse, and foam gushed from her mouth. I left Taylor in her high chair and rushed to Dolly screaming, "No Dolly, no!"

I knew my precious pet needed help, but it was too early for the vet's office to be open. I left both Taylor and Dolly in the kitchen and ran to the bedroom, dropped my robe and pajamas on the floor and threw on a pair of jeans and a sweater. I could hear Taylor starting to cry, and I hurried back to the kitchen. Dolly was still thrashing around on the floor, and Taylor was stretching her arms toward me wanting to be released from the high chair. I was torn, but knew Dolly had the most need. I went to her side and sat next to her. The convulsions were quieting and I cradled her head in my hands,

"I'm sorry girl; so sorry. When this stops, I'll take you to the doctor. Please, please be OK. I need you."

Taylor's cry turned to a demanding wail alternating with screams of, "Mommy, Mommy." Dolly was calming and I picked her up and cuddled her in my arms. She opened her eyes, looked into my face, took a deep breath and was still. I had hoped she would recover, but as her body stiffened, I knew she was gone and I'd lost her. Tears streamed down my face, and I held her for a long time. Taylor's cries turned to whimpers, and eventually the room was quiet.

I didn't know what to do so I carried Dolly to her bed, laid her in it for the last time. I was apprehensive about calling Bernie, but I did. She was on my doorstep in less than an hour, and took over just as I knew she would.

First, Bernie made sure I'd eaten something then she told me she'd take Taylor to the playground, and I was to lie down for a while. I tried, but I just couldn't sleep or even rest. I went to Dolly's bed, sat next to her on the floor and wept for a very long time.

An hour or two later, Bernie found me there and helped me up. Taylor hugged me and asked, "Why Mommy crying?"

Bernie said, "These children will need an explanation and closure. I imagine you'll need some closure too. We should plan a funeral for Dolly. I think the frost is out of the ground now so while Taylor naps, why don't we dig a grave. I know someone who can do that for us."

Less than an hour later, the doorbell rang and Bernie ushered in a short slender man with a handle-bar mustache that curled up on the ends. The mustache was the same color as what was left of his hair, and I suspected that both were dyed. She introduced him simply as Ralph. When the grave was finished, I offered to pay Ralph for the work, but he refused and said it was a favor for Bernie. He offered his hand, and as we shook hands I looked into his eyes. I might have been looking into a cup of coffee. His brown eyes were opaque, there was no light, no sparkle and no life in them.

I called Phoebe, Hannah and Abagail and asked them to come at 5:00 with their families for the funeral. They were all surprised, and said they'd be here. I left a message for Ben at his office and asked him to come home as soon as possible.

When Taylor woke from her nap, Bernie insisted that we drive to a lawn and garden store she patronized. It was the right place; we bought fresh flowers and a large garden statue of a dog with a basket in its mouth. The owner promised a one-day delivery for the statue.

Ben called when he got my message, and I told him what had happened. He stopped at the school to pick up Grant and was home by 4:30. He attempted to explain Dolly's death to Grant, and he helped me take off her collar and wrap her in one of Taylor's baby blankets. Grant was inconsolable and was sure that if we waited just a little longer, Dolly would wake up.

Our guests arrived with enough food to make dinner for all of us. I was shocked when Ralph came in with the guests but was too distraught to ask why he was there. Grant led the funeral procession carrying a picture he drew for Dolly. He was followed by Ben, carrying Dolly's body. Taylor and I were last. Taylor held the bouquet and I carried Dolly's bowls; gifts from the Bridge Club, her name painted on the side of each one.

Abagail's son, Ryan had played with Dolly since I'd reluctantly adopted her, and Phoebe's family lived with us for a few months during their move. Each of them spoke of their memories of time spent with her, and their fondness for her. Rob quoted several Bible verses and delivered a very long prayer.

I was surprised when I noticed Ralph standing close to Bernie during the service and holding her hand. When he came to dig the grave, I assumed he was Bernie's employee; perhaps her gardener or home repairman.

After Ben laid Dolly in her grave, the children and I placed our items with her, and we all marched into the house for drinks and dinner. It was comforting to have my best friends around me. I knew they understood my pain, and they did their best to comfort me.

Later, I glanced outside and saw Bernie standing by the grave as Ralph filled in the dirt. I said to Ben, "Oh, that must be why Ralph's here."

Ben remarked, "Who is that guy anyway?"

I answered, "Your mother told me that he's a friend but I think he probably works for her."

A week or so later, Ben came home with some news that gave me instant indigestion. He said, "I drove to my Mom's house to talk about some investments and that Ralph guy was there."

"Doesn't he work for her? Maybe he was just there doing some jobs."

"Tammy, there was one of those Winnebago things parked in the side yard. It was old and rusty and the utilities were hooked up to her house."

"Maybe he just stopped there on his way to somewhere else and he'll be gone soon."

"Oh no. No, Tam. That's not it!" Ben shook his head in disbelief. "The dinner table was set for two, and he was sitting in the living room in his stocking feet." Ben stood by the kitchen counter with his back to me...I think he didn't want to face me because he had tears in his eyes. When he turned, he said, "That man was sitting in my father's chair swilling down a glass of Dad's Scotch."

I wanted to say something comforting or offer a logical reason that Ben shouldn't be worried about this discovery, but I had to agree with him. I was well aware that Bernie had been lonely since her husband's death, and this news was alarming. I was so distressed the day he came to dig Dolly's grave that I barely paid attention to him, and I thought I'd probably never see him again. Now, it was clear that we needed to know more about this man.

The next day, I was on a mission: call Bernie and find out as much as possible about Ralph. I was determined to be subtle and diplomatic, but that, simply, was not my style.

After we'd said hello and exchanged a few pleasantries, I dove into deep waters and said, "Bernie, how do you know this Ralph person?"

Bernie's tone of voice changed and she seemed a bit hesitant. "Ralph called one day and asked to talk to Ben senior. I told him that Ben died some time ago. He said he'd joined the Army as a very young man and had been under Ben's command. He really admired my husband. Ralph told me Ben took him under his wing and taught him how to be a really good soldier...even saved his life in Korea. He was pretty sad to hear that he'd lost his last chance to see Ben, and he said he'd heard so much about me; he wanted to meet me and give me his sympathy in person. "

I asked, "How much do you know about this man and what's his last name?"

Now, Bernie really raised her guard, "I know all I need to know. He's fixed a lot of things around the house, and he's very supportive. Ralph Massey is a good man."

* * *

I was relieved that I'd be playing bridge at Phoebe's house that Thursday. My friends always seemed to have solutions to a lot of problems, or at least, a different point of view. Sometimes they just offered sympathy, but that was welcome too.

Phoebe led us to the screened porch at the back of her home and offered us glasses of Sangria. She stood in the doorway and said, "I hear you all had lunch with my sister Marcia."

No one spoke, and I put my glass on a table. From the tone of Phoebe's voice, I thought the Sangria might be poisoned. I was relieved when she smiled and continued, "At first, I was insulted and very angry. I suppose every mother thinks her child is perfect and is defensive when even the kindest and best-intentioned advice is expressed. Marcia could say nothing to calm me down, but it was Ariel, herself, who understood that your suggestions went directly to the heart of the matter. She knows you want the best for her, and she's working hard at the first step: weight loss. She and Jeff are running early each morning and she's given up ice cream and junk food. I have to say, they're both looking great."

Abagail seemed to speak for all of us, "We weren't offering criticism, just advice to help you achieve success and happiness for Ariel. Phoebe honey, you know we love you and your family."

"I know you do, and I realize this must have been difficult for you, but I appreciate your thoughtfulness and your effort. Our summer will be filled with recovery from surgery, and Ariel can't wait for her trip to New York."

Abagail said, "Reservations are confirmed and appointments are being made. I can't wait either."

Over lunch, everyone was surprised when I talked about Bernie and Ralph. All of the women saw Ralph at Dolly's funeral but, like me, they thought he was there just to handle the grave digging and filling. Most thought he was too young and too small to be a romantic interest for Bernie. Abagail said he gave her the creeps.

I was eager to find out how Abagail resolved her problem with Stan's boss, and I said, "Ab, speaking of creeps, have you been able to avoid Martin Anacott since our last meeting?"

Abagail said, "I couldn't tell you then, but Stan and an attorney he's worked with are planning to open a firm of their own combining tax and legal services. They've leased office space, hired a few people and they plan to announce their opening in the Sunday newspaper."

Phoebe said, "How did the parting with Anacott go?"

Abagail said, "I was really proud of Stan. He was totally professional and made no reference to Martin's advances toward me. He said that Martin said nothing and merely nodded when Stan told him he was leaving. There was a time when Stan might have cussed him out or even given him an uppercut to the jaw."

When asked about her job search, Hannah told us that she'd had a change of plans. She said, "I'd like to go back to school and get a degree in some kind of computer science. I already have two years of core courses, and the registrar thinks I could finish in a year and a half if I go to summer school. As usual, money is the problem. This probably means I'll have to get a job and save for tuition. I feel guilty because tuition money should be for my sons and not for me."

I said, "What about bridge…what would we do without you?"

Hannah said, "I'll try hard to do something part time or something flexible. Being with all of you is high on my priority list…along with…with… one other thing I do." No one asked about "the other thing". We all assumed it had to do with Rob or the children.

Phoebe asked, "Why computers?"

"I've been advised by people in business that computers are the coming thing. That field is where the well-paying jobs will be in the very near future."

Phoebe was skeptical, "A friend paid several thousand dollars for one of those machines, and all she uses it for is to balance her check book. I can do that for free."

Hannah said, "I've been reading articles in business magazines. They predict that within ten years there'll be a personal computer in every home."

Abagail said, "Hannah, don't do anything until you hear from me. I have contacts at the university, and I'll see what I can do about a work-study program.

At three o'clock we were still sitting at the lunch table and hadn't even thought about bridge. I had to pick up my children so I excused myself. As I drove away, I thought, *I wonder what the other thing is Hannah does?*

HANNAH CONWAY

Anne Elizabeth Fordyce passed peacefully from this world a little over three years after my affair with her husband began. I learned of her death from a large ad in the paper announcing the closure of the Fordyce Auto Agency for the day of her funeral. In addition to the usual family information about relatives who survived and who pre-deceased her, the obituary was quite long and listed her many educational, charitable and social accomplishments. It unnerved me; I thought, *Now that Hugh is free, he'll be looking for someone like her, someone with a pedigree and a long social resume.*

For six months, I carefully scanned the society pages of the Springfield Sentinel to see if he was photographed with a date at some sort of social event. I did see him pictured twice; each time, his daughters were standing at his side. I knew that every unmarried woman in Springfield would run across a highway in rush hour traffic just to spend an evening with him, and I wondered if I was just a dalliance to keep him busy and happy while his wife was technically alive. I felt that calling him would be intrusive, and I hoped he'd call me when he was ready.

At the start of our affair, we spent a few afternoons in a motel room, but it seemed sordid, and I was relieved when Hugh rented a furnished apartment in an out of the way building. During what I hoped was his period of grieving, I occasionally went to the apartment just to feel closer to him. I'd sit on the sofa, listen to the music we'd enjoyed and remember the happy moments we'd spent there together. Some days, I wondered if I'd ever see him again.

One morning, just after I'd sent my children to school, the phone rang. I was expecting a call from Abagail, but when I answered, the familiar deep voice on the other end said, "Tweety?"

I hoped I didn't sound breathless when I responded, "Four Eyes." Those were the affectionate names we used when we were together, and in that moment, I knew that our relationship endured.

"I've missed you." Hugh said, "Can we have lunch together today."

"Of course, we can. I've missed you too."

Hugh suggested that he pick up our lunches and we meet at the apartment and I agreed. Being seen in public was risky business…although now, just for me and no longer for him. I was well aware that there'd been a change in his status and that it would change the nature of our relationship in ways I couldn't foresee.

The joy I expected at our meeting was replaced by intense emotion. All of my doubt and fear of the past few months seemed to fuse with Hugh's sorrow and fatigue. We shared a strong sense of guilt and apprehension over what the future would hold for us. We mostly just talked and held each other.

In a lighter moment, I noticed that Hugh wasn't wearing his glasses. He said his daughters urged him to try contact lenses; he liked them and planned to continue their use. I asked if I needed to change his name to Two Eyes. He said, "No Tweety Pie, I'll always want to be Four Eyes in your eyes."

When we parted, Hugh held me close and said, "Hannah, at some time we'll need to have a serious talk about our relationship and the future." He rarely called me by my real name, and I shuddered thinking of the upheaval that our decisions might cause.

Hugh and I agreed that it was only safe to meet one or two times a month, and I threw myself into projects that would keep my mind off of him and on my family. I felt that I was cheating them, and I probably was. I tried hard to make up for it by painting Faith's bedroom her favorite shade of pink and making curtains with lots of ruffles for her. I was a room mother for Matthew's class, and I helped coach Peter's soccer team. Abagail often called and asked for help with events she was chairing. I took a minor role but enjoyed the camaraderie, and the idea of helping others seemed to relieve my sense of guilt.

* * *

As our finances dwindled, Rob's desperation increased and his religious fervor expanded to an absurd level. He would walk around our backyard with his arms extended heavenward, praying aloud. Sometimes he would spend hours at the river property, and I assumed he was doing the same thing there. Before bed, our family spent at least half an hour on our knees praying for buyers for the property.

It was apparent that my sons were tiring of marathon prayers and the constant recital of Bible verses that seemed to accompany every conversation, whether it was about athletics, grades, or friends. They would never confront their father, but they constantly brought their complaints to me. I tried to talk to them about tolerance, patience and respect. I feared that their father's extreme actions would turn them off on religion totally. I have to admit, that despite my feelings of guilt about my affair and my growing annoyance with Rob's need to display his faith, I still had a deep belief in God and all the teachings of our church. Rob's outward demonstrations convinced me of the need to internalize and keep my religious convictions private.

I did pray, I prayed a lot for a solution to my situation; something that would allow me to make a life with Hugh without inflicting major pain on my family. Sometimes, when I looked in the mirror, I thought I could see the scarlet letter, "A" attached to my chest and I would trace it with my finger.

*   *   *

The day Rob came home with an answering machine tucked under his arm, I wondered why he would buy such a luxurious item when we were so strapped for cash. He was in a buoyant mood, and when I questioned the need, he said, "This is the latest thing. Soon, everyone will have one of these, and I can't take a chance on missing a business call."

When I questioned the expense, his answer was, "I've renegotiated our loans, and we'll have enough money to carry us through the year."

"Are you working with that friend at the Savings and Loan Company?"

"Yes, but the Savings and Loan was bought out by First Guardian Bank and Trust, and now he's a loan officer."

"I've never heard of that bank."

"It's small and locally owned, but they're sharp and aggressive. They'll do very well, and my friend has a great future."

I said, "Should we be using some of that money to begin grading roads at the property?"

"Look, Hannah," he said, "I've told you fifty times; interest rates are at sixteen per-cent and gas is over a dollar a gallon. No one is going to be interested in moving that far out of town. Interest rates are going down and, when the time's right, money will roll in, and I'll be able to pay off the loans. Leave the thinking to me."

What really alarmed me about the recorder, was that when a call came in and recording began, a speaker broadcast the voice of the caller. So far, Hugh and I had an easy system of communicating, but this new development concerned me. I called Hugh to warn him about the machine, and we agreed that in the future I should just call him on his private line. He suggested we meet at the apartment the next day.

*   *   *

I loved the Buick that Hugh arranged for me, but on my way to meet him, it began to make a knocking noise. I told him about it when we met at the apartment and he took it for a test drive. He returned with bad news. "Your car is ready for the scrap heap. You're going to need to trade it in."

I had to take a deep breath. "That means we'll have to involve Rob. I'm not sure I can handle being in a room with both of you."

Hugh took me in his arms and said, "I'd like to put you in the best car in my showroom. Maybe it's time to think about divorce."

I pulled back and met his steady gaze; I could tell he was serious. I had to admit, I'd thought about divorce but thinking about the pain that it would cause made me nauseas. "I don't know, I have to think about it."

"Hannah darling, I love you, and I think you love me. If you don't, what are we doing here?"

"I never knew what love was till I met you, but I also know what pain a divorce would inflict on my children, and long ago, I promised Rob I'd stay till death do us part."

Hugh held me closer and said, "My dear, you've already broken the cleave only to each other part of the promise, and I've put asunder what God joined together. I have no regrets; I've loved you from the moment I drove over that hill and saw you standing in the snow."

"You were married then; what about your feelings for your wife?"

"The person Anne was died and was gone the day of her accident. The girls and I were left with a body, and it was our duty to treat it mercifully as long she continued to breathe. I knew she wasn't coming back, and I'd already had time to mourn her loss."

Later, Hugh returned to the topic of divorce. "I'll get a good lawyer and pay for a divorce. I can give your children many advantages and good educations. Hell, I'll even pay off that flimflammer you're married to; finance his whole development if that's what it takes. It hurts me to see you live so minimally when I want to give you everything. I want to kiss you goodnight and wake up next to you every morning."

Tears began to run down my cheeks; I might have taken offense at what Hugh said about Rob, but I knew he was right. I so wanted to say, "Yes," but I just couldn't; not at that moment. I asked myself Where did you think this was leading? You can't go on like this. You're going to have to devastate one of these men; which one will it be.

As I was preparing to leave, Hugh told me to take the car to his service department and he would arrange to have a loaner waiting for me. Then he said, "I've had to take on some foreign car franchises and I have a Honda that's low mileage and will work for you. Have Rob call me tomorrow and we'll work something out." Then, he took me in his arms again and whispered, "Promise me that you'll give divorce serious thought. We need each other and we'd be so happy together."

*   *   *

I did think about divorce day and night. For weeks, I was on an emotional roller coaster. As the coaster car slowly climbed the rails, I pictured a life with Hugh, the man I truly loved. At the top of the coaster, I could see a life of love, serenity and stability spread before me. Then, there was a jerk and as the car descended at a dizzying rate of speed, I saw my children, hanging on for dear life, looks of fright, shock and horror on their faces. Finally, even before the car coasted to a stop, the three of them were thrown out and lay motionless on the ground. I was well aware by then that I didn't love Rob, but I did have a sense of commitment and responsibility to him, and I simply couldn't bear to break up the family.

I hoped to tell Hugh, face to face, that I couldn't get a divorce at this time. He arrived at the apartment with flowers in one hand and champaign in the other. The hopeful look on his face made it even harder to tell him about my decision.

Hugh sat down on the couch and covered his face with his hands when I told him that I couldn't face a divorce, and I thought it was unfair to him for us to continue seeing each other. After several minutes he looked at me and said, "Hannah...Tweety...I've been too aggressive...pushed you too hard... please, please say you'll continue seeing me. If and when you're ready for a divorce, you tell me; I'll never mention it again."

I gave in, and we continued to see each other. When Hugh's daughters went away to college, we began to spend our afternoons at his home. We'd meet in a mall parking lot, and he'd drive me to his home. We tried to live a full life there in just a few hours. We cooked together; Hugh often played the piano and sang to me. We drank champagne and danced in the dining room. Each time we met, I wondered what kind of magical experience we'd have together.

* * *

As the years went by, the double life was taking a toll on me. I was always in elegant homes when I was with my friends. Phoebe passed on her wardrobe from the previous year; sometimes the items even had price tags still attached. Because of her height, I couldn't wear Abagail's clothes but she made sure that I was well supplied with designer accessories. Even Hugh always had luxurious gifts for me; always something small that I wouldn't have to explain. It might be chocolates, a billfold, bath salts or a bottle of perfume. Once he insisted that I take his microwave oven home with me. I told my family that I bought it at a yard sale with grocery money. I was beginning to feel like a parasite and wanted to give back to all of them, but it seemed impossible.

It was then, that I began to think about getting some kind of job. Rob occasionally got a contract to build a new house, but his future seemed bleak. The boys were old enough to take care of themselves and look after Faith while I worked, and I felt I needed to find a way to provide economic stability for my family.

It was Hugh who persuaded me to consider the computer field. He believed it would be worthwhile for me to invest some time in school in order to get a better paying job. He offered to pay my tuition, but I told him that would be too difficult to explain. He said, "You could say it's a scholarship." Since our affair began, I'd become an expert in the art of lying, and I wanted to stop. I'd already taken too much from too many people, and I was determined to take care of myself and try to pay some of them back

The bridge club seemed skeptical when I told them about my plan to go into the computer field, and I lost some confidence in my decision until I went to the grocery store and found a new computerized check out system. The checker sang the praises of passing groceries across a screen and having the price automatically entered into the register. She patiently explained how it reduced errors and controlled inventory. That experience reinforced my confidence in my decision.

A few days after I announced my career plans to the Bridge Club, Abagail called to tell me that the university had an opening in a work-study program, and she gave me the name of a person to call for an interview. The interview went well and within a week, I was enrolled in two classes in summer school. Happily, the work part of the program paid my tuition and fit with my field of study.

The work portion of the program took place in the library, converting the card catalog to a computerized system. I was required to work twenty hours a week, and I could set my own schedule. That meant I could still play bridge with my friends and meet Hugh regularly.

I barely discussed my decision to go to school with Rob, and I didn't ask his permission; I simply laid out my plan. He wanted to know about the cost, and when I explained that I'd be working for my tuition; he lost interest.

I found the classes to be stimulating, and the tasks I performed at the library helped reinforce and extend my class work. The library was so quiet and orderly; I loved being there. It was a wonderful place to study, and I often stayed for hours when I'd finished my work.

On the day of the Bridge Club luncheon, I was in the shower when I noticed a bump on my right breast. I first thought it was a pimple or a bug bite. Later, I decided it was only a fibroid tumor that I needed to check occasionally.

ABAGAIL GRAY

euben sandwiches and potato salad were on the menu for the
Bridge Club luncheon. Phoebe was the first to arrive. Tammy
and Hannah arrived together, and after the sandwiches were
grilled, we sat down for lunch. I'd chosen a shady spot on my patio and the
temperature was perfect for an afternoon outdoors. We decided we'd stay out
there for bridge when we finished eating.

A few days earlier, I talked to Tammy about her mother-in-law, Bernie,
and Bernie's new friend, Ralph. I hoped she wouldn't bring up the subject,
but when Hannah inquired about Bernie, Tammy was like a volcano starting to erupt. "You wouldn't believe what happened last night." We all stared
at her expectantly. Tension rolled over us like a heavy fog. She continued,
"During dinner, we heard a car horn honking in our driveway. Ben went
out to see what it was all about, and there was his mother, sitting behind the
wheel of a new red BMW convertible."

I was curious, "And?"

"That Ralph guy was in the passenger seat, shirt unbuttoned halfway down
his chest and sporting a heavy gold necklace." Then, the old Tammy emerged
and she said, "He was wearing a shit-face grin and had the strangest looking
damn animal on his lap. Honest to God; I couldn't tell what this thing was.
It had no hair on its tan body and a bunch of long straight white hair on its
head, tail and feet. If it was a dog, it was a really strange one."

Phoebe asked, "What about the car?"

Then Tammy had a full-scale eruption and spewed out her full story. It was
like hot lava running down a mountainside. "Ben asked where the car came

from and Bernie told him that Ralph had a salesman friend at the BMW dealership who sold it to them. Ralph said, 'Yeah, got us a real sweet deal.'"

By that time, the children and I were standing with Ben, and I pointed to the animal and asked, "What is that?"

Ralph said, "This is a rare Chinese Crested Dog. My friend is a breeder, and he threw the dog in on the deal."

"Bernie smiled, reached over to pat the dog and said, "We've named her Chop Suey but we're going to call her Suey."

Phoebe said, "This sounds like trouble."

Tammy kept going; her voice louder and her frown deepened. "Yes, there was a little bit too much talk of 'we' and 'us' to suit Ben. Ben asked Bernie if she traded in her Jeep on the convertible, and Ralph said, "We'll need that for winter weather. But this girl," he patted Bernie's shoulder and continued, "this girl needed something real nice."

All the time the adults were talking, Grant was pulling on my arm. Finally, When I bent down, he said, "Mommy, I want to ride in Grandma's car."

Bernie heard this, and she said, "Sure honey, anything for you; hop in."

Ben said, "Just a minute, I'll go too," and he got into the back seat with Grant."

Phoebe interrupted, "I take it that they came back."

"They did, and Ben was so angry. He said he never wanted our children out of our sight when Ralph was around. He told me that he hadn't wanted to tell me, but he drove to his Mom's house the day before just to check on her, and the utility lines that led from the Ralph's Winnebago to the house were disconnected. This means that Ralph has very likely wheeled his way into the house."

I wanted to change the subject and let Tammy calm down, so I asked Hannah about her school plans. She was rather abrupt, said she was enrolled, had started classes and was working in the library. It was clear; she was not going to offer any more details. She did thank me warmly for arranging the work-study program for her and said almost nothing the remainder of the day.

Phoebe gave us an update on Ariel's progress. She said her daughter had lost twelve pounds and was looking great. An added benefit was that Ariel loved running so much, she hoped to go out for track and specialize in cross country when school started again. Her surgery was scheduled for the following week, and the running would have to be put on hold until she healed. She once again thanked all of us for caring so much about Ariel.

Hannah was very quiet and was the first to leave. This behavior was so unlike her; I suspected she was just having a bad day. Why wouldn't she? It might have been a school problem, a money problem or something that religious fanatic husband of hers had done.

* * *

By the next day, I'd completely forgotten about the Bridge Club. My son, Ryan, was facing the next step in his life, and he needed to concentrate on choosing the college that would suit him best. Stan was totally preoccupied getting his new firm up and running so the job of visiting schools and making applications fell to me. Actually, it wasn't a job. What could be better than traveling around the country with your son, touring beautiful campuses and talking to eager recruiters?

Earlier, we enlisted the help of my nephew, R.J., and he had already given Ryan some good advice. Basketball coaches from several state schools had been in touch, and it was apparent that Ryan could take his choice, and, perhaps, get a scholarship. Still, basketball was of minor importance compared to academics, and we needed to find a place that offered a strong program in Ryan's major as well as good athletic opportunities. The problem we faced was that Ryan had not yet settled on a major. Based on R. J.'s recommendations, I made arrangements to visit Princeton and Notre Dame, as well as Syracuse University, R.J.'s alma mater.

Our trip began at Notre Dame, then we moved on to Princeton and made our final stop in Syracuse, New York. Since this process was new to both of us, Ryan refused to form an opinion until he'd seen them all. I knew immediately that if the decision were mine, I'd have chosen Princeton, but I kept my mouth shut. R. J., on the other hand, was pushing Syracuse. It was his alma mater and he thought it would be an advantage for Ryan to have family close by. He and his wife even invited Ryan to live with them during the school year if he wanted to.

Ryan liked Syracuse best of the three, but he felt it wasn't just exactly what he wanted. He said, he'd prefer a men's school and he didn't want to be in an urban location.

When we discussed these points with R.J., he said, "You know, I have a friend who went to Colgate University. It's a good liberal arts school; only about forty miles from Syracuse. It's been an all-male college but went co-ed just three years ago. I doubt there are many females on campus yet. I'll see if I can make an appointment and, we can drive up there in the next day or two. It's pretty remote and the winter weather is fierce."

From the moment Ryan stepped on campus, he knew he'd found his collegiate home. We climbed a very steep hill to a quadrangle anchored by a charming century old chapel. The traditional dormitories and classrooms were surrounded by newer contemporary styled buildings. An interview with the basketball coach went well. Ryan said that he liked him more than the other coaches he'd talked with.

R. J. said he'd help with the application process and could see no reason that Ryan wouldn't get early acceptance. He did recommend that Ryan also apply to Syracuse and Princeton just as backups.

On our trip home, I came to a new realization. In just one more year Stan and I would have an empty nest and I asked myself What will I do then?

TAMMY YOUNG

On July 3, Phoebe and I were preparing for our annual 4th of July holiday cookout. Phoebe's home at Robin Hill was the perfect location to celebrate the holiday. A few years earlier the Farleys and the Grays built a joint pool on their property line and each year the Bridge Club and their extended families gathered there for a cookout and a front row seat for the Country Club's spectacular fireworks display. This year, Abagail asked that we include Stan's partner, David Kaiser and his wife, Audrey.

Phoebe was speculating about the number of guests we could expect. Most of the teenagers still came, but a few preferred to spend the day with friends. Phoebe asked if Bernie and Ralph were invited, and I said, "Yes, I left a message, but I'm not sure that we're even on speaking terms. When Bernie invited our children, Grant and Taylor, to spend the night at her house, Ben told her that she'd have to visit the children at our home as long as Ralph was living in her house. She hung up on him, and we haven't heard from her since. Ben is very upset and is thinking of hiring a detective to find out about Ralph's background."

Phoebe asked about the nature of their relationship, and I told her that Ralph was definitely living in the house, but Bernie claimed he occupied the guest room. Ben was concerned about Ralph's access to Bernie's financial records and her safety.

Just then, Phoebe's daughter, Ariel, joined us. Even though, her nose was bandaged and her face was swollen and bruised from plastic surgery; she seemed confident and more positive than she'd been since she entered puberty. Phoebe warned her about being in the sun, but she told us both she only came out for a moment to tell me about her experience with Ben. She raved about his surgical skill and his bedside manner. She said, "Dr. Young says I'll only look like this for a few more days. The bruising will be the first thing to go away, and I'll have swelling for a couple more weeks. By mid-August, I'll be healed and looking good when I'm in New York with Abagail."

I told her that Ben said her surgery went well, and she could expect wonderful results. She did a little happy dance, and her mother said, "Settle down. Remember, no strenuous activity for a month."

* * *

Temperatures soared to record highs that next day. We delayed our picnic till after seven o'clock, and even then, grilling was unpleasant and eating hot, heavy food lost its appeal. We only nibbled around the edges of steaks and burgers, but salad and watermelon disappeared early.

Most of us waded in the pool or sat on the edge and sipped cold drinks. No one complained about children splashing in the pool. I made a trip into the cabana to get extra towels and was followed by Hannah. I was surprised when she asked me to get a glass of Sangria for her. She said, "It looks so good, and Rob wouldn't approve." I didn't want to tell her that Rob was so preoccupied doing a property sales job on Audrey and Dave that he probably wouldn't even notice.

I stayed with her while she drank the wine, and we talked about her classes and her work experience. She seemed happy about both. When she finished, I asked if she'd like another and was surprised when she said, "Yes."

We'd stored the food and cleared the table by the time Bernie and Ralph showed up. To everyone's complete surprise, Ben's fourteen-year-old daughter, Melissa, was tagging along behind them. My relationship with her had been strained from the very beginning of our marriage. Because her mother had initiated the divorce action, and Ben and I didn't meet until the divorce was final; she had to know that I had no part in the break-up of her parents' marriage. Still, she chose to spend her time with Ben alone and showed no interest in her half-brother and sister, Grant and Taylor. I suspected envy was the reason.

Just before the fireworks began, Bernie walked around, and chatted with everyone except Ben and me. Ralph opened a beer and settled into a lounge chair by the pool.

Melissa did come to talk with us. Ben asked why she was with her grand-mother, and she said, "Grandma invited me for the holiday weekend so Mom went out of town with her boyfriend."

"You know," Ben said, "you could have stayed with us."

"Yeah, I know, but this is more for Grandma than it is for me."

"Is everything going OK?"

"It's Ok, but I'll be glad when Mom gets back."

Ben said, "Look, if for one moment, you think it's not OK, you call me or you call Tammy and one of us will be there to get you. I worry about this Ralph guy and I'd rather have you stay with us."

This situation was classic Bernie. Ben wouldn't let her have the younger grandchildren, so she brought another grandchild along to show him who was in control. I could see Ben's fist clenching and unclenching.

Although the fireworks were dazzling and merited a lot of ooohs and aaahs, the evening seemed a little flat. I hoped it was mainly due to the weather.

*   *   *

The Monday following the Fourth of July weekend, I got an alarming call from Ben's daughter, Melissa. She was so panicked, I hardly recognized her voice. She said her friend brought her back to Bernie's house after her tennis lesson, and she found Bernie unconscious on the floor. I asked if her grand-mother was breathing. Melissa said, "Yes, I think so. I can't get hold of my Dad, and I don't know what to do." Then she said, "Get away from me."

I said, "Are you talking to Ralph?"

Melissa said, "No, I'm talking to this dumb ugly dog. She won't stop jumping on me."

"Where is Ralph; is he there?"

"I left early, before anybody was awake. Now, the garage door's open and the convertible's gone. I don't think he's here."

"Call 911, and when they pick up Bernie tell them to take her to Memorial Hospital. You ride with her in the rescue vehicle. That's where your Dad is. I'll meet you there."

"This weirdo dog has wet and pooped on the carpet. What shall I do with her?"

"Make sure she has food and water and leave her there. We'll deal with the mess later."

Melissa was waiting in the hospital lobby, and even before I walked through the door, she ran outside and threw her arms around me. I had Grant and Taylor in tow; Taylor was confused and hugged Melissa's leg. I'm not sure if it was a gesture of comfort or if she thought we were having a group hug.

When she'd recovered a bit, Melissa said, "Dad is in the emergency room with Grandma. They won't tell me anything."

I asked Melissa if she saw any injuries on Bernie or if she was bleeding. She told me that Bernie's face seemed twisted but there was no blood anywhere.

We met Ben outside a curtained area in the emergency room, and he guided us to a quiet place in the hallway. Then, he began to question Melissa about the previous evening and events of the morning.

"Dad," she explained, "I went right to my room when we got home last night. The last thing I heard was the TV set going on. The house was quiet this morning, and I didn't want to be late for my friend. I got up early, ate a couple of donuts and drank a glass of orange juice. I didn't see Grandma or Ralph."

"Was the BMW there?"

"I dunno; the garage door was closed, but it was open when I came back and the car was gone."

I asked, "What's he done to her?"

Ben said, "I'm not sure he's done anything except run out on her. Mom's had a stroke."

Melissa and I spoke at the same time to ask about a recovery.

Ben explained, "It may not be good. If she'd had immediate help her chances would be better. We have no idea how long she was on the floor."

Mellisa said, "Let me think…my lesson lasted an hour, half an hour ride each way, and I sat around with my friends for about another half hour. I was gone roughly two and a half hours. Oh…if only, if only…I could have come back earlier."

Ben looked discouraged and said, "However long she was alone; it was too long."

Melissa seemed genuinely distressed and possibly even guilty. I thought she needed a distraction, and I said, "Melissa, why don't we go back to

Bernie's house and pack a bag of personal things for your grandmother? We also need to deal with that dog."

On the drive to Bernie's house, I had second thoughts about the trip. What if Ralph is there? What if he played some part in Bernie's stroke? This is potentially dangerous, and I've got three innocent children with me.

I said to Melissa, "If the BMW is there I'm not going to stop. We just don't know about Ralph and his part in Bernie's stroke." I was relieved when we drove to the front of the house. The garage door was still open, and no red convertible was in sight.

Mellisa agreed to stay outside with the children. I entered the house, let the dog outside and climbed the stairs. Two steps into the master bedroom told an entirely predictable tale. A purse was open on Bernie's unmade bed, and an empty billfold lay next to it. On the dresser, Bernie's jewelry box was mostly empty. I sorted through the remaining pieces and found only costume jewelry.

Ben answered the hospital page almost immediately. After I told him what I'd found, he said, "I think it's time to call the police."

I quickly tossed a few things in an overnight bag and hurried outside. I stopped in my tracks when I saw Melissa and the children rolling in the grass with Bernie's dog. I realized it was the first smile I'd had all day. I loaded Melissa and the children into the car, and promised the dog we'd be back soon. As we drove, I said to Melissa, "Do you remember if your grandmother was wearing her diamond ring this morning?"

Melissa said she was certain that Bernie wasn't wearing any jewelry when she found her.

At the hospital, Bernie had been transferred to a private room. Ben told us that she was still unconscious and there had been no improvement. He added that the police were looking for Ralph and the car.

I asked Melissa if she wanted to go to her mother's house, and she surprised me when she said, "I'm not even sure she's back yet, and I'd rather go home with you, and Grant and Taylor."

* * *

It took two days for the police to find and arrest Ralph for car and jewelry theft. Ben's meeting with the police was disappointing and revealing. A detective told him that the car was not registered to Bernie, but to a Dwight

Kurtzenburg. Fingerprints and a driver's license revealed that the man we knew as Ralph Massey was actually Dwight Kurtzenburg. Dwight had a record for petty theft but no serious crimes. The police said that Dwight or Ralph claimed that Bernie gave him the car, and they found no jewelry on him, so they were unable to charge him with anything. He and the car were gone.

Bernie regained consciousness two days later; unable to speak and partially paralyzed. Soon after, Ben had her moved to a rehabilitation facility for physical therapy. We decided it was best to look at the loss of the BMW as a bad experience and be thankful that nothing worse happened. We also stopped asking ourselves if Ralph did something that brought on Bernie's stroke; accept things as they were and do our best for Bernie.

We had the Winnebago towed to a junk yard and closed up Bernie's house; hoping she'd be able to return.

Nothing is seldom all good or all bad. The one good thing that came from this experience was that Melissa and I became friends, and she asked if she could stay with us until school started. Her mother had no objections and actually seemed happy about the situation.

Melissa and the children were thrilled when we brought the ugly dog home, and they bonded in an effort to keep her. Beside her looks, I hated the name Suey and explained, "It's a hog call; if we go outside and call soooey, sooey, a pig may show up."

My thoughts drifted back to Dolly, the dog I didn't want, and originally named Stinky. I remembered how much she meant to me, and I gave in on the condition of a name change. Suey answered to her name and we thought Suzy was similar and she might not even notice the difference. Ben was not totally on board with the whole idea and suggested we call her Baldy.

Ben felt he needed to know how Ralph knew so much about his father, and he found a way to check out military records. The records showed that neither a Ralph Massey nor a Dwight Kurtzenburg had ever served in the Army.

HANNAH CONWAY

As the summer wound down, student life became increasingly difficult. It wasn't the classwork or the tests but, week by week, getting around campus seemed harder. Finding a place to park was always difficult and was usually followed by a long walk to class. The path from my classrooms to the library was even longer. At least, I found a bench on the way where I could rest. I often wondered how I'd have the strength to make this walk during the winter when the air would be cold, and I'd have to walk on snow or ice.

I realized that I was privileged to have the opportunity, and I worked as hard as I was able to take advantage of what I'd been offered. My grades were very good, and my job performance rating was excellent, but it took all the energy I could muster to keep up with both and take care of my children. I think I'd have had more energy if I ate more, but I really didn't have much of an appetite. I was still able to go to the Bridge Club meetings and to see Hugh on a regular basis. We'd agreed to table the talk of divorce until I finished school, but he'd begun to nag me about my weight loss and my seeming lethargy. I blamed it on the pressures of school.

* * *

In late July, I entertained the Bridge Club at my house. Faith was such a trooper and was so supportive. We cleaned the house together and she helped me set up the card table and make a tuna salad. She's a constant inspiration and a reminder of the power of faith.

Abagail was in New York with Ariel completing the promised makeover. We were all eager to see the results. When I last saw her, Ariel was so much thinner and her plastic surgery was healed. Even without professional beauty services and new clothes, she was a knock-out. I was thankful for Faith's natural good looks. We could never have afforded all the advantages that Ariel had. I wished I were able to buy better clothes for Faith but I'd recently noticed that she and Ariel were now the same size, and I hoped for some hand-me-downs.

Abagail's friend, Audrey, was filling in for her. Having her here made me nervous. The homes of my friends were so grand and mine was barely average; I worried about what she'd think.

During lunch, Tammy told us that therapy had not been helpful for Bernie and depression was part of her problem. She was regretful that she'd allowed Ralph or Dwight or whatever his name was into her life, and she was embarrassed by her foolishness. The doctors advised Ben that Bernie would never be able to return to her home and would need a long-term care facility.

Tammy said, "Bernie wants to go home, and she's really resisting the idea of being in some kind of institution. Ben and I have toured at least half a dozen of those places and I can't say I blame her. They're appalling and if any of you have heard about some place pleasant where she'll get good care, please let me know."

Phoebe asked Tammy about the dog that she'd taken from Bernie's home. We all expected complaints, but Tammy said, "Well, we've named her Suzy and we're keeping her. She's affectionate, playful and a damn good watch dog. All three kids love her and she's growing on me too. Sometimes I think she's so ugly, she's cute."

Phoebe said, "Three kids?"

Tammy told us that Melissa was so happy with her "new family" that she'd asked to stay indefinitely. Apparently, her mother had no objections.

I noticed that pretty much everyone watched me eat, and they all tried to be extra helpful when lunch was over, and it was time to clear the table. I'm sure they knew, or at least suspected, that I was sick. I wouldn't have been surprised if they went out to lunch to talk about me, and someone showed up at my door to do an intervention.

* * *

The lump in my breast was a bit bigger, but what bothered me more, was the dull ache that was always there. While working in the library, I'd read some medical books and was almost certain that I had cancer.

I looked at this just as I did with Faith's birth. Whatever God willed would be what would happen. If He wanted me here on earth then He'd cure me. If He wanted me with Him in heaven, He'd take me. I saw this as a test of faith, and I needed to be ready for either answer.

Just as I turned to the Bible for guidance and comfort, Rob stopped quoting scripture and relating everything that happened to God's plan for us. It seemed as though we'd reversed roles. I felt I couldn't discuss my health problems with him. Life with Rob was a daily grind; he'd become distant and spent a lot of time going over his ledgers. He rarely talked to me or the children but we still had lengthy prayers at bedtime.

During the weeks between the end of summer classes and the beginning of the fall semester, I met with my college counselor and signed up for a full load of credits. I hoped I'd feel better by the start of the semester, and I believed I could push myself to handle the course work and do my library job.

My afternoons with Hugh were becoming an effort. I knew he was aware of my lack of energy, and my weight loss worried him as well. For a while I tried to convince him that I had anorexia, but he wasn't buying it. He begged me to see a doctor and even said he'd arrange to have one come to the apartment to examine me. I said nothing about my decision to leave my health in God's hands; I just didn't think Hugh would understand.

On a particularly difficult day, I turned to the Book of Psalms for some comfort and some hope. Instead of comfort or hope I found a passage that spoke directly to me and gave me an answer, but not the one I wanted."Because of your anger my whole body is sick; my health is broken because of my sins. My guilt overwhelms me—it is a burden too heavy to bear. My wounds fester and stink because of my foolish sins. I am bent over and racked with pain. My days are filled with grief. A raging fever burns within me, and my health is broken. I am exhausted and completely crushed. My groans come from an anguished heart. Psalms 38: 3-8"

It was as if an electric shock went through me. I knew in that minute, I was paying the price for loving Hugh, and if I had any hope for God's mercy, I'd have to stop seeing him. Besides my children, my relationship with Hugh was what I cherished most in life. I'd always said that I would gladly pay any price for our affair, but this disease…this misery was far beyond anything I could ever have conceived. Now, I had to deal with the consequences of my actions. If I had any hope of making reparations so that God would find me worthy, I'd have to give up Hugh. I realized then, how desperately I wanted to live.

* * *

The question of how to break off our relationship haunted me day and night. Should I do it gently, reassure Hugh of my love, but let him know that my conscience demanded that we not see each other or should I try to be cruel; hurt him in some way so he would know that my decision was final and he wouldn't want to see me? I knew that if I confessed how sick I was, he would have insisted on getting medical care for me.

Then, there was the how, when and where. I could see him in person, perhaps in the mall parking lot where we usually met to go to his house or meet him at the apartment. Other options were a letter or a phone call.

I ruled out the last two options. For all he meant to me…all that we meant to each other, he deserved better. I have to admit, I did want to see him one last time; see his handsome face, and look into his deep blue eyes even though I would know what pain I was about to inflict on him. Long ago, when we first talked of divorce, I recalled saying to myself No matter what happens, You're going to devastate one of these men which will it be? Now I had my answer; the one I least wanted to hurt.

Finally, I decided I'd have to meet Hugh somewhere semi-public to break off our relationship. I recalled the time he first suggested divorce. I'd told him then that we should stop seeing each other, and he'd persuaded me to continue our affair. I knew I'd need some place where I could walk away and there would be no opportunity for him to try to change my mind. He seemed reluctant when I asked for a morning meeting at the mall parking lot. I always had more energy in the mornings, and I knew I'd need extra strength to carry out my plan.

We parked next to each other in a crowded area of the parking lot. As always, Hugh held the passenger door of his car open for me; something Rob never did and I so enjoyed. I stood a few steps from his car and recited my well-rehearsed speech. "Hugh, you know I love you, I always will, but I just can't handle the strain and the lies anymore. Divorce is out of the question…"

Hugh interrupted me with, "Hannah, listen…why is…"

I kept on talking, "I can't see you again, please, please let's end this now and cherish the memories of the time we've spent together; it's what I need."

All of this time, I'd been drinking in the sight of the man I so loved as I watched his lips turn down at the corners and his shoulders sag. He seemed to be folding up, and he sat down in the passenger seat of his car. He looked up at me and said, "No!"

I wanted to hold him, comfort him and see him smile, but I could bear no more. I returned to my car and drove away. It was the worst day of my life. At home, I collapsed on my bed and pulled the covers over my head wondering if I'd ever be able to get up again.

* * *

Faith kept watch over me for three days and tried to comfort and feed me. I forced myself to eat the toast and drink the tea she brought to me, more for her sake than for mine. The boys were concerned and checked on me several times a day, but I only saw Rob in the morning before he left for work. He would stick his head in the door and say, "How are you doing today?" He was sleeping on the couch, and I have no idea what he did in the evenings.

Of course, I'd lie and say, "Better." Then, I'd cover my head and pray for forgiveness for that lie and the thousands of others I'd told in the past decade. I wondered if the need for deception would ever end. I also prayed for the courage to tell Rob that I had cancer, but I was fearful of his reaction. Would he want to get medical help for me even though we had no insurance and no money to pay for it or would he turn to the Bible and hours of prayer? He seemed not to notice my weight loss or other symptoms, and I asked myself Would he even care?

On the fourth day, I drug myself out of bed, recruited Faith and Peter for house cleaning and sent Matthew to the grocery store. The opening day of school was only a couple of weeks away, and I didn't want them to be distracted or worried about their home life. I convinced myself that a clean house and a full refrigerator made life seem normal.

With the children's help, I prepared a decent dinner for my family. After dinner, I asked Rob to come into the bedroom for a serious talk. We sat on the side of the bed, and I didn't beat around the bush nor did I try to soften the blow. I came right out with it. "Rob, you should know; I have cancer."

Rob grasped his head with his hands, laid back on the bed and moaned, "Jesus, God." He laid there for a while and when he sat up he said, "How do you know? Have you seen a doctor?"

"I did research in the library, and I have all the symptoms of breast cancer. Maybe you didn't notice, but I've spent the last three days in bed."

"I thought it was some kind of flu that you'd get over. What are we going to do?"

"I've been praying a lot and looking for answers in the Bible. I'm relying on faith. If God wants me in heaven, then he'll take me. If not, then I'll be cured, but I'm not hopeful."

"I thought you looked a little peaked lately, but I guessed it was just strain from school. How long has this been going on?"

"I noticed a lump in the spring and I've been going downhill pretty fast. Every day, I seem to feel worse."

"Hannah, what about medical care? There's no insurance and I haven't wanted to worry you with your school and all, but I've got financial problems...big time."

I knew I finally had Rob's attention when he asked, "Do the children know?"

"No, they know something's wrong, but they don't know how serious this is; at least, I don't think they do."

"Hannah, it's all our problem; the whole family. What'm I gonna do with a sick wife and three kids? What if you die, what'll I do then?"

"I thought that you, more than anyone, would understand my actions. I Pray...read the Bible. That will be my salvation; one way or another."

I was waiting for a comforting arm around my shoulder or at least the suggestion of prayer, but none of that was happening. I said, "This is my problem. I'll handle it."

Rob stood and said, "If faith was the cure for cancer, everybody'd be using it. I need to think about this." Then, he turned and left the room.

Sitting there alone, I thought What a fool I've been; all he cares about is himself.

The next day, I called the head of the work-study program, and told him I wouldn't be returning to classes in the fall.

PHOEBE FARLEY

A stranger seemed to inhabit our home after Ariel returned from her trip to New York. The moment two stunning women walked out of the airport jetway, our welcoming group was amazed. When the trip was proposed, I worried that the New York experts would turn my daughter into a glamour girl, but there she was, suddenly beautiful in a wholesome, age appropriate way. Her formerly mousey brown hair now grazed her shoulders in a mix of lighter shades of brown blended with blonde highlights. If she was wearing makeup, it was undetectable, but from the rosy glow of her face, I knew that something was quite different. She wore a simple black blouse and a smartly cut pair of white slacks that revealed her now slender body.

Abagail too, looked different in an updated way. She'd had her hair lightened and cut into an ear-length page boy style. Her face had the same wonderful glow that I'd noticed on Ariel, and she wore a triumphant smile that told me she was pleased with the outcome of her effort.

The change in Ariel's attitude and her demeanor was deeper and far more significant than the outward changes. As the boxes of new school clothes arrived, I expected excitement and squeals of delight. After all, her wardrobe was every high school girl's dream come true. All of the pieces were so beautiful—I even felt like squealing. Yet, Ariel unpacked her selections in a detached sort of way, inspected everything carefully and demonstrated how she could mix, match and layer her clothes. A day later, she showed more interest when the cosmetics arrived, and I began to wonder what the trip was all about.

When I questioned my daughter about her experiences, she seemed more excited about New York than about her new look. She told me she and Abagail had seen a few museums, visited tourist attractions like the Empire State Building and the Statue of Liberty. They'd eaten in fashionable restaurants, ridden the Subway and she was really excited when she described standing on the sidewalk watching Jane Pauley host the Today Show.

Ariel seemed somewhat disinterested in her appearance, and when I asked if something went wrong on her trip, she surprised me. She said, "No Mom, it was the most wonderful week of my life. I loved New York so much; I didn't want to leave. Watching the Today Show from the sidewalk was thrilling and made me want to crash through the doors and be a part of the show. Abagail and I toured the Columbia and NYU campuses. That's where I want to go next year and major in communications."

During her previous year of school, Ariel had no direction for her future. She was a good, but not outstanding student, and she'd planned to attend Springfield University, live at home and begin college with an undeclared major. Our goal of transforming Ariel's appearance had converted the desire for popularity into purpose. For a while, I thought we'd wasted our money and effort, but we'd inadvertently achieved something far different and more desirable, something of far more value.

Jeff was thrilled with my report about Ariel's plan and promised to arrange interviews and trips to both Columbia and NYU. I was excited about the prospects of a trip to New York and thought I might book appointments with some of the experts who'd made such a difference in Ariel and Abagail's appearances.

A few days before school started, I found Ariel standing in front of the mirror dressed in one of her new outfits. I said, "You're going to get lots of comments and compliments when the new-you walks into that building."

Ariel turned to me with a worried look on her face, "I know, Mom, and I'm not sure how to handle it. A year ago, I'd have wanted all that approval, but now, I see things, especially, all my popular classmates differently, and I'm not so sure I care what they think of me."

I didn't know if Ariel had regrets about her transformation or if the process had given her self-confidence a huge boost. I suggested that when students complimented her, she accept the remarks graciously and ask questions about their summer or change the subject to something relevant and neutral like classes or teachers.

* * *

Abagail needed a big thank you for arranging the trip so I invited her to lunch and bought tickets for her and Stan to see a Celtics road game that would be played in Springfield. I'd also hoped that Abagail could unravel the mystery of what had happened to my daughter and I was not disappointed.

When we'd been seated at our table, Abagail actually thanked me for giving her the opportunity to spend a week with a "wonderful young girl." She said, "I've always wanted a daughter, and if I had one, I'd want her to be just like Ariel. Be careful; I just might steal her from you."

"Abagail, the girl who left my home is not the same one who returned to us. Which one are you talking about?"

"There's really no need to be concerned, Phoebe. No one knows better than I do than when changes take place on the outside, there'll naturally be some on the inside too. You've got a smart girl; she'll adjust.

"Last year she was so eager to be accepted by the popular crowd. I guess I just thought she'd come back wanting to use her appearance to fit in and win their approval."

"She's had a look at the wider world, and now she knows there's a lot more to life than the pecking order at Springfield High. It's much like what happened to me on my first trip with Cynthia."

* * *

On Ariel's first day of school, I think I was more nervous than she was. At noon, the mail delivery brought what I thought would be a pleasant distraction. A large white envelope addressed in gold italic handwriting reminded me that Jeff's law partner's daughter was soon to be married. While I carefully opened the beautiful gold lined envelope, I imagined dancing to live music, drinking champagne and wearing my new best dress. I knew no expense would be spared, and I was excited until my gaze drifted to the bottom of the invitation. My happy day-dream gave way to outrage. The reception was to be held at the Javier Ruiz Alumni Center, and the address on the line below was identical to the one I'd used for most of my life.

Since the day my sister, Marcia, and I said goodbye to our family home, I'd been able to avoid even driving past the replacement building that caused such upheaval in my life. Now I'd be forced not only to look at the building, but to enter it and spend an entire evening there. I threw the invitation on the kitchen counter and said, "Damn it."

I really didn't know what to expect when Ariel came home from school, but I hoped she would be pleased with the reception set in motion by her changed appearance. What I didn't expect was anger bordering on rage. Ariel stormed into the house, dropped her books on the couch and sat down with crossed arms and a pout on her now lovely face.

"Well, Ariel, I take it things didn't go well."

"Mom, it was so insulting. Some girl came up to me and actually said, 'Ariel, what did you do to make yourself look so much better.' She might as well have said 'Wow, you were really ugly before.' I could tell word was spreading and some kids seemed to go out of their way just to look at me."

I said, "That doesn't sound so awful."

Ariel slammed her fist on the couch and said, "My favorite teacher asked my name and when I told her, she looked like she didn't believe me. All through class, she kept staring at me."

"Did anything positive happen?"

"If you could call it that. The cheerleaders invited me to sit with them at lunch, and the head of the squad told me I just had to try out for the team."

"Did you sit with them?"

"By lunch, I was so sick of the stares and the comments that I sat in a toilet stall in the locker room."

"How did you treat the people who complimented you."

"I followed your advice, but I really wanted to turn around and run out of the building."

Help was definitely needed and I wanted to keep Ariel busy so I could call Abagail for advice. "I'll bet you're hungry." I said, "How about a sandwich? A new store just opened called Honey Baked Ham and I bought some of it to try."

Ariel nodded, and I headed for the kitchen.

Five minutes after I hung up, Abagail was at our front door. I whispered, "Pretend you just dropped by."

Abagail sat down at the kitchen table with Ariel and said, "I just couldn't wait to hear how your first day went."

I stepped out of the kitchen door, still within hearing range but out of Ariel's view. I felt like such a snoop, but I had to know what Ariel would say.

Ariel said, "Not well, there was just too much attention. I suppose some of it was well meant, but a lot of it was either insulting or phony. It all seemed so shallow."

"What outcome do you want from this school year?"

"I wish I could just skip the year and go directly to college, far away, with a lot of strangers where not so much attention is paid to my looks.

"Think about this, my dear; you could gain some weight and send the clothes back to New York. Dr. Young could probably reverse the surgery. Would you want that?"

There was a long moment of silence before Ariel said, "No, definitely not."

Abagail said, "There's a price to be paid for everything good and this is your price. You're quite a beauty now and wherever you go, you'll always get attention for that, but the shock value won't be there."

"I guess I just don't know how to handle this. I know I wanted to be popular, have people want to be with me, but now all I want is to study hard, run track and get into Columbia or NYU. This is going to be a long nine months."

"Fortunately, other things will happen for your classmates to talk about, and by Halloween, they'll forget you ever looked any different. You need to think long term."

"I thought I was."

"Here's the thing about college applications; grades and sports are not everything. My Ryan has been applying to a couple of schools and they look at things like activities and leadership as well. You'll need the good will of your classmates to get those things going for you, and you don't have much time."

"How do I do that?"

"Play them…make it a game. Pick out the leaders, befriend them and tell them what you want. If you want an office in a club tell the faculty sponsor and ask for their help. You'll be surprised how easy it is."

"Is that what you've done…I mean…you're an important person in Springfield."

"I don't care much about a lot of the organizations I've headed or raised money for, but it's good for Stan's business and I have the influence to get things done, such as helping Hannah get into a a work-study program so she could go back to school. That's my reward, and yours could be getting into the college of your choice."

About that time, I tiptoed into the living room. When Abagail left the kitchen, I hugged her and said, "Thank you, now I really owe you."

She said, "You were behind the door, weren't you?"

"You know me too well."

"I would have done the same thing. Don't worry; this will all work itself out."

*   *   *

Jeff must have had a bad day and was not at all sympathetic to the events of my day. He expected that Ariel's return to school would be thrilling and triumphant.

When I told him that she was freaked out by her classmates' reaction to her new and improved appearance, he was genuinely annoyed. He scoffed at my concern for her, "Good God, Phoebe, think of the effort we've made and the money spent to get what she wanted, and now she's not happy about it… She needs to grow up."

I should have saved the wedding invitation for another day or just waited until after dinner, but I thought Jeff would share my reluctance to return to the site of my former family home. When I showed him the invitation, he lashed out at me, "That broken down, worn out pile of bricks provided us with the money for this lovely up-to-date home with cash left over. I'd say the university did us a favor. Ariel is not the only one who needs to grow up, you both need to get over yourselves."

I said, "You lost a case, didn't you?"

"Yes, it was a big one."

Dinner that evening was very quiet. Jeff must have been looking for some good news, and he asked Adam about his day.

Adam said, "We have a Tarantula spider in science class."

Jeff said, "That sounds scary. Aren't they dangerous?"

Adam replied, "No Dad. They're gentle but when they're mad, they kick their back hairs at you like a porcupine. If they do bite, they have less venom than a snake. They're so neat. I want one of my own for a pet."

Ariel said, "You want to bring a creepy killer spider into our house? No way!"

Jeff stood, threw his napkin on his plate and stomped out of the room.

*   *   *

The wedding reception left me with mixed emotions. I was relieved to find the drive leading to the new building had been straightened and changed. Except for one ancient oak tree the familiar landscape was gone. The building itself was vastly different from my former home. It was a one story, flat roofed, angular structure in some sort of smooth cream-colored masonry. As we approached, we could see that neither the front nor the side had any windows. I thought it looked like a giant mausoleum. When you think about it, the design was entirely appropriate on many levels.

Directly across from the large double entry doors, hung a life size portrait of Javier dressed in his academic robe. It was so lifelike; I had to hide my reaction when Jeff paused to study it. I tried for a blank stare and hoped the tear drop forming in the corner of my right eye wouldn't run down my cheek. One of the university regents approached us and remarked, "It's a very good likeness."

I asked, "Who is the artist?"

He replied, "The head of the art department painted it."

Jeff said, "He did a marvelous job."

The Regent said, "Yes…yes, she did," and walked away.

I found myself just the tiniest bit jealous. Whoever painted that portrait knew Javier very, very well. When I was able to excuse myself to go to the ladies room, I looked into the mirror and saw a woman a decade older than the man I'd seen in the portrait and I realized he'd be there forever young, while I'd turn into an old crone. I said to myself Perhaps then, I'll be able to forget him.

ABAGAIL GRAY

Early on an autumn morning a call from George Mason, the university registrar, upset me more than it surprised me. He said, "Mrs. Gray, I know that you highly recommended Hannah Conway for our work-study program, and I thought you might know why she's not returning for the fall semester."

"I'm sorry," I said. "I wasn't aware of the situation."

"Hannah worked into the program so well, had good grades and was loved by the library staff. Her counselor wondered if someone or something here at the university caused her to drop out."

"George, I'll certainly look into this and get back to you."

"Please tell her we'd welcome her back if she changes her mind."

Maybe I combed my hair, but I'm not sure. A chill was in the air and I did take time to grab a jacket, but I wore no makeup or lipstick when I drove to the Conway residence. Thank God the children were in school and Rob was away at what he referred to as work. I almost didn't recognize the woman who answered the door. She was so thin, not much more than bone covered by skin; her hair was dry and matted and her skin color was a pale gray.

I said, "Hannah?"

The stranger at the door took a step back and replied, "Abagail, come in."

I stepped inside a home in disarray. Dirty dishes were stacked in the kitchen, and a layer of dust covered the furniture. Hannah was obviously weak. I led her to the couch and as we sat down, she started to sob and more or less collapsed in my lap.

We must have sat there for half an hour or more and between sobs she muttered, "I'm sorry," several times. When she'd recovered, she said, "I liked school so much, and I wanted to make you proud of me." Then, she began to apologize over and over.

Finally, I said, "Hannah honey, I'm not worried about school. Tell me what's wrong. What's happened to you?"

She blurted out, "I have cancer, I think breast cancer. I loved school; I wanted to go back, but I can't. No matter how hard I try, I just can't."

Questions poured out of me…"How long have you known? Who is your doctor? What kind of treatment are you getting? Why didn't you tell us?"

At first my inquiries were met with a wall of silence. I didn't give up and I finally said, "Hannah, I'm your friend; talk to me. I want to help you."

The answer to all my inquiries was faith and Faith. If I'd had time to think about it, I might have guessed the answer to those questions. Because Hannah and Rob had relied on God's will during Hannah's pregnancy with Faith, they believed they could do the same with any medical matter. Hannah said, "God is my doctor, prayer and the Bible are all the treatment I need."

"What kind of nonsense is that? Even if you have no insurance, your friends can help you. Ben Young can find doctors who'll work with you without a charge and I'm sure all of us can handle other expenses. Please, please, let us help."

Hannah stiffened and said, "I'm atoning for my sins and hoping God will find me worthy of living. I've brought this on myself, and now, I have to deal with it. Please respect that."

This was unthinkable, and I said, "Hannah, you're the best person I know. Isn't God supposed to be merciful and all about forgiveness? Just maybe…He sends us doctors and medicine to work His miracles."

Hannah said, "You have to go now, I'm tired and I need to go to bed."

I said, "You shouldn't be alone. Let me call Rob. He should be here with you."

"No, please, I just need to lay down; then, I'll be all right." As I opened the door, she threw her arms around me and said, "I love you."

* * *

I may have run a couple of red lights on my way to Phoebe's house. I was frantic and felt as though something should be done immediately. Phoebe answered the door in her robe, coffee in hand, and when she saw the expression on my face she said, "Abagail, what's happened?"

I rushed past her and said, "Call Tammy, we've got a big problem."

She stammered, "What…why…is something wrong with Tammy?"

"No," I shouted, "It's Hannah…she has cancer."

"How do you know?"

"She told me…I was just at her house…she looks like a skeleton! I'll tell you all about it when Tammy gets here."

Tammy arrived at Phoebe's front door with her daughter, Taylor, in tow. She said, "I was just going out the door when you called. What the hell is happening that I had to drop everything and rush over here?"

"Hannah has cancer."

"Is she having surgery…chemo?"

"That's the problem; she's praying and reading the Bible. I don't think she's even seen a doctor. She diagnosed herself."

"You're kidding!"

Phoebe chimed in, "I wish Abagail were kidding, but this is exactly how she and Rob handled a scare before Faith was born."

Tammy said, "If money is the only problem, Ben can find a clinic that will get her the treatment she needs."

I said, "I doubt she'd accept it. She's talking about paying for her sins."

Phoebe said, "Sure, what kind of sins would Hannah commit? She might have blown on her soup or stuck her gum under a table, but I seriously doubt she's done anything worse than that."

We all sat down at Phoebe's kitchen table, and our trio suddenly fell silent. Eventually, I said, "If you'd seen how awful she looks, you'd know something has to be done."

Tammy surprised Phoebe and me when she said, "What Ben and I learned from our experience with Bernie, is that people are going to do what they do, even when it seems dangerous or stupid. Logic just isn't enough. If it makes you feel better, you can call it destiny, fate or even karma. Sometimes all loved ones can do is stay close and be ready to pick up the pieces."

I said, "No matter how good your intentions are, I suppose you can't invade someone's home and tell them how to run their…" I looked at Phoebe and stopped in mid-word.

Phoebe smiled and said, "Sometimes it works, but I doubt this is the same sort of situation." She added, "We are Faith's Godmothers and it's our duty to take care of her. What we can do is visit often, take meals to the house and, if they'll accept it, get a cleaning service. The boys also need to know that we're available if they need any kind of help."

We all agreed that was a plan we could live with and if Hannah or Rob wanted to talk about medical help; we'd be ready to step in.

Tammy needed to take Taylor to nursery school, and when Phoebe and I were alone, I asked if Ariel had adjusted to her school situation. Phoebe said, "Yes, she's doing much better. Her counselor changed some of her classes and made arrangements for her to work on the school newspaper and to be on the yearbook staff. The students she works with are more serious and less social. It's a much better fit for her."

*   *   *

Rob Conway easily accepted our offer of a weekly cleaning service even though he had to overrule Hannah's objections. Four evenings a week a hot dinner was delivered by one of us to the Conway family. We also brought cereal, bread and fresh fruit for easy preparation of other meals.

Soon Hannah began to gain some strength and to look a little better. She even felt good enough to go to a hairdresser with Tammy. On one of my dinner delivery days, she seemed to be in better spirits and when I commented on it, she said, "I think I've found the answer."

I was wary of approaching the subject of medical intervention but I wanted to see if that's where she was heading. I said, "What might that be?"

"I've found two Bible verses, one from John and one from Ezekiel, and they're in agreement on God's promise for life. Here let me show you." Hannah picked up her Bible and turned to a well-worn page in the Old Testament. She read, "Ezekiel, Chapter 47, Verse 9 It will come about that every living creature which swarms in every place where the river goes, will live. And there will be very many fish, for these waters go there and the others become fresh; so everything will live where the river goes."

She looked up at me and said, "That's not all." She turned to a marked page in the New Testament and once again read aloud, "John, Chapter 7, verse 38 He who believes in Me, as the Scripture said, 'From his innermost being will flow rivers of living water.' You see, Abagail, both the Old and New Testaments agree. This has to be right; the river and the water are the answer."

"Hannah," I lied, "these verses are very interesting but just how do you think they'll help you?"

"I don't know yet, but I'm sure they're the answer, and I have to think and pray about this a bit more. It could be God's will that we own property on the river."

The minute I got home, I phoned Phoebe and repeated the conversation to her. She said, "I can see why you're disturbed. Would she try to go live by the river that runs through their property?"

"Not with winter coming on; I'm afraid she might just want to drink the water."

Phoebe speculated, "If that's the idea, she'd better hurry. Temperatures are dropping and the river will soon be frozen. Do you think the cancer has spread to her brain?"

"That could be…just reading the verses seemed to improve her spirits so much. It was almost like being with the old, healthy Hannah. Maybe just the idea or the promise is all that she needed."

*　*　*

As much as I hated leaving town at that time, Stan had made arrangements for our family to visit Colgate University with Ryan. We flew into Syracuse and spent two days with my nephew, R.J., and his family. His children were beginning to treat Stan and me as grandparents which we both liked very much.

We checked into the delightful Colgate Inn and spent two days on campus. The admissions office made arrangements for Ryan to spend his time with a member of the basketball team. They attended classes together, and Ryan was even able to suit up and practice with the team. During that time, Stan met with the bursar to talk about tuition and other expenses.

On the flight home to Springfield, Ryan told us that he'd found his college home and was ready to start the application process. Later, Stan told me about the costs involved, and we both swallowed pretty hard. I had hoped for a scholarship, but Colgate doesn't give athletic scholarships and Stan's salary from his previous year with Anacott & Associates disqualified us from any other financial aid. Stan's new partnership wasn't quite off the ground yet and he said, "It looks like we'll have to tighten our belts for a while, but we'll do it."

By the time we collected our luggage and drove home, it was nearly midnight. While we were away, the temperature in Springfield dropped well below freezing. I was cold and tired and wanted nothing more than to crawl into my bed but the light on our answering machine was flashing steadily. My first inclination was to ignore the messages and deal with them in the morning, but the rate of flashes seemed to convey a sense of urgency.

When I pressed the play button, a series of messages from Tammy and Phoebe guaranteed me a sleepless night. First, Tammy told me she had a call from Hannah's son Peter saying that Hannah had a relapse and was in great pain, wasn't eating and couldn't get out of bed. Next, I heard from Phoebe who said that Rob was not to be found, and the children were helpless and frantic so she called Tammy for help. Finally, Tammy's call was the most distressing of all. She'd taken Ben to the Conway house to examine Hannah. Hannah would have no part in it and refused to even let Ben take her temperature. He offered her a prescription for pain medication, and she turned that down as well. She said she'd taken the cure and would be better soon. It was too late to call or do anything, but I went to bed with a feeling of an impending crisis.

TAMMY YOUNG

Assisted living was a new concept in Springfield and Bernie barely qualified, but she finally accepted the inevitable. A new, well-equipped wing had been opened in an institution a few miles from her former home, and she realized that place was as good as it gets and resigned herself to it. Ben and I only visited on weekends. My week days were filled with chauffeuring children, doing what I could for Hannah and getting Bernie's house ready for sale.

When school started, Ben's daughter, Melissa, asked to stay on with us. Her mother agreed on the condition that Ben would continue to pay child support. Melissa was happy to be in our home, and I found her to be a plus in my life so we agreed to the payment. Melissa pitched in as we cleared out Bernie's home and also helped me prepare meals for Hannah's family. Melissa liked music and insisted we listen to the radio while we chopped and sautéed. Often, we'd dance through the food preparation. The children loved it and sometimes joined in.

Melissa usually went with me when I delivered the meals, and I suspected she had a crush on Peter.

Hannah's relapse unnerved me. One day she was doing so well, and the next it was as if she'd had a complete collapse. Despite her pain and weakness, she seemed at peace, refused medical attention again and told us that she'd be better soon.

There was something a little off…no…there was something way off about this whole situation. Until now, the boys had always been open and willing to discuss Hannah's condition, but now, they were evasive and couldn't even seem to look anyone in the eye. Then, there was Rob's absence and his seeming indifference to his entire family.

* * *

Our November Bridge Club meeting had to be moved up a week due to the Thanksgiving holiday. Since there were only three of us, we chose to skip the game and simply have lunch together. I was scheduled to be hostess which worked better for me because I could put Taylor down for her nap and didn't need a sitter. Of course, the main topic of conversation at lunch was Hannah and her condition. We all sensed that something had happened to account for Hannah's children's odd behavior, but we couldn't figure out what it was. We were also upset about Rob's daily absence and how the children seemed to have all the responsibility for their mother's care.

Phoebe said, "If we seem too curious and interfere too much, they may ask us not to come back."

Abagail disagreed, "Someone should to talk to Rob. Tell him that he needs to be involved, take control and to stay home and help the children with Hannah's care. I could probably try that."

Phoebe said, "Tread lightly."

I suggested, "Melissa is closer to Peter's age and they seem to get along pretty well. Maybe, she could get him to talk about Hannah's relapse and why he thinks that happened." They all agreed and thought it was worth a try, if Melissa agreed.

The conversation moved on to Thanksgiving and our personal plans as well as what could be done for the Conway family. Abagail announced, "My nephew R.J. invited us to Syracuse for the weekend. We'll probably spend some time on the Colgate campus so Ryan can confirm his decision. I get nervous when I say that because the empty nest is a bit scary."

I told my friends that our family would be traveling to Arizona to spend the holiday with my former in-laws, Millie and Boots.

Phoebe said, "That means I'll be the only one here. My sister, Marcia, has reserved a big party room at The Collonade, and we'll be celebrating with her and fifty other guests. What would you think about ordering a dinner from there and having it delivered to Hannah's home?"

Everyone agreed, and Phoebe volunteered to make the arrangements.

As we were breaking up, I asked how Ariel was doing.

Phoebe said, "Ariel is doing very well. She's studying hard and has found her niche in school social life. Three boys asked her to the homecoming dance, one of them is a popular football player."

I was so happy and excited for her, I asked, "Did she go with him?"

"No, she went with the editor of the school paper. He's good looking but shy and a little nerdy. She actually asked him, but they seemed to have had a really good time. Abagail, I know how you feel. I hate to see Ariel leave too, but I still have Bug Boy."

I asked, "Bug Boy?"

Phoebe smiled and said, "That's what Jeff and I call Adam. He's crazy about bugs. He has an ant farm in his room and is begging for a Tarantula."

*   *   *

Melissa was uncomfortable with the idea of questioning Peter about his mother's condition, but said that if he opened the subject, she'd pursue it. When we made our next dinner delivery to the Conway home, Melissa turned on their radio and asked Peter to dance. When he said he didn't know how, Melissa insisted on teaching him. I took Taylor and Grant to Hannah's room with me to see how she was doing.

Not five minutes later, I heard a door slam and a loud, angry voice say, "What's going on here?" I rushed into the kitchen, to find Melissa and Peter still as statues. All the blood had drained from Peter's face, and he was white as a sheet. Rob looked at me and barked, "How dare you bring this Jezebel into my home to lure my son into the ways of the devil?"

I was close to unloading on him, but I kept thinking of Hannah's welfare and I didn't want to disparage Rob in front of his son. I said, "Rob, they're children, please, let's not go overboard with the religious references."

"Dancing is the gateway to sin, and I'll not have it in my house."

"Caring for the sick and the needy is God's work, and that's what we're here to do. If you don't like it, you should spend more time at home yourself."

"You…you, with your rich doctor husband and your big house; what could you know about my life and what I have to do every day just to survive and to take care of my family. I have more problems than you or anybody could possibly guess so don't go judging me, lady."

Before things could get any more heated, I gathered the children and left.

PHOEBE FARLEY

The Collonade served a sumptuous Thanksgiving dinner. Afterward, Marcia and a few cousins gathered at our home to play bridge. It was past midnight when Jeff and I finished cleaning up, and I looked forward to sleeping late on Friday morning. Daybreak was arriving later and later as autumn turned to winter, and it was barely light when the phone rang at 7:45. I said to myself This can't be anything good, so I let Jeff answer the call.

I heard him say, "Wait a minute, slow down and say that again." There was a pause and I heard Jeff ask, "For what?" twice and then he said. "I'll try to take care of this. Now, I'm going to give the phone to Phoebe, and you do whatever you think is right." As Jeff handed the phone to me, he said, "It's Matthew Conway. There's big trouble and I've got to go. He'll explain."

I took the receiver and heard an hysterical Mathew Conway say, "Mrs. Farley, everything is going crazy. Please help me...I don't know what to do."

I said, "Mathew, can you tell me what's happening. Is it your Mom?"

Matthew started to sob and I only picked up a couple of words which I could barely believe. The first was "Jail" and the second was "Strange man".

I said, "Try to calm down, Mathew. I'll be there as soon as I can."

Matthew said, "I'm not at home."

"Where are you?"

"I'm at Memorial Hospital. Mom is really sick."

"Okay, you hang on and I'll see you soon."

At that moment Jeff walked out of the closet, tie and belt in hand and he said, "Rob was arrested around three o'clock this morning. Matthew thinks

186

it's for bank robbery but this doesn't sound right. I know that the police would take him in for questioning…probably during the day."

I said, "Maybe they already have and that's why he's never home."

"You could be right, but I'm going to make a couple of calls before I go anywhere."

When I'd finished dressing, Jeff returned to the bedroom and said, "The police don't have Rob. It's not robbery; it's bank fraud and the FBI has him. This is much worse. I'll go to their office and see what I can do. Are you going to the Conways?"

"No, Hannah's finally in the hospital where she belongs, and the children are there too. I don't know how that happened but I intend to find out." I left a note for Ariel and told her to take care of Adam and that I'd call later to make sure everything was all right with them.

*   *   *

At the hospital, I was directed to the intensive care floor. I found the three Conway children, standing in the hallway, staring into their mother's room through a large glass window. There was a man in the room with her. At first, I thought he was a doctor, but as I watched, the man adjusted her pillows, kissed her fingers and brushed Hannah's hair from her face. Each time she opened her eyes, she looked at him and smiled faintly.

I took Matthew aside and said, "What happened? How did you get here?"

Matthew said, "I don't know. He, that man, was banging on our door around seven…"

I interrupted Matthew and said, "Let's sit down in the waiting area away from Peter and Faith. Then you can start from the beginning and tell me everything."

When we were settled, Matthew said, "Men were pounding on our door around three this morning. Dad answered and they said they were arresting him for stealing from a bank and several other things. I thought it was a joke or something. They were wearing suits, not police uniforms. They asked me if there was another adult in the house and, when I said, "Yes," and tried to tell them how sick my mom was they didn't pay any attention. They had handcuffs out, but Dad begged them not to cuff him in front of me, and they didn't. Then, they marched him out the door."

"Who else saw this?"

"Just me; everyone else was still asleep."

"Why didn't you call us then?"

"I didn't want to wake you up in the middle of the night. Then, I heard Mom moaning and I made some toast and tried to get her to eat. She was having a lot of pain and I thought it was better not to wake Peter and Faith."

"Now tell me about that man with your Mom. Have you ever seen him before?"

"I think he's a car salesman. Mom and Dad bought…Oh, oh…now I remember. He's the man who rescued us when we were in the blizzard. When he put us in his car this morning, I had the strangest feeling that all this happened before."

"Matthew, that's called déjà vu, but go on."

"Anyway, a little after six the doorbell started ringing; I thought maybe it was the police again. When I opened the door, this man said, 'Is your mother here?'

"I said, 'Yes, but she's sick.' He brushed past me and ran through the house calling her name. It woke up Peter and Faith.

"When he opened Mom's bedroom door, he looked at her, stopped in his tracks and said, 'Oh my God.' He looked back at me and asked, 'How did it get this bad?'

"I said, 'She has breast cancer.'

"He asked how long we'd known and what kind of treatment she'd had. When I told him none; he went to the side of the bed and took her hand. She looked up at him and said something but I couldn't hear it. Then he told us we were going to the hospital and to get dressed.

"I didn't know what to do, but I wanted to get help for my Mom so I went along with him. She couldn't walk very far and he picked her up and carried her to his car. While we were getting ready to go, he called each one of us by name. It was so weird; all that car stuff happened a long time ago. Faith was a baby and Peter and I were just little kids."

I asked if Peter and Faith knew about the arrest and he said, "No. They keep asking where Dad is. They're already confused and I don't know how to tell them."

I said, "Thank you Matthew. I'm sure you know you have friends who'll help you. I'm not going to lie to you, but your family may never be the same again." I could see tears welling up in Matthew's eyes and I continued, "Try not to let yourself feel desperate. Your family will be taken care of."

"What about my Dad?"

"We'll do the best we can for him, but he's in serious trouble. Let's wait just a little bit before we tell Peter and Faith."

*   *   *

Matthew and I walked back to Hannah's room just as a nurse was going in. The man came out and said to the children, "Your mother's getting medication, and she shouldn't be in as much pain." Next, he asked, "Are you hungry?" Peter and Faith nodded. Then, the man turned to me and said, "You're Phoebe." He extended his hand and said, "I'm Hugh Fordyce. Let's take these children to the cafeteria."

After we'd seated Hannah's children at a table with their food, Hugh nodded toward a booth out of their hearing range. He asked what I'd like, and I said, "Coffee, black." When he returned with two cups of coffee, I was wishing I could order a bourbon and Seven up. I couldn't have known then that when our conversation was finished, I'd want a double. I had so many questions for him; I surprised myself when I only said, "How do you know my name?"

Hugh said, "I've heard so much about you. I'd have known you anywhere; you and Tammy and Abagail. There's no reason for secrecy anymore, and I think you should know that Hannah and I have been in love for years."

"Hannah...our Hannah had an affair. I'm assuming it was an affair?"

Hugh nodded and said, "Yes, for ten years. You may call it an affair, but it was more than that, much more. I know how close the four of you are, and I'm surprised that no one even suspected."

"You're the man who rescued her in the blizzard."

"Yes, I fell in love with her the moment I saw her. Later, I invested some money in Rob's land deal. She handled the exchange of paper work, and that's how our relationship began. I only invested to get to spend time with her."

This was incredulous, and I asked why there was never a divorce. Hugh said, "I begged her to divorce that...that...man she married. I think she was on the verge when she got sick, and that's when she stopped seeing me. She had a lot of hang-ups about the children and the vow she made years ago. I would have taken care of the children and paid for a divorce. When she started to lose weight, I begged her to get medical care and offered to make arrangements and pay the bills. I didn't know until today that it was cancer."

"What made you go to her home today and weren't you concerned that Rob would be there?"

"I was listening to the radio on the drive to work, and I heard that the FBI had taken Rob and another man into custody for some phony loan scheme. According to the news report, they'd been under investigation for some time. I knew Hannah would be alone with the children, and I wanted to help her if I could."

I said, "How are you going to explain yourself to the children?"

He said, "I'm an investor with their Dad, and, I'm saying I'm a close friend of their parents. Rob's in jail and Hannah can barely talk. It's a half truth, and someday they'll probably figure it out; for now, it's enough."

The children had finished eating and gathered around our booth. Hugh said, "Let's go see how your mother is doing. He rose and extended his hand to help me up."

I said, "Thanks, but I need another cup of coffee. I'll see you in a few minutes."

* * *

I was spellbound during Hugh's confession and still staring into my empty coffee cup when I heard a familiar voice say, "Penny for your thoughts."

I looked up and saw Jeff standing next to me. I said, "My thoughts are worth more than a penny, maybe a million dollars. How did you know I was here?"

"I went to Hannah's room and Matthew told me you were in the cafeteria."

"What's going on with Rob?"

"He's in deep doo doo. It seems he's mortgaged property that he doesn't own and his co-conspirator, a bank loan officer, has been taking kick-backs on every loan. Right now, that guy has a good attorney and is spilling his guts for a plea deal. Rob will probably take the fall. He needs a criminal attorney; probably two or three good ones. At the moment, I'm Rob's attorney of record, but I only handle civil law, and I'm not experienced enough to take on a case of this kind.

"I suspect that right now, Rob can't even afford a cup of coffee. How can he pay for good counsel?"

"Maybe pro bono, but he might have to settle for a public defender. I'll ask around and see what I can find for him. By the way, who's that man with the Conway kids?"

"That's the million-dollar question, and the answer is a bombshell."

Jeff sat down and said, "Now, it's your turn to spill your guts."

I said, "Fasten your seat belt. If you think Rob's activities are shocking; wait till you hear what our Hannah's been up to." As I repeated what I'd learned from Hugh Fordyce, Jeff leaned farther and farther across the table. I could see he was fascinated by what he was hearing.

When I finished, he sat back in the booth and said, "Hannah…Hannah had an affair? "

"Yes, she did."

"It's always the quiet ones to look out for." I was surprised when Jeff burst into a very long, very loud laugh. I gave him a quizzical look and he said, "I'm happy for her."

I so wished that Abigail and Tammy were in town to help, but I couldn't get hold of them and even if I could, I didn't want to ruin their vacations. I said to Jeff, "Those children can't go back to that empty house alone; we'll need to take them home with us."

Jeff agreed, and suggested that after lunch we take them back to their house, let them pack a few things, and relax with us at home during the evening. I said, "They've been through so much; they need some time to just be kids without responsibility for a sick woman. Faith and Peter don't know what's happened to Rob; maybe we can find a way to break it to them gently."

* * *

Faith and Peter were willing to go home with us, but they continued to ask about their father. Matthew wanted to stay at the hospital and said that Mr. Fordyce would drop him at our house when visiting hours were over. Jeff finally decided we couldn't keep Faith and Peter in suspense about their father, and he was very straightforward about the situation. He told them that Rob had broken a law, and he was in jail. They both cried and Jeff promised that he would try to arrange a visit for them.

It was good that he did tell them the truth, because when we reached the Conway home, it was swarming with men searching every corner of the house.

Jeff confirmed that they had a warrant and persuaded the searchers to allow the children to pack some clothing and personal things with supervision.

The remainder of our day alternated between hospital visits for the children, and a movie to take their minds off the situation. Every time we went to the hospital, Hugh Fordyce was there. He sat on one side of Hannah's bed and Matthew on the other. She had minutes of consciousness followed by hours of drug-induced sleep. Hugh told us that the hospital staff didn't have much hope for her, but he had arranged for a specialist to see her on Monday. He still hoped that some specialized treatment could give her a little more time.

*   *   *

When we were finally able to go home, Ariel met us at the door. She looked like she was ready to explode until she saw Faith and Peter. After she glanced at their overnight bags, she seemed to calm down and said, "Mom, I need some help in the kitchen. Can you come in there with me?"

I could tell Ariel didn't want to talk in front of the Conway children, and I asked Jeff to show them where they'd be sleeping. When we were finally alone, Ariel said, "Where have you been? You've been gone all day, and I've been worried to death."

I said, "Hannah Conway's in the hospital, and we've been there most of the day."

"Did you know that Mr. Conway was arrested?"

"Yes, your Dad's been trying to get some help for him."

"It's all over TV. Did he rob a bank?"

"Sort of, but not with a gun. He and a bank employee just kind of helped themselves to some money."

"Well, the phone's been ringing all day. Everybody wants to know about it. The Pastor from church even called."

"I'm sorry I didn't check in, but we've been dealing with a lot."

"Oh yes, Tammy Young called and said that she's back in town. They came home early because Dr. Young's mother had another stroke, and they're moving her to some other place where she'll get more care."

"Does Tammy know about Rob's arrest?"

"She didn't mention it and I didn't either. She sounded really stressed, and she was in a hurry."

"Anything else important?"

"Mrs. Gray left a message. They're staying in Syracuse a few extra days. Ryan wants to look at Cornell before he makes his final decision."

Learning that I was all alone with responsibility for three extra children put me under some stress as well. At least, I was relieved that Hannah had good care. I said to Ariel, "Can you help me with dinner? We have two or three extra mouths to feed, and it may be that way for a while."

While we cooked, Ariel said, "I just don't understand all of this. Stealing is a sin and Mr. Conway is so religious. How could he do that?"

I was happy that Ariel didn't know the whole story, but as it turned out, neither did I.

ABAGAIL GRAY

The weather in Syracuse turned nasty and our plane was delayed for several hours. Even though our ride to Springfield was turbulent, we were thankful that our plane was able to get off the ground. It was after ten o'clock when we arrived at our home, and I wanted nothing more than a hot shower and a soft pillow.

Early the next morning, the phone roused me out of a deep sleep. I hoped that Stan would answer, but when I looked at the clock, I realized that he had already gone to work and Ryan to school.

Phoebe's voice sounded muffled and she said, "Abagail, I need your help. Can I come over now?"

I tried to stall, "I'm still in bed. I just woke up."

"Throw on your robe, I'll be right over."

I had to ask if what I'd been dreading had happened. "Did Hannah die?"

"No, she's in the hospital, but that's not the bigger problem, I'm on my way."

I answered the door wondering what could have upset Phoebe so much. Her first words were, "I don't know where to begin."

"Start at the beginning. What's the problem?"

"Rob's in jail, and Hannah's in the hospital."

A hundred questions flooded my brain and all I could say was "Jail?"

"Yes, he was arrested for bank fraud. Jeff's talked to him and to the FBI and it seems he'll go to prison for a long time."

Phoebe sat down at the kitchen table and when she had spilled out the events of the last two days; I wanted to go back to bed and pull the covers over my head.

194

Finally, I said, "Hannah and Hugh Fordyce…I know him from the Country Club. He's a catch; handsome, nice and successful. I've wondered why I never see him with a woman."

"Believe me, he knows a lot about you too. Hannah's been telling him about us for years. I think he's probably more than nice. Since he took Hannah to the hospital, he's barely left her side; he's paying for her medical care and he's bringing in a specialist today."

"So, where are the children?"

"They're with me and they're traumatized. I can't send them to school; not while Rob's in the news. It's possible they'll be teased and bullied in addition to all their other problems. Matthew is with Hannah most of the time and barely leaves her room. Peter is withdrawn and hardly talks to anyone."

"Is Tammy back yet? Does she know?"

"They came back early, and I haven't talked to her yet, but she did leave a message. All I know is that Bernie's had a massive stroke, and Tammy and Ben are moving her to a clinical care facility."

I said, "What can we do?"

"Rob's beyond help, and Hannah is getting medical care and being looked after, but I need some help with the children. They're confused and scared, and I honestly don't know how to handle it."

"We can't separate them; that wouldn't be good. Could we take them home and take turns staying with them?"

"Jeff says they may not be able to live in their house again; maybe never. It will likely go to the bank or possibly even be confiscated by the FBI."

With that comment, the full weight of the situation dropped on me. Unless there was a miracle cure for Hannah, these three children were going to be orphans, and without intervention, might possibly go into the Foster System.

While Phoebe and I were trying to figure out what to do with Hannah's children, Tammy called. She said, "What's this we're hearing about Rob? Did he really get arrested?"

I said, "Yes, that's true, and Hannah's in the hospital."

Tammy asked, "Where are the children?"

I said, "Phoebe has them now, but we're trying to figure out what to do with them."

Tammy sighed and said, "I wish I could help, but Bernie's in very bad shape. The doctors are only giving her a few days. Melissa's been a trooper about caring for Grant and Taylor, but she needs a break and to spend some time with her grandmother too."

I said, "Do what you have to do and don't worry about our situation. Phoebe and I will work it out. Please tell Ben how sorry we are and we'll be thinking about you and praying for Bernie."

When the call was finished, Phoebe said, "I've got to get back. The children will need breakfast, and after they've eaten, I'll take them to the hospital."

"When you're finished, bring them here. It's time to put up the Christmas tree, and if they help, maybe, they'll forget about their problems for a while. If they want to go to the hospital later, I'll take them."

Matthew chose to stay at the hospital for the day so I only had Peter and Faith to help with the tree. Peter mostly sat on the sofa and stared into space.

* * *

I have to admit, I was pleased to take the children to the hospital in the afternoon. I wanted to see Hannah, but I was more eager to finally meet Hugh Fordyce.

When I walked into the hospital room, Hugh rose and said, "Abagail." It was a statement not a question. I was surprised at his appearance. He had a day's growth of beard, and his wrinkled shirt was hanging out of his pants."

I went to Hannah's bedside and took her hand. I have to admit, she looked much better than the last time I saw her. She opened her eyes, smiled and said, "Abagail."

I started to tear up, and Hugh Fordyce said, "Let's give the children some time with their mother, and he motioned toward the door. Once in the hallway, he said, "I could use some coffee. Let's go downstairs to the cafeteria. By the way, I'm Hugh Fordyce."

I said, "So I've heard."

As we waited for the elevator, Hugh gave me a sideways glance and said, "You know, don't you?"

"Just what I've heard from Phoebe."

"Well, it's all true, and I know all about the three of you. Hannah was very fortunate to have you for friends, and the children are lucky too."

When we'd settled in the cafeteria, I said, "I don't much care about what happens to Rob, but I am very concerned for Hannah and the children. Do you know any more about her condition?"

"She had tests this morning, and I was only able to visit with her cancer specialist briefly. He thinks she should have been diagnosed and treated long ago. I'll meet with him tomorrow when he's had an opportunity to study the test results."

I said, "You'll keep us informed?"

"Absolutely."

* * *

About six o'clock Stan rushed into the house and said, "I was listening to the news on my way home. What the hell is going on with Rob Conway?" Before I could answer, he noticed that our dining table was set for six, and he said, "Are we having a dinner party?"

I said, "Shhh, the Conway children are here and Ryan is upstairs studying. Phoebe is picking up the children after dinner and I'll tell you all about it then."

"Okay, but I've gotta know…is that Conway con-man in jail or not?"

"Yes," I said, "but it's worse than anything you've heard on the news."

Stan said, "I need a drink. Can I fix one for you?"

"I'll save mine till we're alone. You may need another by then."

Except for the fact that Rob had been arrested, Ryan was in the dark about the rest of the story, and he tried to make light conversation with the Conway children at dinner. Faith seemed to be taking all of this better than her brothers, and only she made an effort to communicate with our family.

After dinner, I was alone in the kitchen when Matthew walked in. I said, "How are you doing?"

"This is very hard, but I'm OK. I really appreciate everything you and the Farleys are doing for us; especially for my Mom and Dad."

"No matter what happens, you and your sister and brother will have a home."

Matthew teared up and said, "My Mom is going to die."

I said, "We don't know that for sure. Let's wait to hear what the doctor has to say."

"I already know. He came to her room late this afternoon to talk to Mr. Fordyce, and he said she only has a week or two at most."

"I'm sure you know that we all begged her to get medical attention, and she just wouldn't do it."

Then came the big question, "Mrs. Gray, is Mr. Fordyce my Mom's boyfriend?"

"All I know, Matthew, is that Hugh Fordyce rescued all of you in the blizzard and invested in your Dad's property. Phoebe, Tammy and I are your mother's best friends, and the only time she ever talked about him was after the blizzard incident."

I knew there would be more questions, but I thought Hugh Fordyce should be the one to answer them. I had a question of my own, and I said to Matthew, "Is Peter all right? I'm worried about him. He seems so depressed and withdrawn. I don't know what we can do to make him feel better."

Matthew said, "We're all depressed, but Peter is dealing with some stuff and isn't handling it very well."

Even the skeptical Stan was shocked by the details of the what I'd come to think of as the Conway Family Saga. When I'd finished telling him about my day, he said, "I've played golf with that Fordyce guy and thought he was pretty nice. But...but I just don't know what to make of this. Is he the hero or the villain?"

In my opinion, he's Superman, all he needs is a cape. He saw a problem; he flew in and saved the day. Think about it...would any of us have had the nerve to take Hannah to the hospital against her will or would we have been willing to pay for a specialist? Without him, she'd be back in the house racked with pain and cared for by three frantic children.

"You may be right, but all this is going to take a lot of explaining."

PHOEBE FARLEY

My awakening was slow; rather like floating up out of deep water. My eyes were still closed when I surfaced. I reached out to see if Jeff was still in bed. The sheets were cool, a clue that he'd been up for a while and had probably left the house. Thank God, I thought. I need some time alone to wrap my head around the dream I've just had.

I'd never had a dream that vivid; I'm sure it was a dream, but it seemed so real. I was standing on a street corner and my friends were there, frozen in place, as if they were all mannequins. In the distance, I saw a man approaching on a bicycle. As he drew nearer, I could see that it was Javier. He looked just as he did when I last saw him at the university. He was wearing a silky, short sleeved shirt that almost glowed. The color was aqua, a little more green than blue, but yes; definitely aqua. He stopped the bicycle near us, said nothing, but just observed the scene. I looked at him, but we didn't speak. After our eyes met, he pedaled away, and all my mannequin friends came to life, began to move around and speak among themselves.

In the bathroom, I found a note from Jeff telling me that he would feed Ariel and Adam and drop Adam at school. I knew that Matthew, Faith and Peter would be wanting breakfast soon, so I reluctantly dressed and started for the kitchen; still unable to shake the dream. Just when there were so many important decisions to be made, I needed to be able to concentrate and deal with all the problems in my real life. I asked myself *Why this? Why now?*

As I was setting the table, I thought about how long it'd been since I'd seen Javier, and I began to calculate how long he'd been gone. As I did the math, I stopped in mid-step. Today was December 12, Javier's birthday. Normally,

I always thought about him on his birthday, but with all that was happening lately, I'd lost track of the dates. I recalled that once, in the early morning, when I was still in the twilight zone, my lips felt as if they'd been kissed. Javier's kiss was soft and warm and always left me with a tingly feeling; that's what I felt on that day. I had to wonder if this man was haunting me.

* * *

A call from Tammy jolted me out of my dream world and back to reality. She said, "I should have called you sooner, but Bernie passed away around noon yesterday. Ben and I spent all afternoon making funeral arrangements."

I said, "I'm sorry," and half meant it.

Tammy said, "It was a blessing. She was totally unresponsive and had no hope for recovery. Bernie always let us know what she wanted and she was very vocal about her dislike of funerals. Long ago, she said she wanted a graveside service and no open casket."

I asked about the time and place, and Tammy said, "The funeral will be Monday, the fifteenth at the Mortengate Memorial Cemetery. She'll be buried next to Ben senior."

I half-heartedly said, "Is there anything we can do for you?"

"Yes," Tammy said, "could you call Abagail and tell her about the arrangements? It sounds like you two have your hands full with the Conway children; and how is Hannah doing?"

"She's hanging on; I don't think there's a lot of hope, but we'll be hearing from a specialist today."

"A specialist? How can they afford that?"

I suddenly realized that Tammy didn't know about Hugh Fordyce or the circumstances of Hannah's hospitalization. I said, "You need to concentrate on Bernie's burial, and when your life is back on track; we'll talk about Hannah."

"You make it sound so mysterious."

"It's just complicated. Please give our sympathy to Ben and take care of business; then we'll talk."

* * *

I'd just finished my phone call with Tammy when Matthew walked into the kitchen. I asked if Faith and Peter were awake, and he said, "If it doesn't mess up your schedule, it would be better if Peter could sleep as long as possible. He had a hard time last night and didn't go to sleep until late."

When he finished eating, Matthew said, "Mrs. Farley, do you think that Mr. Fordyce is my Mom's boyfriend?"

I thought it was a legitimate question, but I needed to find out more about what Matthew already knew. I asked, "What makes you think that?"

First he said, "Investors and family friends don't stay all night at the hospital and they don't pay all the bills." I didn't respond. Then, Matthew said, "When I've been just outside of the room, and Mom is conscious, Mr. Fordyce kisses her and calls her Tweety. She seems to like it."

I said, "Look Matthew, when Faith was born, that didn't mean that your Mom had to take love away from you and Peter to give to Faith. I'm sure she loves all her children the same but in different ways and for different reasons. We all have an infinite, unmeasurable amount of love in us, and we can love a lot of people in different ways."

Matthew said, "I know my Dad did a bad thing, and he didn't take very good care of my Mom, and I hate him for that; but he's my Dad, and I still love him too.

"Matthew, it's OK for you to feel both love and hate for the same person. One thing I'm sure of is, whatever your Dad did, it was for his family. I know he didn't want to break the law, but he didn't know what else to do and, he more or less, sacrificed himself for your welfare. He did the best he knew how to do. Remember that and when you're older, you'll be able to sort it out."

I turned away so Matthew wouldn't see the tears streaming down my face. I'd just voiced all the thoughts that my dream had stirred in me, and I thought, *What are you telling this boy? You're older and you still haven't sorted it out. Besides that, you've just made a perfect case for infidelity.*

I just couldn't take any more, and I sat down, cradled my head in my arms on the table and sobbed. Matthew was starting to say something but stopped when Peter walked into the room.

Peter said, "What's going on? Why is Mrs. Farley crying?...Matthew, did you tell her?"

I grabbed a napkin from the table, wiped my tears, blew my nose, looked up and said, "Tell me what?" and I stared at Peter.

He collapsed into a chair, and said, "My Mom is going to die and it's our fault; we've killed her; Matthew and I did it."

I looked at Matthew, and he couldn't meet my eyes. He said, "We did what Mom wanted. She said we'd be saving her life, and if we didn't go to the river, she'd die for sure. She seemed better, and we thought she could maybe be getting well. We couldn't understand why she wanted to go to the river."

Peter said, "It was so cold. At first, we said no, but she ordered us to do it, and finally, she got down on her knees and begged us."

"What did you do?"

Matthew said, "We told her the river was frozen and she couldn't do anything?"

She told us to get a piece of rope and an axe to take with us.

Peter added, "When we got there, Matthew told her the ice was thin and wouldn't hold anyone, but she insisted that he crawl onto the ice a little way and chop a hole to the water. I tied the rope around my brother's waist in case he fell in but he was able to do it."

I could see where this was going, and I was feeling more and more nauseous.

Matthew said, "All the time we begged Mom to let us take her home, but she was so determined. She tied the rope around her own waist and crawled onto the ice; pulled up her sweater and put her bare breast into the freezing water. I thought she'd just let the water wash over her and come back, but she laid there for what seemed like forever. Peter and I finally pulled her back with the rope, and all the while she was screaming, 'No, no, I need more time.'"

I said, "That's when she had the relapse?"

Peter said, "When we got her back to shore, she was shaking so bad and her lips were blue. Matthew and I had to wrap her in our coats and carry her to the car. She's been getting worse ever since."

I said, "It's that damn Bible verse…that's why she wanted to do it."

Both boys stared at me and Peter said, "How did you know?"

I said, "She showed it to me, and she believed it was the answer."

I said to Peter, "Is this what's had you so upset?"

He looked down at the table and said, "Yes." Shame was written all over his face.

I said, "Have you told anyone else about this?" They both shook their heads, and I continued. "I'm promising you that I will never repeat what you've just told me to anyone ever and I want you two to give me the same promise. This stays with us. Understood?"

Matthew nodded, and Peter said, "I promise."

*   *   *

A phone call from Hugh Fordyce was a relief from this conversation. He told me the cancer specialist would be in Hannah's room at 11:00, and if Abagail and I wanted to speak with the doctor, we were welcome to come.

As Abagail's phone rang, I was desperate for her to answer. When she picked up on the sixth ring, I told her about Hugh's call, and said, "Could you pick up the children and take them to the hospital. I've had a very bad morning, and I can meet you at there at 11:00."

When I was finally alone in the house, I laid on my bed. Too many things had come at me in too short a time. The long-buried feelings stirred by my dream, news of Bernie's death and Matthews suspicions about Hugh were all stored in my subconscious. I knew I'd have to deal with them in the future, but for now, all I could think about was our darling Hannah lying on thin ice, both literally and figuratively; desperate for life and forgiveness. I felt total revulsion, and I hoped that anyone who knew and loved her, would never have this picture in their minds. No wonder Peter was racked with guilt. I felt a need to talk to him about that and wondered if he'd need professional help to get over it.

Not unexpectedly, the cancer specialist was nearly an hour late. He talked to Hugh, Abagail and me in the hallway while the children stayed in the room with their mother. The doctor used a lot of medical terms to describe the type of cancer that Hannah had. I was not surprised when he said that the cancer had been in Hannah's body for at least three years and early diagnosis and treatment could have extended her life indefinitely. He said, "By the time the lump was big enough to feel, it was already too late for treatment." He summarized by saying that Hannah had only about a week left and added, "All we can do now is keep her comfortable."

I asked the doctor to speak to the children and urged him to emphasize how long the cancer had been in their mother's body and how long ago her case became hopeless. Hugh and Abagail looked at me as if I were crazy, but

I wanted Matthew and Peter to know that Hannah was already beyond hope when they took her to the river, and their actions didn't cause her relapse or her death.

Cooking for seven people was wearing me out, and I decided pizza was on the menu for our dinner. I asked Peter to ride with me because I wanted a chance to talk to him privately. When we drove into the parking lot of the Pizza Hut, I turned off the engine and said, "Peter, we need to talk about your Mom."

"Yeah, I guess."

"When the doctor told you about how long your Mom's been sick, how did that make you feel?"

"Mrs. Farley, it made me mad."

"Who are you mad at?"

"My Dad and my Mom; she should have gone to a doctor right away. Even if we didn't have the money…there had to be a way."

"Do you understand now that you and your brother did nothing to cause your mother's relapse and what happened at the river was simply an act of faith on her part."

"Maybe, but I'm really mad at God. He promised a cure and when she did everything the Bible said to do; he let her down. If that's what he does, I don't want anything more to do with him."

I didn't have an answer for that, but I said, "You have nothing to feel guilty about. You obeyed your mother and tried to help her, but it was already too late."

On the way home, I switched on the radio hoping to distract Peter from the serious discussion we'd just had. We were both jolted by a news alert saying that John Lennon had just been shot on a New York Street.

* * *

Despite the unending coverage of Lennon's death, when all of the children were settled for the night, Jeff sat me down for a serious discussion. I was so tired, that was the last thing I wanted. He began, "I know these children need help, but this situation has really gone too far. You're so focused on them; you don't know what's going on with your own children. Besides that, you're a mess. Look at you; your eyelids are drooping, and you can barely hold your head up."

"I know… I know but I'm too tired to even think about this now. Can we talk about it in the morning?" I couldn't explain the extra stress of learning about Hannah's trip to the river, and the guilt both of her boys were suffering, and then, there was my dream. That too, had increased the pressure I was already feeling.

Jeff took my hand, guided me upstairs and helped me into the shower. When I came out, he dried me with a towel and rubbed my back till I fell asleep. The last thought I could remember was, *I hope Javier will leave me alone tonight.*

The alarm woke me at six o'clock. Jeff turned on the bedside lamp and said, "Feel better?"

"I will when I've had some coffee."

"The pot is brewing, and I'll bring you a cup as soon as it's finished."

Jeff said, "I don't want to put any more pressure on you, but are you aware that Christmas is less than two weeks away? We have no decorations, and as far as I know, no gifts either."

Truthfully, I hadn't even had time to think about Christmas, and Jeff's announcement made me feel awful; but with Bernie's funeral coming up and the extra cooking and driving children around, I honestly didn't know how I'd work it in.

When Jeff returned with my coffee, he sat down on the side of the bed and said, "You know Phoebe, Hannah's children belong in school. It would take their minds off of things and relieve you of dealing with them all day."

"Abagail and I thought that news of Rob's arrest could cause teasing and bullying, and along with their mother's illness, they don't need anything more. Christmas vacation begins in a few days and they can go back after New Years and have a fresh start."

"That may be true, but news of Lennon's death is getting constant coverage. It's all people talk about, and there's hardly a mention of Rob's arrest. These children are falling behind in their studies. Matthew is a senior, and he needs passing grades to graduate. The news reports on the arrest didn't say anything about Rob's family, and it's possible that no one's even put them together. Rob has decided to take a guilty plea so there won't be all the publicity usually surrounding a trial."

"Why did he do that?"

"We can't find an attorney who'll take his case pro bono, and Rob will have to use a public defender. I think he hopes to spare the children the publicity of a trial."

Jeff continued, "Of course, it's all part of God's plan."

I said, "How much time do you think he'll get?"

Jeff rolled his eyes and said, "Probably, twenty years, but that's no problem. Rob is planning to serve his sentence doing prison ministry."

TAMMY YOUNG

ernie's funeral was scheduled for 11:00 and I needed to find a suitable place for a luncheon to follow the service. But so close to Christmas—it seemed that all the private dining rooms in Springfield were reserved for office parties. I was getting desperate for a location when Abagail saved the day! She was able to reserve a small private dining room at The Springfield Club.

God bless Millie and Boots. They left Arizona to brave our winter weather and help out. Millie cooked many meals and took care of my children while Boots decorated the house and did a lot of our Christmas shopping.

The morning of the funeral, Phoebe called to tell me that Hannah was failing, and if I wanted to see her, I needed to do it soon. She said she needed to talk to me first and suggested we meet for coffee in the hospital cafeteria the day after the funeral. I kept asking myself, "What's the big damn deal?"

A sleet storm hit Springfield the morning of the funeral. The mortuary limousine nearly slid off the road, and the hearse had a difficult time climbing the steep hills of the cemetery. It seems that Bernie had only fair-weather friends, and a small band of mourners huddled under a tent at her graveside. The minister displayed the quality of mercy and conducted a very brief service. Ben gave a short eulogy in which he spoke about his mother's parenting skills and her devotion to her grandchildren. I couldn't help but think *the funeral for my dog, Dolly, was more heartfelt.*

*   *   *

The Springfield Club outdid itself and served comfort food that was perfect for a stormy winter day; creamed chicken on tea biscuits and apple pie a la mode for dessert. During lunch, I noticed that Phoebe looked pale and tired and, Jeff was unusually attentive. Abagail, too, looked sad and serious, and I knew that she wasn't grieving for Bernie.

After lunch I found Jeff standing outside the ladies lounge. I said, "Phoebe's not herself and she doesn't look good either."

"I'm worried about her, Tammy. She's got Hannah's three children full time plus our two. She's worn out, and we've done nothing for Christmas. I haven't told her, but I'm going to take a week off to help and at least do the Christmas shopping."

I felt terrible about not being available, and I said, "Look Jeff, this is like history repeating itself. We've spent Christmas together before and Millie and Boots are here. Millie's cooking and Boots has decorated the house. Please, plan to have Christmas dinner with us."

"Counting the Conway children, that's seven extra mouths to feed. Are you sure?"

"Absolutely, don't worry; we'll work it out. This has been a sad time for all of us and it will be good just to be together."

"Thank you and count us in. I'll tell you what, I'll organize all the children into a clean-up crew, and we'll take care of that part of the meal."

Phoebe still hadn't come out of the lounge, and Jeff asked me to check on her. I found her stretched out on a chaise lounge sound asleep. I was reluctant to tell Jeff, and when I did, he reacted just as I suspected he would. He brushed past me and rushed into the lounge. He gently woke Phoebe, and although she was still groggy, he said, "Come on Sweetheart. I'm taking over now, and you're going home to bed."

Abagail walked in just at that moment and said, "What's going on?"

When they had gone, I told Abagail that Phoebe was exhausted and Jeff was planning to take time off from work to help her. I said, "I'm supposed to meet her at the hospital tomorrow before I see Hannah, but I wonder if that's going to happen."

Abagail said, "You don't know, do you?"

"Know what?"

Abagail said, "Come with me. I'm going to buy you a drink."

"What's the big mystery, and why do I need a drink at 1:30 in the afternoon?"

Abagail said, "Trust me." I followed her and we were seated in two large leather chairs in a lounge area mostly occupied by overweight, white-haired men, drinking whiskey and reading newspapers. When two martinis had been served, Abagail said, "There's no way to say this gently or talk around it; Hannah was having an affair."

She caught me in mid-sip, and I was so shocked, that the old Tammy resurfaced. I spewed out a mouthful of gin and said loudly, "No shit! An affair!" Several of the men lowered their newspapers and stared at us. As I tried to wipe the liquor off of my jacket, I looked around and in the same tone of voice said, "I'm sorry." Before the men raised their papers, I noticed a couple of them grinning.

I took a moment to process this information, and found I had about a hundred questions. *How do you know? Who knows about it? How long had this been going on? Who is he? And why does this matter now that Rob's in jail and Hannah's dying?* It took a second martini for Abagail to tell me the whole story, and for the first time in a very long time, I was speechless.

Abagail assured me that Hugh Fordyce was taking good care of Hannah, and that I'd like him when we met. Out of the corner of my eye, I caught Stan and Ben approaching, and I asked, "Do the men know about this?"

"Yes, but I'm not sure how much Rob knows, and I'm not sure that it matters. Hannah will be gone, and he'll be in jail for a very long time."

"What about the children? Will they become wards of the state?"

"It's possible, but we can't let that happen."

*   *   *

The following morning, I made a list of thank you notes that needed to be sent and put it aside promising myself that I'd take care of it after Christmas. When I arrived at Hannah's hospital room, I stood outside and just watched for a moment or two. I found Matthew engaged in a quiet conversation with a very good-looking man. Faith and Peter were sitting on the other side of their mother's bed. Hannah's eyes were closed and she seemed to be sleeping peacefully. I studied the man with Matthew carefully and thought, Wow, no wonder Hannah couldn't resist him.

The man turned, caught a glimpse of me and came into the hall. He extended his hand and said, "I'm Hugh Fordyce."

I said, "It's nice to meet you, Mr. Fordyce. I'm Tammy Young."

"Please, it's Hugh. I understand there's been a loss in your family and you have my sympathy."

"Yes, and I believe we're about to have another loss," and I tilted my head toward Hannah's room.

Hugh said, "Why don't we go to the cafeteria. I'd like to talk to you privately."

When we were settled, Hugh said, "I imagine you know about my relationship with Hannah."

"I only learned of your existence yesterday, and I'm still in shock."

"Our connection is deep and long term. I begged Hannah to divorce Rob and marry me. I wanted to take care of her and her children. I'm grateful to have that opportunity now even though it's brief."

I said, "How are the children accepting this situation?"

"We don't discuss it, but I'm sure Matthew knows and understands. We seem to get along very well. I think Peter suspects, and Faith is completely puzzled about me, but relieved that her mother is being cared for."

I said, "Circumstances were very bad before Rob's arrest, and I'm sure that all three children are relieved and so are her friends."

"Hannah has only a few days left, and then some decisions need to be made about the children. When all of this is over, I'd like to meet with you and Phoebe and Abagail to discuss different possibilities."

"We're Faith's Godmothers and we take that seriously. We'll do whatever is in their best interest."

Hugh said, "I know."

Before leaving the hospital, I spent some time at Hannah's bedside, but she didn't wake up. I hugged the children and tearfully told them how much I loved them and their mother. I wished I could have relieved Phoebe and taken them home, but I had my own children and Melissa to care for and many jobs to wind up Bernie's affairs.

* * *

That evening, I didn't want to bother Phoebe so I called Abagail and told her about meeting Hugh Fordyce. She said that she and Stan were taking the Conway children for a few days to relieve Phoebe. Stan had checked them into a hotel with a pool and restaurant to give them a chance to relax and to give her a break from feeding them. I invited her family for Christmas dinner, but she said her nephew R. J. would be in town and they planned to celebrate the holiday with his family.

Even though Millie served a wonderful Christmas dinner, the meal was subdued. Matthew decided to remain at the hospital, but Faith and Peter joined us. Only the young children were excited about the holiday and their gifts. Adam Farley was ecstatic as he described his new Tarantula. He felt his pet needed a name and asked for suggestions. Boots said, "Why not call him Charlie."

Adam looked puzzled and said, "Charlie?"

"That way, he'll be Charlie Farley."

Adam said, "That works for me." And, at last everyone smiled and some even laughed. It was the last light moment we'd have for the foreseeable future.

* * *

The following day, we were told that Hannah had slipped into a coma and it was only a matter of hours. She died the night of the twenty-sixth surrounded by her children. Hugh stood in the back of the room and Phoebe, Abagail and I watched from the hallway.

The day after Hannah's death, Hugh asked to meet with the three of us at his place of business. Jeff asked to come in case there were legal questions. First we discussed final arrangements. Hugh wanted to have Hannah cremated and have a memorial service, mainly to give the children a sense of closure. We all agreed and no mention was made of Rob or what his wishes might be.

Hugh's other reason for the meeting was to decide what should be done with the children. No one wanted to see them in foster care. We all knew they should be together, but who would be willing to raise three children; certainly not me. I already had two of my own and a step-child. Jeff told us earlier that Matthew was eighteen and, in our state, could legally become the guardian for his siblings. Whether he was financially or emotionally qualified didn't really matter as long as it was legal, they wouldn't have to go into the Foster System.

Hugh said he and Matthew had spent so many hours together and had discussed in depth the best course for the family's future. Matthew was college bound, but thought he should stay in Springfield and go to Springfield

University. Peter would graduate the following year. Hugh said that he would be willing to take care of their tuition and anything else they needed.

Phoebe said, "What about this school year? There may be teasing and bullying, and depending where they live, they may not even be in the same district."

Hugh said, "Matthew is a strong young man and he wants to graduate with his current class. He's not at all concerned about what might be said about his father. I've made significant contributions to a private school that my daughters attended, and I'm sure they would enroll Peter and Faith when this vacation ends. They could all live with me, but I'm a stranger to them and I don't know how they'd feel about that."

Jeff said, "Matthew could act as legal guardian. The state will want to verify that Peter and Faith have acceptable housing and attend school, but that's where governmental involvement ends. Peter will be eighteen and considered an adult in just over a year and a half; leaving only Faith as a minor dependent."

Hugh said, "When you consider their ages, caring for them is actually short term. It's not like taking on babies or young children. They've been through so much, I'd like to see them get a decent start and have enough education or training that they can take care of themselves. It's what I wanted to do for Hannah and the least I can do for her now.

Our meeting ended without resolution and, in the end, we all wanted to think about the situation and to see what the children wanted. Until this time, we were thinking on a day-to-day basis and concentrating on Hannah's condition and her care. Having to deal with this question brought the reality of Hannah's death to each of us.

* * *

God bless Jeff; he volunteered to visit Rob and inform him of Hannah's death and to reassure him that his children would be cared for. Later, Phoebe told us that Jeff said he spoke in general terms, and Rob had little response but did say he'd pray for Hannah's soul. Jeff was grateful that Rob didn't seem to have any interest in details such as who paid for Hannah's medical care and funeral expenses and who would care for his children. No explanation of Hugh Fordyce was needed.

A funeral service was conducted in the chapel of our church with Hannah's ashes and two small snapshots of her on the altar. Unfortunately, there were no professional photos taken of her or her children. A few women from our former church Circle and some of Hannah's classmates attended.

Hymns were sung, prayers said and tears shed, as many for the children as for Hannah although they were not aware of it. I was weary of death and sadness and often found myself mindlessly staring into space. Hugh Fordyce stood in the back of the church and left before the service ended.

* * *

The following day the Farleys, the Grays and I met with Hannah's children and Hugh to discuss where they would live. They were determined not to be separated, and Hugh offered a home to all three of them. Matthew seemed to welcome the possibility and Peter neither accepted nor rejected the proposal. He said, "I guess it's OK, as long as I'm with Matthew."

Faith was appalled at the possibility. She wept uncontrollably and threatened to run away if she was forced to live with "him". We explained the possibility of foster care to her and promised that living with her brothers in Hugh's home could be on a trial basis, and she finally agreed.

* * *

I was still feeling like a slacker because I'd not been able to help with Hannah's children so I arranged an adult New Year's Eve dinner at my home. We were eager to welcome a fresh new beginning and to bid farewell to a difficult year. After cocktails, we all gathered around the dining table and agreed to hold hands and have a moment of silence to remember Bernie and Hannah. My dog, Suzy, was under the table and the moment that the room fell silent, she began a long mournful howl that continued until we dropped hands and someone spoke. It was something she'd never done before or ever did again.

1999-2002

Shakespeare wrote, "In calm seas all boats alike show mastery in floating. Only in a storm are they obliged to cope." The wisdom years bring many storms: widowhood, loss of friends, changes of residence, loss or changes of jobs. These are usually viewed as inevitable miseries of old age, rather than as opportunities to see what we are made of. The lifelong pessimist who respond to these changes can learn to be resilient. The woman who loses her husband can find that an entire new and exciting life opens up to her.

Perhaps the greatest gift of the wisdom years is a renewed understanding of how important a network of close friends is to your health, happiness and longevity. The woman who feels isolated either because she has recently left her job, friends behind or because her spouse has passed away has an important opportunity to reevaluate her circumstances and reweave herself into the web of life.

Joan Borysenko, Ph.D.   A Woman's Book of Life

The Bridge Club survived Hannah's death, but the bridge game did not. At each of their official monthly meetings, Phoebe, Abagail and Tammy fondly toasted Hannah and her memory. The ladies successfully launched the younger generation into the world, cared for the older generation as they left the world, and learned to cope with the issues of the aging process. Since we last saw them, they have witnessed the Gulf War, been horrified by the bombing of the Oklahoma Federal Building and faithfully followed the murder trial of O.J. Simpson. More importantly, they have all mastered the internet, communicated by email and they marvel at the possibilities of the cell phone and that new thing called Google.

PHOEBE FARLEY

The Farley household expanded when Ariel left New York, accepted an anchor position with a Springfield TV station, divorced her husband and landed on their Robin Hill doorstep with her two sons. Soon after, Phoebe and Jeff found their retirement paradise on the Gulf of Mexico and Phoebe's sister, Marcia, shocked her with an eye-opening surprise relocation of her own.

ABAGAIL GRAY

When Abigail graciously retired from her life as a community leader, she had no idea that she would be accepting a role as full time caregiver for Stan. Abigail resisted the temptation to move to Syracuse to be near her son and her nephew and chose instead to stay with her friends and the community that meant so much to her.

TAMMY YOUNG

Strangely enough Tammy and Ben found a retirement home on the property once owned by Rob Conway. Ben's forced retirement from his practice took Tammy by surprise and brought her closer to her step-daughter, Melissa.

TAMMY YOUNG

My husband, Ben, usually needed to go to bed around eight o'clock to be fresh for early morning surgery, and he slept soundly all night. During one of my increasingly frequent late-night trips to the bathroom, I noticed a light in our den and found Ben sitting straight up in a chair staring at his hands with his fingers spread wide apart. He was totally unaware of my presence until I asked, "Are you all right?"

A startled Ben quickly folded his hands and moved them to his sides as if to hide them. He hesitated a moment before he said, "I was just thinking about a case. Go back to bed; I'll be there in a few minutes." I laid awake but pretended to be asleep when Ben returned over an hour later. This was a scene that repeated at least weekly, like a bad recurring dream.

* * *

Our Bridge Club never replaced Hannah, but Phoebe, Abagail and I continued to meet monthly over lunch, and we still referred to ourselves as the Bridge Club. Sometimes we met in homes and other times in restaurants. It's never too early to make plans for a significant event like the millennium and we met at my home for that purpose. We all wanted to mark the milestone with a destination celebration, but first, we spent a little time catching up.

Phoebe told us that Ariel was tiring of behind the camera jobs on morning network shows, and, even though she loved New York, she was thinking of interviewing for a news anchor job in a smaller market. I asked about Bug Boy and learned that he felt so guilty about killing bugs that he sold his successful extermination business and was lecturing in the entomology department at Cornell University.

Abagail was just beginning to talk about Skyping with her grandchildren when I heard the garage door open, and a few moments later, saw Ben walking from the kitchen to the den. I knew that he had scheduled a full day of surgery and couldn't guess why he wasn't at the hospital. I excused myself and rushed to see what brought him home in the middle of the day. I found him on the sofa, curled up in the fetal position. I knelt down on the floor, put my arms around him and whispered, "Tell me, what's happened."

Ben said, "Maybe later; I can't talk now."

I returned to my friends and said, "Ben is home and doesn't feel well. You can stay if you like, but I need to see what I can do for him." I was relieved when they chose not to stay and left immediately.

I returned to the den and found Ben sitting up in a chair; his hands covering his eyes. All sorts of things crossed my mind, first of all, I feared that something awful happened to someone in our family. I said, "Please…please, tell me what's wrong."

Ben uncovered his eyes and said, "I was shaking so badly during surgery, I had to step aside and let a resident finish. I stayed to oversee it, and she did a good job, but I can't operate again, not ever."

"Maybe, you're not getting enough sleep; maybe, this is temporary and will stop if you just take a break."

"I haven't known how to tell you, my dear, but I have Parkinson's Disease."

"Are you sure…shouldn't you see a doctor?"

"Tammy, I am a doctor."

I argued, "I'm sure you know what they say about lawyers who defend themselves and have a fool for a client. I would guess the same applies to doctors who diagnose themselves."

We hardly spoke for the remainder of the day. Ben was mainly on the phone arranging the cancellation of his upcoming appointments and setting up a meeting with his partners. It seemed they'd heard about his failed surgery and had a good idea of what was coming.

Over dinner, Ben told me about his first partner, Dr. Hendricks, who was removed from the operating room under the influence of alcohol. He said, "The first clue was that Hendrick's hands were shaking, and I feel I need to reveal my medical condition so this doesn't seem like history repeating itself."

When we did have a specialist's diagnosis and retirement details in place, what Ben worried about most, was not the progression of his disease, but what he would do with his days. I'd heard about Dr. Hendricks suicide following his removal from the operating room and that's what concerned me most. I kept a close eye on Ben for some time, but I need not have worried.

* * *

Unlike most retirees, there were no vacation plans for us nor did we think about pursuing interests or hobbies. Almost daily, Ben's mobility seemed to decrease and we concentrated on just getting through each day.

Strangely enough, Rob Conway's property was purchased by a large successful developer who turned it into an updated version of Rob's dream. The city had grown, and the once rural land was eventually surrounded by stores and services of all kinds. A luxurious retirement community was built at the crest of the hill overlooking the river. Ben offered no resistance when I suggested a move to what was now called The Overlook.

Our new home served a dual purpose; medical care was available for Ben; I was free of maintaining a large home, and I had a safe place to live when Ben was gone.

ABAGAIL GRAY

Two decades after I began my climb to the top of the Springfield social ladder, nothing much had changed. Socially ambitious and aggressive young women, were invading the organizations I'd once chaired. I saw myself in them, and I graciously stepped aside. I took my final bows and handed my resignation to each board, club and foundation with which I was still involved.

Like Phoebe, I'd used the services of Dr. Ben Young more than once and although I still looked younger than my chronological age, I was tired. By the early night-teen nineties, I felt old and jaded; done it, seen it, eaten, drunk and worn it all, and finally, couldn't get excited about much of anything. Early on, every experience, every possibility seemed shiny and available, and I was reveling in it all. I'm glad I did; I needed those memories to keep me going through the difficult days that were to come.

* * *

Shortly after I retired from community service, I noticed that Stan was starting to repeat himself and while driving he often missed turns. He seemed to be displaying road rage on a regular basis, and I told myself, That's Stan... that's just the way he is.

It was computer technology that convinced me something was very wrong with Stan. He was reluctant to convert ATLS, the company that he and David Kaiser founded in 1980, to a computerized system. David, in truth, had already been using word processing for some time in the legal department of the company and insisted that computers would be needed in the accounting area just to remain competitive. Stan seemingly agreed, and while he could advise clients about their practices and procedures, he couldn't cope with the actual work of filling out tax returns or preparing spreadsheets on a computer. He declared that using a keyboard was woman's work, and at first, refused to even try to learn. As computers appeared on every desk in the office Stan made an effort to learn, but his frustration often led to angry outbursts.

Eventually, David Kaiser insisted on buying Stan's share of the business, and he offered a very fair price, plus a percentage of the profits for the following five years. An elegant retirement party was given at The Springfield Club.

The morning after the party, Stan insisted that he go to his office. I thought he needed to say thank you for the party or to pick up personal items. I was told that once there, he began making calls, and he attempted to do some work. This went on for nearly two weeks, and Stan's former colleagues showed a lot of patience. Finally, I was able to book us on a two-week cruise hoping Stan would be distracted and make the transition to retirement. When we returned, he once again announced that he was ready to go back to work. I hid his car keys but he called a taxi.

It was a crushing blow, but Stan finally understood when David Kaiser, reluctantly, had security respectfully escort him from the building. Ryan and, my nephew, R.J., tried to help, but were often unable to leave their law practice in Syracuse.

I made a strong effort to keep Stan at home, but he was a large man and was growing increasingly hostile. As walking became difficult for him, I was forced to place him in the memory care unit of a nursing facility. By that time, I felt that Robin Hill was too large and lonely. Ryan and R.J. urged me to relocate Stan to Syracuse and to move there to be near them and especially my grandchildren. I felt I needed to be in a familiar location and near my friends, so I settled for a condominium in a high-rise building downtown near Springfield's concert hall, museums, and the convention center where professional and college basketball games were played in season.

* * *

When Stan passed away in 1996, I was tempted to move to Syracuse, but I felt so tied to my friends and the community that I simply wasn't ready to leave. However, my downtown location was becoming risky. There had been some shootings and muggings. I often felt threatened when I attended concerts or basketball games after dark, but the building doorman was always available to walk with me. I would phone him when I was ready to come home, and he'd meet me and walk back to my building with me. It was not a satisfactory situation.

Tammy thought life at The Overlook offered more security and other benefits and she strongly urged me to move there. I have to admit, that when I saw people arriving at games and concerts in an Overlook bus, I envied the convenience and the safety that they had. After I was shown a lovely fifth floor unit with a sensational view of the river and the hills beyond, I sold my downtown condo and came to terms with the aging process.

PHOEBE FARLEY

We were all pleasantly surprised when, my daughter, Ariel's job search brought her back to Springfield, and she was hired by a local television station to anchor two evening newscasts. Her marriage had been shaky for some time, and the move made a split inevitable. When she and her two son's Mitch and Noah moved into Robin Hill with Jeff and me; we all thought it was temporary.

* * *

Shortly after Ariel's and her sons arrived, Jeff stepped down from full time practice but remained with his firm as Senior Counsel. We suddenly had an opportunity to travel with no concern for the security and care of our home and we revisited many of the locations we'd enjoyed on vacations and thought we might want for a second home. Possibilities ranged from coast to coast, dessert to mountains and even the island of Hawaii. Finally, we settled on Sanibel Island, a place where we'd enjoyed several vacations. We purchased a spacious condominium on the beach and looked forward to escaping Springfield's harsh winter weather.

* * *

When I told my sister, Marcia, about our purchase, she surprised me with an announcement of her own. She said, "That's great news. I'll love spending time with you there, and I hope you'll be able to visit me in Santa Fe.

I asked, "Is that just seasonal?"

Marcia replied, "No, it's a relocation. Debbie and I are planning to move there permanently and open an art gallery."

"I know you and Debbie have known each other for a long time, but that's quite a commitment to make with a friend."

Marcia couldn't conceal her amusement and she said, "Surely you've guessed; Debbie is much more than a friend."

I tried to cover up my naïveté, but Marcia wasn't buying it. She said, "Sis, you never guessed, did you? Didn't you ever ask yourself why I didn't have a man in my life or even act like I wanted one?"

I was so caught off guard that I said, "I just thought you hadn't met the right man. You've always been so pretty and so..so...feminine." I stopped right there and said, "I'm sorry. I'm saying all the wrong things. I just want you to be happy, and I guess you are."

Marcia hugged me and said, "Yes, yes, I am and I hope you'll accept my choices and learn to love Debbie as much as I do."

I knew I'd try to accept the choice, and I hoped I'd succeed, but one thing I knew for certain; I'd never love Debbie.

It was past midnight when Ariel came home from her news broadcast, but I waited up for her. I was usually asleep when she came in and she was somewhat surprised to see me. "Mom is everything all right?"

"Well, yes… I guess. Marcia was here today, and she told me she's moving to Santa Fe."

"Good for her; that's an art mecca, and I know she'll enjoy it."

"She's moving there with Debbie, and they're planning to open an art gallery."

"And you stayed up this late to tell me. Do you have a problem with that?"

"No, not exactly, but going so far away and starting a new business with… Oh what's the use. Marcia is gay."

Ariel burst out laughing and said, "Did you just figure that out?"

"No, Marcia had to tell me. Did you know?"

"I knew by the time I went to college."

"Why didn't you tell me?"

"I thought you knew. It was pretty obvious." Ariel patted my shoulder and said, "I'm really beat, I'll see you tomorrow."

The following morning, Jeff suggested we go out for breakfast. After our food was served, I took a guess and said, "Jeff, how long have you known that Marcia is gay?"

"Pretty much since we started dating." Jeff took a bite of his pancake, put his fork down, stared at me and said, "You just figured that out, didn't you?"

I could tell he was holding back a laugh, and I said, "How could I not have known? Everyone else did!"

"My dear, your innocence is endearing. It's one of the things I love most about you. Now that you know, how do you feel about Marcia and her gender preference?"

"It just seems odd. For all the years since we've been married, I wondered why Marcia was so happy for me. I thought maybe deep down inside she might have been jealous that I had a wonderful husband and children and she didn't. I just think it'll take a while for me to absorb the whole idea."

TAMMY YOUNG

The first time I saw Ben walking with Canadian crutches, I wanted to cry. I fought hard to keep back the tears so that he wouldn't see them. Our children, Grant, Taylor and Melissa lobbied him endlessly for physical therapy. He refused any kind of treatment. and in a few months a walker replaced the crutches. Within a year and a half of his diagnosis he was confined to a wheel chair.

Our step-daughter Melissa, now a clinical psychologist, and our son, Grant, a resident in psychiatry, were in close contact and conferred constantly hoping to find ways to persuade their father to help himself. They told me that he seemed to have lost the will to live; I alternated between desperation and anger. I asked myself, *was I and our wonderful marriage, not enough to live for and what about our children; all three successful and a source of pride? Didn't he want to see them marry and meet his grandchildren? Was rearranging the faces of aging women all that was worth living for?* I asked him that and he had no answer; apparently it was.

As Ben's ability to move his body declined, we spent more time together and grew closer. It gave us an opportunity to discuss our thoughts on nearly everything and to review all the special moments of all the years we'd spent together. He even confessed that he was not willing to take the measures needed to lengthen his life. His decision had nothing to do with leaving his medical practice but was based on his reluctance to burden our family with his care. Nothing I could say would change his mind.

Our daughter, Taylor, was living in Chicago and going to law school, but Melissa and Grant were always available when needed and looked in on their father several times each week. Although Ben's death was devastating for all of us, he seemed relieved as he neared the end and died peacefully.

PHOEBE FARLEY

Shortly after Jeff and I returned to Springfield from our winter in Florida. I hosted the May meeting of the Bridge Club at Robin Hill. Tammy, Abagail and I were excited about the millennium and eager to plan a memorable, exciting celebration. Since Tammy and Abagail were now widows, Jeff and I thought we should host the party.

While Tammy seemed very satisfied with her home at The Overlook, Abagail was having second thoughts and seemed a bit depressed. When I suggested that we celebrate the year 2000 at our Sanibel Island home, she seemed to brighten and responded to the idea with a level of enthusiasm that I hadn't seen in a very long time.

We spent the afternoon planning our dinner and thinking of ways we could incorporate the tropical setting into our celebration. We knew that caterers would all be booked, and we decided to cook the meal ourselves. The menu included steak, lobster, asparagus risotto and, of course, the dessert would be a decadent key lime pie. From previous New Year celebrations, I knew that the island would be glowing with fireworks, probably more spectacular than any others we'd seen.

When I mentioned that we had an invitation to an Atwood Vineyard wine tasting on December 30, Tammy was thrilled. She said, "Wine Enthusiast magazine rates them as one of the best boutique vineyards in Napa."

Abagail remained unimpressed and said, "I've just never learned to appreciate wine. As you know, I'm a martini girl.

Our guest list was easy. Children of the Bridge Club were scattered across the country, but we hoped they'd all be able to come. Hugh Fordyce was on the list as were Hannah's children.

Peter Conway earned a degree in computer science and was working in the field. We had all hoped to see him, but he later sent his regrets and said he would be working through the New Year holiday due to Y2K concerns.

My sister, Marcia, was also on the guest list which meant that her partner, Debbie, would have to be included. I thought I should give my friends a heads up about their domestic situation. By now, I should have realized that no explanation was needed, but I made one and no one seemed shocked or even surprised. Here I was, the closest to Marcia and, seemingly, the last to know. Before the afternoon ended, Tammy and I each sampled a glass of Atwood Chardonnay and we made a martini for Abagail.

*   *   *

Wonderful as our plan sounded, fate intervened. We were all notified shortly after Christmas that Hugh Fordyce died from a heart attack on December 26th, the exact anniversary of Hannah's death, and his funeral was to be held on December 30. Out of respect, we cancelled the celebration. Tammy and Abagail remained in Springfield to attend the service. On New Year's Eve, my family gathered at our Sanibel home and had a quiet dinner together. Tammy told me that the attendance at Hugh's funeral packed his church. All the Conway children and Hugh's twins were present. We never did know how Hugh explained his involvement with the Conway children to his daughters, but apparently he pulled it off, and they seemed to accept Matthew, Peter and Faith.

AFTERWORD

Part of alleviating the fear is the knowledge of the right to die with dignity, surrounded by loved ones to whom we have made our wishes clear. The opportunity for thanking one another, forgiving one another and finding new levels of meaning in the years that have been shared is facilitated when seriously ill patients discuss their wishes about the dying process.

Joan Borysenko, Ph.D. A Woman's Book of Life

MELISSA YOUNG

My biological mother was a beautiful, promiscuous, alcoholic narcissist. As a clinical psychologist, I can say that with authority. I've spent most of my adult life studying psychology in an effort to understand her, and, yes…myself as well. Looking back, I can see that she planted the seeds of dislike for my stepmother, Tammy, and watered those seeds until they bloomed into a garden of contempt.

As an adolescent, I made no effort to conceal those feelings and avoided my half-siblings whenever possible.

Strange and sad as it may seem, my grandmother's stroke may have been the most fortunate event of my life. I was forced to spend time with Tammy, and when I saw what a normal family life looked like, I wanted to be part of it. The contrast between my mother and Tammy was so sharply defined that I began to see my mother for what she really was. Tammy gave my father absolute support and showered selfless love on her children and, later, on me. I began to thrive when I became a full-time member of their family.

How do you say thank you to someone whom you treated with disrespect and, in return, that person gave you unconditional love and made you an integral part of her family?

When Tammy was diagnosed with lung cancer, our family was devastated as were her friends. The disease had advanced to stage four without diagnosis. A series of six chemotherapy treatments was recommended, but after three Tammy said she could stand no more, and she died peacefully two weeks later. From diagnosis to death, she lasted only six weeks.

My younger sister and brother were both out of town, but Abagail and I mainly took care of her. Phoebe had hip problems and used a walker but stayed with Tammy as often as she was able. We made sure that Tammy was never alone and along with Grant, Taylor and the ladies of the Bridge Club, we were with her when she died.

I kept in close touch with Phoebe and Abagail until Phoebe died two years later during surgery after a fall in her home. She was still living at Robin Hill and no amount of reasoning would persuade her to move to The Overlook. She said it was because of the river. We could never understand Phoebe's aversion to the river. While most residents insisted on apartments with the river view, Phoebe said she couldn't bear to look at the river.

Now there is only Abagail. She's in assisted living at The Overlook and still looks beautiful. She is certainly the best dressed woman in the facility and insists on Botox shots every three months. Ryan has retired, moved to Springfield and spends a great deal of time with her.

DR. MATTHEW CONWAY

My father phoned me the day he was released from prison. I had never visited him nor had my brother Peter. Faith saw him twice but couldn't go again. She said his conversation was peppered with Bible quotes that related to his prison ministry, and he tried to engage her in one of his marathon prayers. She said she attempted to tell him about us and our lives, but he seemed to have no interest in any of his children. He did ask about the river property and, when she described the new development, he pumped his fist and said, "Six more months; six more months was all I needed and everything would have been fine. We'd be rich now and I'd never have gone to prison."

After a brief description of the difficulties of prison life, my father came to the real purpose of his call. He said he had a plan, needed a loan and asked to stay with me, until he got on his feet.

In a way, I felt sorry for him and nearly agreed to give him a home but knew my wife wouldn't agree and, quite frankly, I didn't want my children subjected to the endless prayers. I did give him money, not as loan, but I stressed that it was a one-time gift and there would be no more. I said, "This is God's plan for you…and also mine." I never heard from him again.

Now, I think I can speak for my brother and sister when I say that all three of us think of Hugh Fordyce as our father. He was the strongest influence in my life and during the time we spent together in my mother's hospital room, my vision for my future changed dramatically. I was so deeply touched by the commitment and the skill of the hospital staff, that I was inspired to become a cancer specialist. I was also impressed by Hugh's devotion to my mother and his generosity to all of us. We had some deep and personal conversations during that time, and I came to see him as a man of integrity and character. He could have had a carefree life and pursued his many interests, but instead, he chose to raise three children not his own. He saw that we all had good educations and were well settled in our adult lives. I don't like to speak in religious terms, but my sister, brother and I were truly blessed.

Besides Hugh Fordyce, the ladies of the Bridge Club were an immense blessing to me and my siblings, but especially to my mother. They cared so much about each other through all of life's stages that their bond lasted to the very end of their lives and it exists yet today in my generation. Soon after Hugh's funeral the three of them, Peter, Faith and I met at the cemetery and scattered my mother's ashes over his grave. It seemed the best and only place for her. I think it was the last time the ladies of the Bridge Club were all together.

*　*　*

Abigail and I sometimes have lunch, followed by a trip to the cemetery. She pauses before the men's graves: Jeff, Ben and Stan, but she lingers longer at Phoebe and Tammy's graves. We bring a bouquet and place a red rose on each grave. On our last visit Abagail said to me, "Matthew, soon I'll be here too. Don't bring flowers for me. Bring a martini and pour it on the ground: Bombay gin, very dry and a little dirty."

Lightning Source UK Ltd.
Milton Keynes UK
UKHW010642280521
384539UK00001B/25